Carnival Creeke

Book 2

Angela Foy Davis

This is a work of fiction. The events and characters described herein are imaginary and are not intended to refer to specific places or living persons.

CARNIVAL CREEKE: BOOK 2

Cover and illustrations by Angela Foy Davis

ISBN: 978-0-578-59307-4

Printed in the United States of America

To my beloved Fellowship of Creative Nerdiness:
My husband, Jeremy, Andru the Author, my Mom, and my Dad.
You inspire me, you stoke my fire.
You were endlessly willing to read my wordstuffs.
And you never let me stop writing.

KEEP YOUR EYES OPEN...

If you spot one of these little symbols, visit www.CarnivalCreeke.com and check out the “Easter Egg Hunt” to unlock goodies, bonus creature artwork, or listen to the song that’s playing in that scene.

HAPPY HUNTING!

1

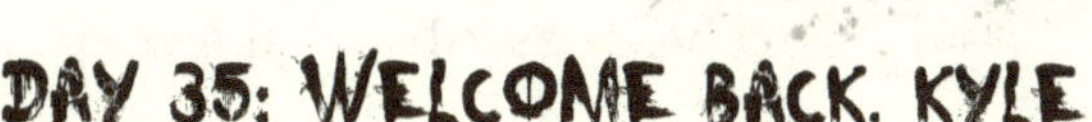

DAY 35: WELCOME BACK, KYLE

My name is C. Kyle.

What's the 'C' stand for? Beats me. I can't remember. Pretty sure it's C-L-something... But I'm not really worried about that right now. I'm running through a moonlit cornfield and my main concern is the scarecrow that's trying to murder me. It's Mr. Brown's scarecrow. Usually the big straw-stuffed dummy is slumped on a post, neither alive nor murderous, but today it's both. And as an added bonus, the straw that it's stuffed with is also razor sharp.

Thunk-thunk-thunk!

Blades of straw whiz past my cheek like tiny needlepoint daggers, impaling a cornstalk two inches from my head. I freeze for a beat, then I plunge in the direction that the attack came from, whacking the crispy stalks aside with my heavy battle axe. One of the stalks slingshots back and a fat ear of corn clobbers me in the face.

Yowch. That's going to be a gorgeous black eye later.

I can't remember anything before waking up here in the cute little town of Carnival Creeke and finding out I was reliving the same day over and over. Friday, October 20th. Again and again,

skipping like a bad record. But there's a catch. Each day, there's a fun new surprise.

A wildcard.

How can I best describe what a wildcard is? Picture the most inconvenient thing you can think of. It's raining. Your Twinkie fell on the floor. Now multiply the weird factor by a thousand. Acid rain that turns people inside-out. A Twinkie with fangs that's trying to kill you.

Usually, I have to hunt down the wildcard. Sometimes, it'll hunt me. Like that day that I coughed up my evil twin. Then sometimes the wildcard involves no hunting at all, like when the entire town was covered in ice, people and all. Fun times.

Whatever the wildcard, the finish line is always the same: Neutralize the wildcard before the day resets, or it sticks. For good. Rain *keeps* on turning people inside-out. Twinkies remain bloodthirsty forever. Me and Carnival Creeke, stuck on that day forever, but now with the wildcard sealed as our new reality. And let me assure you, I've never met a wildcard that you'd want as reality.

Those are the rules. That's the game.

Hang on tight, now.

I've reached the edge of the cornfield. I grasp the old wooden fence, my chest heaving, an indistinct moan rustling the cornstalks behind me as I duck between the fence posts.

Who am I? And why did *I* get chosen to play this never-ending game? There's only one person who knows the answer to that: Rascal Holliday. The obnoxiously beautiful Irish jerk who ripped out my heart (literally), stuffed it into a tin canister, and then dropped me into this crazy hamster wheel game. He's got answers. But he's not telling.

Just as my foot touches the grass, the scarecrow bursts out of the cornfield behind me like a drunken zombie farmer, eyes like two cherries in a bowl of melted ice cream and wet leather.

I've decided to name him Bloodshot.

I do a helter-skelter backwards somersault into the road and the hulking brute comes windmilling after me, swinging its L.L. Bean flannel-clad arms.

It's still coming at me when the flatbed truck slams it out of its boots. Its stuffed body blows apart like a sack of tissue paper, limbs spiraling in every direction. I have to shield my head from a hail of straw-needles that rain down hard enough to sink into the asphalt. The scarecrow's torso rolls up the windshield and bounces onto the pavement as the truck roars off toward town.

I walk slowly toward the body, down the center of the moonlit road, axe in my hand. The limbless torso twitches, rolling itself over. Grunting, it starts using its chin to drag itself toward me.

I stop walking.

"Hey big fella," I say. "No hard feelings. We've actually got a lot in common. I've got no heart, you've got no brain… It's been a fun day."

The scarecrow is still inching itself laboriously toward me like a giant, straw-filled slug. Its red eyes burn through the dark at me, a high-pitched gurgling sound emanating from its stitched-shut mouth. This thing is tenacious.

I check my watch. Ten minutes to one o'clock.

With a sigh, I tromp over and plant my boot on the scarecrow's burlap forehead.

"Say hey to the wizard for me."

It's amazing how easily a well-sharpened battle axe will slice off a stuffed straw man's head.

All in a day's work. In ten minutes, this day will reset, and I get to wake up and do it all over again. Lather, rinse, repeat.

For how long, you ask?

However long. Forever long.

Only way out of this bonkers game is to figure out a way to *stop* time from skipping.

Suggestions? I'm wide open.

I've got time.

I've got all the time in the world.

DAY 36: MIRROR, MIRROR

I'm sprawled on the ground on my back beneath the water tower, blood pouring from my nose. Holliday sits on my chest, heavy despite his slim frame. An angel dipped in black leather, his combat boots grinding my arms into the soil. I swallow repeatedly, struggling to push words out and keep the vomit down as I lay there in the dirt. Trying to keep calm, even though every bone might be broken.

Holliday pulls some kind of brushed metal cylinder from the duffle bag slung over his back.

"What've you got there?" I ask him. My voice would sound downright casual if I weren't shaking like a baby bird.

He averts his eyes.

"Ye seen those things at the bank drive-through window, right?" Calmly, he screws a bulb into the top of the cylinder, attaches three wires like miniscule jumper cables. It's only when he's peeled down the neck of my shirt and I can feel the edges of the cylinder boring into the thin skin of my chest, a ring of tiny drills burrowing into the taut flesh over my breastbone – that's when his black eyes shift down and look at me.

I can't lift my knee. Can't snap my arms wide or buck to throw him off balance. He seems to be predicting my every move, adjusting his body slightly to counter me before I even try. So I do the only logical thing I have left.

I've just worked up a good mouthful of spit when he wags a warning finger at me.

"Shhh, easy, Doc." The jerk grins. "Stop wigglin'. It'll be less than silky if ye tense up."

That open-mouthed leer.

Like a shark, like night itself...

The canister releases a hiss; it's now air-tight against my tented skin.

Here we go.

I brace my back against the soil and swear on all that is and ever was that he will not hear me utter a sound when this happens...

I jolt awake.

My face is smushed into the warm mattress. I must have knocked my frilly pillow off onto the floor in my sleep. I roll over. The little tin clock on the bedside dresser says 6:11.

Always 6:11.

Why 6:11? Because that's when the stupid car alarm goes off outside my window at the Red Rooster bed-and-breakfast every morning. The Quik-Pump gas station is right next door, its garage home to the offending old rust bucket that blasts me out of the booger woods each day. Not my first choice for a wake-up call, but you don't exactly get a say when you're stuck in a repeating day. So...wakey, wakey, eggs and bakey.

Yawning, I methodically press my finger to my neck. Still no pulse. No heart. It wasn't a dream.

I can hope, can't I?

Rubbing the circular scar on my chest, I roll off the bed onto the blue rug and immediately start doing push-ups. I do this every day. My morning routine is a well-oiled machine.

My arms move. My legs move.

The wildcard is just the kind of challenge I like.

Today is my day.

Pants, boots. Toothpaste, toothbrush. Stick to the routine, and you'll never get caught off guard.

Except maybe…*THAT*.

I've just leaned over to spit into the old-fashioned sink basin when I glance up at the mirror. But instead of my reflection, a ghoulish face is staring back at me.

It looks like a sunburnt mummy. The creature's dark skin is withered and pruned, like rawhide stretched over a skull. Staring blindly through hollow empty eye sockets, a few crimped cobwebs of hair sprout from its scaly scalp. Two flabby breasts cling to its skeletal frame like deflated grapes, suggesting that this thing is female. She doesn't mimic my motions, and she's not holding a toothbrush – so I'm relieved that this eyeless ghoul isn't *my* reflection.

No, this crispy creature is actually *behind* the glass.

A wildcard popping up in my room like this, first thing in the morning? I'm hardly ever this lucky.

Trick or treat, Kyle.

Toothbrush still hanging from my mouth, I fling myself across the bedroom and grab the porcelain rooster off my dresser. Holding it by the neck, I smash it against the edge of the dresser, instantly transforming the happy barnyard curio into a jagged, makeshift weapon. Crude, yes – but my weapon options in this room are extremely limited, so Henny Penny works in a pinch. I try to live life without regrets, but I do sincerely regret not stashing a chainsaw under my bed before I began this repeating day.

In response to my rooster-smashing, a muffled voice hollers from the room next door.

"What the ding-dang is going on in there?!"

The creature in the bathroom mirror immediately whips her head toward the shout, sniffing like a blind dog. Then she dives out of sight somewhere behind the mirror.

Oh crud. She's going to kill my neighbor.

The adjacent rooms are occupied by a pair of well-manicured ladies with abnormally pillowy lips and a superhuman ability to talk for an entire hour about Corgis (or poodle-doodles, or Corgipoos, or whatever those dogs are called). Seriously. *An hour*. This is ten percent of why I usually grab my breakfast to go most mornings.

I quickly snatch all my belongings off the bedside dresser. A wad of cash, my "live for today" cookie fortune, and my little plastic 8-ball keychain. Everything I own fits into my jacket pocket. Some might call that sad. I call it convenient.

Locking my door behind me, I hurry down the hall to room three and rap the door with my knuckles.

"Hello? Everything okay in there?"

No answer.

Pressing my ear to the door, I can make out a dull scraping sound. Like a body being dragged across the floor… I take a deep breath and kick the door down. It flings open with a lot more oomph than I'd intended, the antique brass doorknob punching through the wall.

I do a quick optical sweep. This room is identical to mine – rustic four-poster bed, assorted rooster figurines on the dresser, framed barnyard painting on the wall – only instead of my blue gingham, the bedspread and curtains in this room are pine green. Corgipoo Lady stands there wrapped in a towel, wet hair, with both her hands against the wooden dresser. Looks like she was pushing it across the room.

One-hundred percent normal.

Zero percent wildcard.

"Ooh, sorry," I rub my forehead, forcing a nonchalant laugh. "I was just wondering if you knew what time breakfast was at. And yeah, I know I just ended my sentence with a preposition. I'll let you get back to–" I wave my hand at the cattycorner dresser. "Whatever you were doing."

Corgipoo Lady bristles indignantly, her cheeks flushed.

"Oh, don't get all judgy," she snaps at me. "I was just moving this dresser to the other wall. The Feng Shui in this room doesn't spark any joy *at all*."

Behind her, the closet door is open. I see that she's relocated her record player into the closet, sitting on the pile of old records. What a waste. I love my record player. I consider asking which records she has, but quickly veto the idea. I've got a mirror mummy on the loose.

A sudden yelp rings out downstairs, followed by a crash.

That's my cue.

I leave Corgipoo Lady to Feng her Shui and sprint down the carpeted wooden steps, vaulting over the banister.

Down in the dining parlor, Mrs. Moffatt, the tiny Filipino proprietor of the Red Rooster, is crouched on the rug. She's surrounded by scattered buttermilk biscuits, and an overturned silver tray the same color as her bobbed China doll hair. She's staring straight ahead, her expression transfixed in horror.

In fairness, the woman always looks terrified. She's like a rabbit. Once I asked her how she got her waffles so fluffy, and she just stared at me like I was a terrorist.

But she's not looking at me now.

Mrs. Moffatt's wide eyes are locked on the silver tray lying on the floor. There, reflected in its polished metal surface, is the prune-faced creature from my mirror upstairs, peering out at us through those dry, dry, empty eye sockets.

I dart over to the lace-covered buffet table and snatch a saw-toothed bread knife. My emergency weapon option number two, a decided upgrade from the porcelain rooster.

"Get behind me!" I bark at Mrs. Moffatt. I'm only 5'3, but she's as tiny as a doll and fits snugly behind me.

Winning the award for the worst timing ever, the two Corgipoo ladies start clomping downstairs together in their matching yoga pants and headbands.

I point at them with the knife.

"Don't come down here!" I warn. Aghast, they skitter back up the stairs needing no further prompting. As soon as I speak, Pruneface looks at me, swinging her head so fast that her stringy hair flops against her face, sticking there. Even without eyes, I swear she recognizes me. The creature's leathery lips peel back into a grin, revealing a mouthful of jagged, shark-like teeth.

"Breakfast?" I ask, flipping the knife to reverse-grip. "I recommend the waffles."

Pruneface gives me a smirk that cracks her skin like old pottery. Then she vanishes.

What a way to start a day.

*

I assure everyone that the show is over and instruct them to sit back down and eat breakfast, and by the time I'm heading for the door, I've got them all convinced that the face in the tray was nothing but a trick of the morning light. Swamp gas, Elvis in a potato. People are malleable. Tell them what they want to hear, and as long as you serve it up with confidence, they're usually relieved to return to their regularly scheduled lives.

My trek into town consists of an arrow-straight road and thirty minutes of cornfields. A swaying sea of gold, shimmering with early morning dew. I used to loathe this imposed downtime, but lately I've started embracing it. Might as well, right? It's the perfect time to prepare myself for the day. My own little pregame yoga. In my profession, preparation is paramount. You never know when a wildcard will pop up and try to chew your face off.

Welcome to Carnival Creeke.

A chilly autumn fog is draped over the tree-lined Main Street; the sleepy morning sun barely grazing the shopfronts' striped awnings. The town wakes up in stages. Right about now, Merle is firing up the deep fryer, though he won't switch on the diner's neon sign for another hour. Also in the Early Risers Club are the construction workers, eternally patching up the gargoyle damage in the library's cemetery. Perpetually hammering away up on their scaffolding, each clang echoing off the rooftops. A beam of sun spotlights the huge cranberry and orange banner stretched across the street, announcing tonight's homecoming football game and parade.

Perfect Smallville storybook, right?

Don't judge a book by its cover. This cute little Norman Rockwell town is a veritable grab-bag of weirdness. Come sunset, we might be getting terrorized by a big hairy monster, or this whole place could be covered in ice, or slime, or peanut butter. You just never know what you're going to get.

Oh, Carnival Creeke. My never-ending box of chocolates.

And let's not forget, I've got a less-than-friendly mummy chocolate slinking around somewhere this very moment. There must be hundreds of mirrors in town, and countless reflective surfaces. Pruneface could be hiding in any of them. Sure, my Icemaker's wildcard detector could bullseye her in a jiffy...but my shotgun is stashed in the bank vault. And the bank won't open until eight o'clock.

I stop walking, narrowing my eyes at the library.

It stares back at me.

The brick academy building with its Colonial-style portico columns, with its heavy doors and untold secrets, its sprawling courtyard lawn that will be scattered with happy picnickers this afternoon – it all stares right at me, daring me to exist. My eyes move automatically upward, to the gargoyle statue hunched atop the roof gutter. Recessed in shadows, lifeless and non-lethal, a constant reminder of its ugly brother that came alive and nearly killed me on my first day here.

I glance up at the library's steeped bell tower, at the huge, ornate clock. 7:22. I check my watch. I've got it synchronized with the library's clock.

My watch, and my life.

Every day, those glowing Roman numerals seem to oversee my fate. A looming Gamemaster, the deep, heavy tick of the clock's iron hands already counting down to...destruction and doom? Blood and guts? A leisurely steak dinner?

Whatever it is, I'll need provisions.

*

On the General Store's pumpkin-lined porch, the life-sized wooden Native American greets me with his customary scowl. Every time I look at the glowering statue, I can't help but expect Rascal Holliday to be perched atop it again one day. He never is, of course. The only thing sitting on the statue's carved wooden headdress is a Cubs baseball cap.

"Looking good," I give the chief a nod.

The cowbells clatter as I walk in. Sam Dove looks up from the counter, where he's always arranging the pink-and-yellow spiral lollipops in the wooden log next to the cash register. He beams, throwing me a warm smile under his gigantic, wooly Papa Bear mustache.

"Well, howdy-day, young lady!"

I zig-zag systematically through the aisles, gathering my daily survival essentials: A small utility knife, a lighter, antiseptic, medical tape, earplugs, a sewing needle, a bottle of rubber cement, duct tape, and dental floss. This takes me approximately twenty-eight seconds. Then five more minutes for Sam to leisurely scan all my items. In a moment, he'll ask his question.

Wait for it…

"So, if I may ask," he leans toward me with a covert wink. "Do we have a bun in the oven?"

He *always* asks. Because the first time he saw me on Gargoyle Day, I was in here buying a pregnancy test. How was I supposed to know that my dizziness and upset tummy were caused by Holliday ripping my heart out?

Live and learn.

"No buns today!" I sing, throwing Sam a salute and shouldering out the door with my brown paper bag of provisions. As soon as I'm outside, I transfer my items into the pockets of my cargo pants, crumpling the paper bag into a ball.

I've watched Carnival Creeke blow up. I've seen it burnt to the ground. But each morning, it's always back. Good as new, like nothing ever happened. That grill will always fire up. Those workers always back up on their scaffolding, as though a gargoyle ripping off a few roof shingles is the worst thing that's happened to this town. It takes a licking, and keeps on ticking.

Like me, I guess.

And these people, like their town, are not to be underestimated.

On instinct, I glance over my shoulder. Down the street is Tuscany Mill, the historic old grain mill-turned fancy-pants restaurant. The towering shape of its rustic timbers cut an impressive silhouette against the diamond morning sun.

Merrick Cohen is inside that restaurant right now. If it's early morning, and the wildcard has already popped up, sometimes I'll track down Merrick while he's working, waiting tables. But I always feel like a jerk, pulling him away from his job like that. Often I'll wait until afternoon, when I know he'll be at Merle's Diner eating lunch, and I'll recruit him there. Or sometimes I won't involve Merrick at all. It all depends on the wildcard. Depends on the teeth, depends on the danger factor.

Depends on a lot of things.

Okay, it's eight o'clock. Time to go get me a gun.

*

The precocious little hipster in the pink suit jacket leads me down the honeycomb hallway toward the bank vault. Even though I could navigate these halls with my eyes closed, I follow him, yawning, into the small room lined with two walls of silver drawers. I guarantee none of them hold *anything* as wicked cool as my drawer.

Pink Peacock bows with a dramatic flourish then sashays off, his plaid pants swishing around his ankles. As soon as I'm alone, I reach into my pocket and fish out my 8-ball keychain. Holding it to my lips like a microphone, I ask it a yes-no question (*"Will today be the best day of my life?"*). The 8-ball reacts to my voice, obediently cracking open in my hand, spilling out my silver key in a pool of black liquid.

Wiping my hand on my pants, I eagerly unlock my drawer and scoop my compacted Icemaker from the safety deposit box. An electric tingle spasms through me. I swear, every time I hold this weapon it feels like the first time.

"Hey, gorgeous," I whisper. "Did you miss me?"

In its compacted form, the folded-up weapon could easily be mistaken for an old wooden door handle. But like this town, it's more than it appears.

Lovingly, I run my thumb over the button that would spring it open into a Winchester shotgun. Not now, though. Later.

I start to slide the drawer shut.

Like a TV screen suddenly switching on, Pruneface appears in the gleaming surface of the drawer, two inches from my face, her mouth stretched in a wide, jagged grin.

I jerk backwards and automatically go to flip open my Icemaker – but then I freeze.

The security camera blinks from the corner of the ceiling.

I can't be seen waving a shotgun around in a bank. I'd land myself in jail in three seconds flat, effectively putting an end to my day. Sheriff Gammell has managed to throw me into his drunk tank twice already, and that's twice too many. Getting caged like that is the worst monkey wrench you can throw into my ticking wildcard timeclock. One o'clock comes faster than you would think.

As if aware of my predicament, Pruneface responds with a gurgly, snakelike hiss. What I assumed to be jagged teeth I can now see are actually shards of glass, set in her oily black gums.

"You again?" I huff. Wobbling her mummy head back and forth on her reedy neck, she digs one clawed finger down into her empty eye socket. I cringe.

"Hey, if you don't quit picking at that, it's never going to heal."

"Tsk-tsk," she whispers in a voice like dry leaves. *"You're not supposed to be here."*

I frown. "Yeah, well, neither are you."

I've never had a wildcard talk to me before.

Weird...

I scoot back a few steps, out of Pruneface's reach. Her face vanishes. I spin around just in time to see her swipe a skeletal brown arm from the silver wall of drawers behind me. Hot, sharp pain sears my scalp as her hooked claws rip out a chunk of my hair.

"Pulling hair now, huh?" Grimacing, I rub my scalp. "And here I thought we were above those girly-fight tactics."

Get one inch closer, and she'll rip out more than just hair. A teeny flesh wound might be small potatoes to anyone else. But to *me*, it could be mortal. Without a heart, my body can't produce new blood. As Holliday so eloquently put it, I've only got six liters of life juice sloshing around inside me. Probably more like five now, actually. I've been careful, but scrapes are inevitable, and I've lost blood. A squirt here, a splash there… It adds up.

In fairness, the ever-benevolent Holliday *did* leave me with one little parting gift when he ripped out my heart.

Super-fast healing abilities.

Cool, right? Wrong. It's a joke. It's just enough to keep my delicate heartless self on this side of the dirt, just enough to give me a fighting chance of surviving long enough to scrub out the wildcard and win each day.

I slide my heels back a centimeter, to what I'm praying is dead center of the room, mere inches out of range of those fishhook claws that Pruneface keeps slashing experimentally at me. She's alternating walls now, really leaning into each swipe, thrusting her bony shoulders out to try and reach me better. I suck in a breath, running my thumb along the button on my Icemaker.

I *could* do it. Blast her in the kisser. *Boom*. Wildcard done. Then who cares if Gammell arrests me? Let him. What's the worst that could happen? I chill in a concrete cell until the sun sets, and the day resets at one o'clock?

"ONE INCH CLOSER, AND SHE'LL RIP OUT MORE THAN MY HAIR..."

Unless...I miss. Or maybe she regenerates. I've encountered self-healing creatures before. Wildcards aren't always cut and dry. And they sure as heck don't always play by the rules.

Rules, shmools.

Pruneface has stopped trying to slash my skin off, and is now circling the room around me like a panther. An eyeless mummy panther, her hideous face moving from one drawer to another, as if walking from window to window. I pivot, keeping her in view.

Something about the way she moves...

Something almost...*familiar.*

I shrug, shoving my Icemaker into my jacket pocket. "Suit yourself."

I yank the knife from my boot and fling it at her.

It hits her square between the eyes, but does nothing, bouncing off the metal drawer with a loud and harmless clang. Pruneface's grin spreads so wide that flecks of skin peel off as she wheezes uproariously behind her fortress of safety. Good thing I didn't try to shoot her.

I stick out my tongue at her.

"Great, Kyle," I mutter. "Never bring a knife to a claw fight."

But now what? I can't stay in this vault all day...

Or is that her plan? Just keep me contained in here, whittle down the clock? How could she possibly know that?

Abrptly, Pruneface vanishes again. Pink Peacock pops around the vault doorway. He raises one eyebrow, wringing his waifish hands.

"Er, everything alright, Madame?"

My eyes dart to my knife lying on the floor corner. He clearly hasn't spotted it yet. His well-moisturized face remains terror-free.

I spring up from a crouch. "Yep, I'm stellar!"

Shooting me a dubious glare, his coifed head slides out of view. The smile drops off my face. I peer around the empty vault. No sign of Pruneface. My knife gleams on the floor. I inch toward it, keeping one eye on my Icemaker's blank screen. If she jumps out, I'm easily within her reach now. I edge forward another inch, feeling like a delicate unguarded water balloon full of blood and intestines, ready to pop.

Crouching, I slide closer. My knife is inches away from my outstretched fingertips.

Oh, screw this.

I make a decisive lunge for the knife. The instant I do, Pruneface appears, lunging at me so violently that she slurps right out of the wall and tumbles through the air over my head. And for one flickering second I see her entire body, emaciated and ghoulish, a skeleton wrapped in burnt leather jerky.

And she's a mermaid.

From the waist down, where her legs should be, is a fish tail – a spikey, scaly dry husk, striped with ribbons of tattered, translucent fins.

A freaking mermaid.

She falls through the floor like it's not even there and proceeds to swim out into the hallway, disappearing under the carpet.

"Aw, no you don't!" I snatch up my knife and sprint down the honeycomb hallway, skidding to a halt in the lobby.

A lobby that's milling with people.

Twenty souls completely oblivious to the grisly sideshow monster that's sliding like a bullet under the polished marble floor beneath their feet. I shoulder my way across the lobby at a hurried pace, just barely keeping me from looking suspicious, throwing open the double doors and dashing outside.

But she's gone again.

And...can just reiterate...*MERMAID.*

"Congrats," I mutter breathlessly. "You're officially the freakiest thing I've seen all week."

And that's saying a lot.

3 HUMBUG

Merle's Diner, lunchtime.

I allow myself sixty seconds to stand in the doorway, inhaling the familiar burnt-plastic smell of heater and grilled cheese. Clinking plates, soupy buzz of conversation. As usual, Conway Twitty is crooning "Crazy Dreams" from the candy-colored Wurlitzer jukebox in the corner. It's stuck on that song. I've never actually seen anyone put in money and choose the song, but every day, "Crazy Dreams" is playing on repeat, over and over. I guess it's fitting.

Touché, jukebox.

Over the past thirty-six days, I've gotten to know these folk. Over in the far booth – that's Old Dapper Jack, in his bath slippers and Victorian top hat. Dapper Jack is what you'd get if you turned Droopy Dog into a human and crossed him with Ray Charles, then removed a few senility marbles. He always looks so serene, gazing vacantly out the window, munching on his chicken and dumplings. I've sat with him and kept him company a few times.

Then there's the jolly businessman – the one with the donkey laugh, always raving about the rhubarb pie. His name is Phil. Pudgy, balding, and unmarried, he's just passing through Carnival Creeke on his way to Washington D.C. for some consulting pow-wow. Of all days to visit, right? The guy lives off airplane food, which is why he's fangirling over Merle's scratch-made pie. He always runs out of napkins. I usually discreetly slide him a pile of extras.

I spot Merrick and smile. Not that I have to hunt for him; he's always sitting at the counter in his gray hoodie and jeans, turkey on rye, his nose buried in a Douglas Adams book.

With his sunny green eyes and matching set of dimples, Merrick is a super cute nerd. He's a brilliant first-year biochemist, easily the smartest person in this entire town. But he's also brimming with self-doubt, the kind of guy who would never assume anyone would actually find him attractive. So I never have to worry about any cumbersome crushy feelings sprouting between us.

Merrick is safe. Predictable. He always adds up to the same thing, and that thing makes sense. I trust him explicitly. The kid will always do the right thing. Sure, sometimes he pukes – but he's got an open mind, a big brain, and a truck. Just the kind of partner I need. He's proven invaluable more times than I can count. When push comes to shove, I know he'll take the shot.

How do I know?

Because he took the shot *that night*. In the middle of the street, he aimed my Icemaker and blasted Deadhead Kyle right off her dirty little copycat feet. And although I've yet to see another appearance of "Smile-for-My-Boomstick" Merrick, I have faith.

I clear my throat and plop down beside him.

Merrick looks up with a mouthful of turkey. When he sees it's me, he chokes so hard he almost loses his glasses. He does this every day. Thank goodness I've never had to perform the Heimlich on him.

"Hey," I say.

"Hey!" Merrick gulps, straightening his glasses. "Uh, so you're still alive, huh?"

"Looks like."

It's hard not to act too casual with Merrick. But I have to stay consistent. Remind myself not to overstep any boundaries. After all, the kid only met me twenty-four hours ago.

That's what *he* thinks, anyway.

His messenger bag is open and I can see his gold name tag pin, the one he wears when he's waiting tables at Tuscany Mill. I nod down at the pin, playing clueless.

"So your name's Merrick?"

"Oh, yeah," He wipes and extends a hand awkwardly. "Merrick Cohen."

"Call me Kyle," I say like always.

He grins sheepishly. "So, how's the shoulder?"

'The Shoulder' he's referring to would be my shoulder that got dislocated when he hit me with his Chevy Tahoe. That's how we met. In fairness, it wasn't his fault. When I learned that my heart was gone, I suspected that I might be invincible and decided to test my theory by cartwheeling into oncoming traffic. My theory proved false, by the way. Painfully, embarassingly false.

I shrug, pretending to rub my long-healed shoulder.

"Eh, I'm fine. Been better, been worse."

Merle sets my root beer float and a bowl of house chili on the counter with a warm smile and a wink that crinkles the puckered scar on his beefy cheek. Then he ducks his slick black head under the orange-and-black Halloween garland, and lumbers back to the kitchen fryer. I'm glad Merle's not trying to butcher me today. He really is a decent fellow.

Merrick watches curiously as I scoop the ice cream out of my root beer float, dumping it into a bowl.

"Health nut, huh?" He grins modestly at my discarded ice cream.

"I've got a heart issue," I smile.

Took me a while before I could say *that* without snorting in my root beer. The heart thing is true, but I'm also lactose intolerant. Lucky me. Of course, I could ask for my float without the ice cream. But I never do.

"Gee, it's melting." I nudge the bowl toward Merrick. "You like vanilla?"

He looks at the bowl, then at me.

"I nearly made road hamburger out of you...and you want me to eat your ice cream?"

I shrug carelessly. "You helped me out yesterday, right?"

And a bazillion times in between.

Merrick sighs, picking up the ice cream spoon.

"Okay, fine. To your health–"

"And things that go grr in the night." I click my glass against his spoon.

As I'm leaning over my chili, I glance down into my pocket at my Icemaker for the umpteenth time. Lo and behold – a red dot has appeared on the screen.

An elated thrill runs through me.

Spinning my fork on my finger like a gunslinger, I recite my big pitch.

"Listen Merrick, I've got a proposition for you. There's stuff out there scarier than that gargoyle. Bigger. *Wilder*. And it's outside this diner right now."

Yes, we've had this conversation a hundred times. I've got this script down pat. Sometimes I'll toss in slight variations, just to see how he'll respond. It's like a game. Like those old choose-your-own-adventure books. As the clincher, I always slide my folded-up Icemaker from my pocket, just enough for him to see the red dot on the fan-shaped screen. Behind his glasses, Merrick's green eyes widen.

I don't bother hiding my smile.

"So what do you say, Merrick Cohen? Join me for one more adventure?"

I glance down at my Icemaker's screen. The red dot suddenly vanishes. It reappears again, almost immediately, but this time a few streets over. Looks like Pruneface is on the move...

We'd better move, too.

I catch my fork between my fingers and hurriedly extend my hand to him.

"If I go with you," Merrick says slowly. "Will I see another monster?"

"Monsters galore, kiddo."

He's going to say yes, of course. He always does. He can't resist. This boy must think the paranormal follows me around like fruit flies on a melon.

He isn't wrong.

"Yeah," he exhales. "Okay, I'm in!"

He's still gripping my hand mid-shake as I practically drag him out the diner door, headlong to a wild mermaid hunt.

What's next, fairies and unicorns?

Never mind, forget I said that. I don't think any amount of Alka-Seltzer could heal me from the nightmares that would follow a Carnival Creeke version of fairies or unicorns.

*

"Take a left up here."

Merrick puts on his Tahoe's blinker and obediently steers his truck back onto King Street. I'm navigating from the passenger seat, guided by my trusty Icemaker's screen. Rolling the window down, I savor the crisp breeze in my hair, inhaling the warm, buttery aroma of sourdough and rye as we pass the bakery. Diamond afternoon sun dances through the trees, casting bright dapples on the herringbone brick sidewalk. We've been chasing Pruneface all over town, but hey, I've had worse days.

Sunshine. Merrick. Red dot.

"Keep going straight," I tell him.

Practically as soon as I say those words, the red dot disappears from my screen yet again. It reappears, this time on the opposite side of town. I growl.

"U-turn again," I tell Merrick. "Sorry," I add.

"No worries," he says, pulling into a parking lot to turn around. "Monster hunting with you beats waiting tables during the lunch rush any day."

"Lousy tippers, huh?"

"Yeah, I wish." Merrick snorts. "You know after four margaritas Mrs. Grubmueller tells me her middle name and tries to grab my butt?"

"Employee of the month right here, folks." My smile drops as the red dot blinks off my screen. "Rats. She's gone again."

"No worries. So, this Pruneface thing...you said she's only able to travel through mirrors, right?"

"Reflective surfaces, anything shiny."

"Like Bloody Mary?"

"Sort of. Except she's a–" I clear my throat. "A mermaid."

About twenty different expressions cycle across Merrick's face. Finally, he shrugs and nods.

"Okay, I guess I shouldn't really be surprised by that."

That's my boy.

I tap my screen. "And I don't mean sparkly, blue-haired, seashell-bra kind of mermaid. We're talking dried-up razer-toothed Cryptkeeper kind of mermaid."

He chuckles, impressed. "You mean like the Fiji Mermaid?"

"What's that?"

"An old carnival sideshow attraction. You know, P.T. Barnum?"

"Okay." I frown, tapping impatiently at my blank screen. "So how did they defeat it?"

"They didn't." He shrugs. "I mean, it wasn't alive. Just some dried-up dead monkey with a fish tail sewn onto it. A Frankenstein hoax."

"Well, our little mermaid is very much alive out there. And it's clear she wants more than just to be part of my world."

"What are you gonna do when we find her?"

"Shoot her, probably," I say matter-of-factly. "But as long as she's camping out behind glass, I think she's protected. I threw a knife at her earlier, but it bounced right off."

"Hold up. Can we back up to where you said *'shoot?'* As in with a *gun?* Because I definitely don't carry any–"

I press the button on my Icemaker. It springs open in my hand, unfolding into the shape of a Mare's Leg Winchester shotgun.

"Ho-o-o-ly cr-a-a-a-p," Merrick exclaims, the words drawn out into a terrified laugh.

His reaction never gets old. I swear, he is my soul food.

I flip the weapon, running my hand over the sawed-off barrel. The sunlight exposes every scuff and scrape on its weathered walnut forestock.

Merrick chuckles in awe, turning back to the road.

"Seriously, Kyle. What's your story? Avenging angel sent from another dimension? Secret government agent? C'mon, be honest. You've got our town in some manila folder marked 'X', don't you?"

Slyly, I raise an eyebrow. "And if I did?"

Merrick breaks into a shy grin, waving it off.

"Yeah, I know, I know. If you told me, you'd probably have to kill–"

"WATCH OUT!"

My warning shout comes a second too late, because the skeletal brown arm that just shot out from the rear-view mirror is already slashing wildly around the car's cabin, slicing Merrick across the chest. He jerks involuntarily behind the wheel, and I feel my stomach drop as the Tahoe skids into a reckless tailspin.

Battling the centrifugal force, I attempt to point my Icemaker at Pruneface, but my seatbelt has my arms pinned down tight like a python. I fumble for the buckle; my belt finally pops free. Using the butt end of my shotgun, I bash the mirror off the windshield and fling it onto the floor, where it promptly flips over and skitters under my feet, scuttling around like some horrific giant crab, Pruneface's bony arms acting as the legs. I manage to get one good stomp on it – which would have been a victory, except that the Tahoe just crashed head-on into something – and thanks to my brilliant decision to ditch my seatbelt, there's nothing to hold me back as I'm flung forward.

My face smashes into the dashboard, and the world explodes in bright stars. I'm vaguely aware of white marshmallow airbags popping all around me in a symphony of jarring thuds. My face must have switched on the radio, because Queen's "Fat Bottomed

Girls" is now playing. The music veers in and out, weird and warbled. My brain feels thick and fuzzy, torn between needing to protect Merrick and wondering whether this song is a super perfect or super inappropriate soundtrack since we're about to be mauled to death.

But in the end I don't have to decide, because before I can even turn my heavy balloon head to look at Merrick, everything goes black.

*

I spasm myself awake. I'm screaming Merrick's name, but something over my face smothers the sound. I yank it off.

It's a sheet.

I'm lying flat on my back in a dark room, my butt freezing against a metal table.

Wait a minute. Those pineapple-ring fluorescent ceiling lights. A whiff of…is that formaldehyde?

Oh crud –

I'm in a morgue.

And I'm naked as a jaybird.

"Son of a beer-battered monkey fart!" I hiss under my breath. I roll myself and tumble gracelessly off the metal exam table. My bare feet hit the cold floor tiles, bonking my head on a bell-shaped scale suspended from the ceiling above the exam table – the type of scale presumably used for weighing cadaver kidneys, brains, and other squishy bits during autopsy.

Glad they didn't get that far with me. I'd hate to have to punch a mortician, but I will. I like to keep my entrails on the inside. Just a personal preference.

The overhead pineapple-ring lights are all shut off and the morgue is dark, the double doors casting a pair of skewed squares of light across the green-tiled floor. My swoony head tilts the room and I stumble past a tray of surgical tools.

Gripping the edge of the counter, I hastily do a self-check.

Limbs intact. A few scratches, some crusty dried blood in my nostrils (likely from my lovely dashboard face-plant), but aside from that, I don't appear to be leaking blood from any other significant wounds. There's a plastic identification band around my ankle. They've got me labeled "*Kyle, female*."

Sighing and grabbing a scalpel from the tray, I saw the band off and toss it into the trashcan.

Well, I can officially add this to my list of things I never want to do again. Can't believe I'm in the freaking morgue. But *of course* I'm in the morgue. After the truck crashed, Merrick must have checked for my pulse, so –

Merrick!

I dart drunkenly around the small room, checking all the empty exam tables and freezers. None of them say Merrick Cohen. Looks like I'm the only stiff in here – which is a good day for Carnival Creeke, as far as I'm concerned.

Now where the heck are my clothes? And how long have I been snoozing down here? My watch is gone, but there's a clock on the wall.

3:44.

Crap. Nearly three hours.

I'm not itching to spend another minute in this pickle party. I've already lost enough time. Plus, with all these metal tables, and that wall of freezers… There are reflective surfaces everywhere. If I'm not superbly careful, Pruneface could climb out of any of them and eat my soul with hot sauce. Or whatever it is she's so hell-bent on doing to me.

Grabbing the sheet off the floor, I wrap it around my naked body like a toga and shove through the double doors, staggering out into a no-frills brick hallway. Merrick is slumped in a plastic chair, his face in his hands. A clipboard of untouched paperwork sits across his lap.

He's alive. Not ripped into pieces. Relief floods through me.

I clear my throat quietly.

"Hey, kiddo."

Merrick looks up and drops the clipboard, making no attempt to grab it.

"Kyle?!" His already-wide eyes pop seeing me in nothing but a sheet. His face reddens and he spins around, continuing to talk with his back to me. "But how…h-how can you be–?"

Poor kid looks like he's seen a ghost. Which I guess is valid. Hiking my sheet up, I expel a laugh. "Yeah, funny story," I begin, but my confidence suddenly dries up in my throat. "Actually, short version. I'm fine! False alarm."

Merrick's forehead knots in bewilderment. "Kyle…you were *dead*."

"Well, clearly I'm not." Grabbing him by both shoulders, I turn him around and make him face me. Seeing the jagged rip across the chest of his gray hoodie, I frown.

"Did she hurt you?"

"Huh? Oh, no, but I might need a new shirt," he pokes distractedly at the hole. "Listen Kyle, I checked your *pulse. You didn't have one*."

"Yeah, sorry. I have really low blood pressure. Runs in my family."

He just stares at me dubiously.

I laugh again. "It's not like I'm not running around without a heart or anything!"

Because that would be so, so ludicrous.

"Hey, can you sign me out?" I take him by the arm and we start walking toward the check-in desk. Merrick robotically signs his name on the dotted line. I scrawl my initials under his, leaving a smear of dried blood on the page.

Merrick shakes his head, still dazed. "You don't understand...I thought I killed you."

"Listen to me. That accident? It wasn't your fault. We got attacked by a supernatural creature that doesn't like to give a heads-up when she jumps out of a mirror. Don't you dare beat yourself up over it. Besides, it's going to take more than a little bumper cars to finish me off." I thump myself on the chest, smiling broadly. "Still kicking. See? Promise."

Clutching my sheet-toga in one hand, I start shepherding Merrick toward the door.

This is my first time back in this hospital since my initial day in Carnival Creeke. So far, I've miraculously avoided any reason to return. It's not the hospital itself that bugs me. I'm just nervous I'll run into Doctor Fairchild again. If he spotted me, he would *definitely* remember me. You don't forget the psycho girl who held you at knifepoint with a cake slicer. Super embarrassing. Not my finest hour.

One of these days, I need to just bite the bullet and apologize to poor Doctor Mole-Face.

We stop in the hospital lobby and I use the restroom to change back into my living-person clothes and clean the crusted blood from my nose at the sink. Zipping my cargo pants, I press my forehead to the restroom door.

"Hey, Merrick?" I call through the door.

"Yeah?"

I open the door, leaning against the wall. "Did you…have to carry me in here?"

"Well, yeah." He shrugs, a shy smile crossing his face. "You weren't exactly walking."

I blush, smearing my palm down my red face.

I *hate* the idea of being carried. It makes me feel like a useless hunk of driftwood, which is why I classify being carried as "over my dead body." But I guess that's exactly what happened.

"Well…thanks." I mumble. "And sorry I wasn't awake to protect you."

"That's not exactly your responsibility. Besides, the Sea Witch didn't show up again. The car mirror broke when you stomped on it."

So Pruneface can't climb through broken mirrors?

Interesting...

Merrick eyes me worriedly the whole way out, as if still not entirely convinced I'm not a ghost. Fishing out his keys, Merrick tells me to hang tight by the curb while he pulls his Tahoe around. I roll my eyes.

"I told you, I'm not dead!"

"Yeah, I know. If you were dead, I wouldn't be offering. Look, just...stay put, okay? Stay." He raises both hands, as though motioning for a puppy to stay. Rooting myself to the curb and shoving my hands in my pockets, I shoot him a murderous glare that's way too fond to be murderous. Merrick grins, maintaining eye contact for a beat longer before sprinting off into the parking lot.

It's silly...but everything feels better when I'm with Merrick. Like a bellyful of chicken soup. It's moments like this I can't believe I ever considered doing this crazy gig by myself. I strongly suspect that Cl. Kyle had a partner.

Maybe. Wish I could remember...

Sometimes I'll catch little glimpses of Before Kyle. In the way I'll cut a burger in half to examine it first, or the practiced muscle memory whenever I handle my Icemaker. But memory of my former self is like dust in the air. Visible only when hit by sunlight at precisely the right angle, glimmering and swirling, only to disappear as soon as you reach for it.

Standing there under the hospital overhang, watching the tufts of beach grass rustle gently in the chilly breeze, I silently decide that Merrick is the only person I'll ever allow to carry me.

*

We've covered the Tahoe's side and rearview mirrors with duct tape, blacking them out. So far, the thin barrier seems to have deterred Pruneface. Maybe she can't see us.

We're still alive…

There's a significant V-shaped dent crunched into Merrick's bumper grill from our accident. At least it eclipses the me-shaped indentation on his hood, which is probably a good thing.

Pruneface hasn't dared show her face again, but that's fine with me. There's something I need to do, and unfortunately, it doesn't involve food. My too-near-death experience has me starving (and I never got to finish my chili at lunch). But for now, the snacks in my pocket will have to do.

*

I'm munching on my turkey jerky as we exit the Antique Weapon Replicas shop, a Viking battle axe in my hand.

Next to my Icemaker, this axe has become my favorite weapon for smashing wildcards. Not only will it slice and dice nearly anything into confetti, the weight of it has become a familiar old friend.

I hoist the heavy weapon, twirling it in a tight figure-eight.

Merrick eyes the axe, looking equal parts awestruck and scared of me.

"Whoa there, Painkiller Jane. You think it's the best idea to walk around town carrying a battle axe? I mean, it actually looks sharp."

I hesitate.

He's got a point, of course. I don't typically pick up this bone-crunching weapon unless it's an emergency – the kind of emergency where the wildcard has boiled over so badly that no one would look twice at a girl with a battle axe. And granted, this peaceful October afternoon doesn't exactly fit into the "crazy boiled-over" category... But today, I'm making an exception. Something about the way that smug mermaid looked at me. Like she knows me...

Plus, she hurt Merrick.

Nobody hurts my Merrick on my watch.

I shrug. "Would you rather end up fish food? Pruneface is looking to fillet us. I'd rather get the honor first."

Merrick nods. "Okay, fair enough. Just hear me out. I think I know a way that you can carry that bushwhacker around in broad daylight and not look crazy."

A slow grin spreads across his face. He opens his arms as though waiting for a drumroll.

"Halloween costumes!" he announces dramatically, gesturing like a circus ringmaster. I cross my arms and bite my lip, stifling the urge to laugh.

"Yeah, that's a big 'nope' from me."

"C'mon, Kyle! Homecoming parade is tonight. Lots of people are gonna be dressed up. You'd blend right in. Could be fun?"

"I'm not here to have fun. I'm here to kick monster tail."

"I'm sure Sheriff Gammell will respect that explanation."

Merrick: 1.

Kyle: 0.

I growl, unfolding my arms. "Fine, okay. Lead the way."

His grin is over the moon.

Since I just spent most of my cash on the axe, and Merrick is a college student who waits tables, we decide to hit the thrift shop. Racks of Halloween costumes have been rolled to the front of the store. Pretty good selection, and most of them brand new. A plastic shrunken head hanging from the door announces our entrance by launching into a shrill shrieking sound effect. Guess I'm still a bit antsy, because I swing a fist at it.

We immediately locate the mirrored dressing rooms so that we can stay as far away from them as possible. Honestly, I don't expect Pruneface to make an appearance here. I saw how she darted away when Merrick or Pink Peacock entered the room. She seems to want me, and me alone. The milling people in here might actually be protecting *me*. How's that for role reversal?

Tucked behind a black trellis stacked with purses and hats, I finger through a rack of gauzy spider web scarves.

Something is still bugging me about Pruneface. That familiar way she moved...

I can't shake this feeling that I've seen her before.

That I *know* her...

Curiously, I drape a gauzy scarf over a mannequin's face, obscuring its smooth white features. Pruneface is female. So who are the women in town?

In my head, I cycle through the possible candidates.

Timid Mrs. Moffatt? Julie Dove, the high school principal? Or maybe that old police station secretary, Gladys? No, too easy. She already looks like a freeze-dried prune.

Merrick's voice comes from the next rack.

"Okay, so you'll need a costume that looks natural carrying an axe. Harley Quinn? Xena Warrior Princess?"

I roll my eyes. "How about a refrigerator?"

"Nah. Too restrictive." There's a brief rattle of hangers. "Aha!"

He's holding a Joan of Arc costume. With its sleeveless, silver sequined "armor" and Spandex bodice, complete with a bright red velvet crusader cross, it looks like Joan of Arc if Joan of Arc were a bartender at a theme park. At first I think the lower half of the costume is missing, but apparently it's just a really short skirt.

"I still like my refrigerator idea," I mumble, grabbing the costume from Merrick and giving him the mother of all eye rolls.

*

I agree to Merrick's costume proposal on one condition:

He has to wear one, too.

He looks resplendent in his new gorilla suit. He's standing outside the Tahoe, keeping watch while I change in the backseat. He glances around awkwardly, scratching at his furry collar.

"This thing itches."

"Want to trade?" I call from the backseat where I'm wrangling my feet into my costume. I hear Merrick laugh.

"Uh, hard pass. But thanks for thinking I have the legs for it."

I grin at him through the window. He can't see me in the taped-off mirror, not that he would sneak a peek. Merrick is a sweetheart, an endangered breed of gentleman.

I swing the door open, tugging at my sequined sleeves.

"Hey, can you zip me up?"

I pull my hair aside and feel my bodice tighten as Merrick zips it. His face reddens slightly, or maybe he's just overheated in his gorilla suit.

Hopping from the Tahoe, I march out in my combat boots and do an unenthusiastic curtsy. Merrick feigns applause. I grab my jacket from the backseat and throw it on. Screw historical accuracy. I'm pretty sure Joan of Arc didn't wear sequins or a miniskirt either, but at least this getup is a free pass to carry my axe. As long as no one inspects it too closely, that is.

"Alright," I announce. "Let's go make mermaid sushi."

*

Sundown is fast approaching, and we know Pruneface will resurface. But this time, *we're* choosing the location. Somewhere that she won't be limited to one entry and exit point. Somewhere with lots of mirrors, and preferably no people to get in the way or get dead. We've chosen the perfect location.

And this time, we're not letting her escape.

The evening streetlamps have flickered on outside Bobby's Barber Shop, a flame-orange sunset reflecting off the windows.

The shop is dark, and the red and white candy-striped pole isn't rotating. A sign hangs in the window:

"Closed early for homecoming parade. Go Wolverines!"

Lucky for us, most folk still think this town is safe, and they don't bother locking their doors. We click the door open and slip inside, quiet as mice.

Without its usual crowd of wisecracking old men and papa bears, the small shop feels abnormally silent. Six black leather barber chairs sit facing six mirrors – three on the left wall, three on the right. The open space in the center of the room looks like a vacant dance floor, the air still thick with the smell of shampoo suds and spicy sandalwood aftershave.

My eyes fall on a baseball bat fastened to the wall near the front door. I lift the bat off its hooks. A blonde Rawlings, autographed by Mark McGwire. Sweet.

I flip the bat handle-side-up and pass it to Merrick, who accepts it with wide eyes and a tight, tentative nod. Outside, the distant rattling crack of snare drums and thumping tubas float into earshot. The homecoming parade is starting.

On tiptoes, we begin creeping across the creaking floor toward the mirrors. We don't get more than three steps when we hear it. Long and low, a whispering, rattling hiss, echoing from every direction around our heads. We pivot, pressed back-to-back. Over his shoulder, Merrick addresses me in a frantic whisper.

"Which mirror is she in?"

"All of them," I mutter.

"WHICH MIRROR IS SHE IN?"

As if to confirm our dread, a murky shape slithers into view, each mirror blinking dark as she swims past, from one glass frame to the next. Circling the room. Circling us like a shark. My back is still pressed against Merrick's, and I feel him starting to sweat in the thick gorilla fur. I feel bad for making him wear it, but now is hardly the time to ask him to strip. I pop open my shotgun.

"What do you want?" Merrick cries.

Pruneface looks at me. Her jagged grin spreads like black ink as she drags a clawed finger across her gristly neck.

My spine goes cold.

"Okay," I say, clamping my Icemaker's throttle. "Simple and straightforward. I like that."

I point the shotgun at her and release the throttle. A sizzling burst of blue light rockets from the weapon's double barrel, and I shoot her.

Major correction: I don't shoot her.

I shoot the mirror.

Much like my knife earlier, the blue blast bounces harmlessly off the mirror's surface. Not so harmless is the blast itself, which ricochets around the shop like a glowing pinball of death, bouncing off at least three mirrors and sending us diving hard on our bellies. It finally thunks against the far wall, toppling a coat rack, then fizzling out.

I roll over on the floor, grabbing Merrick's shoulder.

"You okay?"

He nods in an "all-things-considered" manner, shoving his glasses back on as we climb cautiously to our feet.

"Where'd she go?"

Pruneface answers that for us. With a loud wet thud, she slaps her body against the center mirror, her arms up, mimicking the teen prankster in a horror movie going for a cheap jump scare. Merrick jumps. But I refuse to scare.

"You said she can't climb out from broken glass, right?"

He looks over at me, gripping the baseball bat. My nod is resolute.

"Light her up," I snarl.

Merrick shakes his head apologetically. "Sorry, Bobby."

Taking a deep breath, he charges forward with the bat, smashing the center mirror in a shower of jagged glass. Pruneface vanishes. I spin around just in time to see her grisly visage pop up again, this time in the mirror directly behind me, her crackling brown lips peeled back in a shark-toothed grin. I swing my battle axe as hard as I can, punching clean through the mirror. My axe blade sinks into the drywall behind the frame.

I swung hard.

Too hard.

I roar, yanking to free my axe, but Pruneface has already lunged out of the next mirror, claws poised for my throat flesh.

"*Duck!*"

I let go of the axe and fling myself in a somersault, rolling backward over the nearest barber chair as Merrick's bat whistles over my head. Pruneface slurps back into the mirror half a second before it explodes in a hundred shimmering shards.

She doesn't seem fazed. In fact, she seems to find this all hilarious. Cackling uproariously, she eggs us on with slow, sarcastic claps of her bony hands, smushing her skullish face against the inside of each mirror, pretending to smear boogers. We continue like this, a haphazard un-choreographed three-body dance, punctuated by jarring crashes and tinkling of glass, until at last, only one mirror remains.

One mirror.

One chance left.

And as long as she's behind her shield of glass, it's hopeless. We need to get her *out* – where our attacks will hit flesh.

Outside, the homecoming parade blares, marching band thumping, cheers roaring. Must be passing right outside now. Decisively, I lunge for the nearest grooming station and grab an electric razor. Holding the plug end of the cord, I toss the razor to Merrick, and I shout, "Stormtrooper in the doorway!"

Acknowledging my coded nerd reference, he responds with an enthused nod. He catches the razor and we pull the cord taught between us, clotheslining Pruneface in the head, momentarily knocking her off balance. Then we skid past each other, switching sides, ensnaring the emaciated creature in the crossed cord. Her slashing claw snags the sleeve of Merrick's gorilla costume, knocking him to the floor. Pruneface wastes no time untangling herself from the cord, and I watch helplessly as she grips the mirror frame and begins scraping herself backwards, back inside.

Last mirror. Last chance…

She won't give us another.

I reel back, hoisting the battle axe and rushing toward Pruneface. She freezes momentarily in the mirror frame, and we meet each other's gaze – but I never swing.

Because that's when I see it.

There, on Pruneface's leathery chest, is a circular scar.

Just like mine.

4 DEEP DIVE

My stomach drops and my legs go numb.

Pruneface skitters backward into the mirror, like a sand crab disappearing into its hole.

Merrick rushes over to me, breathless. "What's wrong? You *had* her!"

With extreme effort, I blink my eyes into focus, gluing myself back together.

"This isn't working." My voice sounds far steadier than I feel. "Smashing glass doesn't do anything but make a mess. We need to get her *out*. In the open…in the real."

Where I can *end* her.

There's a screech of car tires outside, and the barber shop is abruptly flooded with headlights. Red and blue lights flash, followed by two quick whoops of the sheriff's siren. Merrick's head drops, his brow knotted in dismay. He turns to me.

"Listen, I know Sheriff Gammell. Let me go talk to him."

Good luck with that, I want to say. But I know Gammell, too. My best cheesy disarming smile usually works on everyone else in Carnival Creeke, but never on Gammell. I've introduced myself to him as a military consultant, a baker's apprentice, a college student. Doesn't matter. The man always seems to see through me like I'm made of cheesecloth. There's only one thing I've found that grants me a neutral pass in Gammell's book, and that's Merrick. He always vouches for me.

Merrick trudges across the trashed shop, his shoes crunching broken glass, the outline of his wooly gorilla arms raised, silhouetted against the glare of the red and blue lights.

"*Merrick?!*" Gammell's jaw drops. I see him shove his sidearm back into his holster, shaking his head. "What in Sam-hill are *you doing* here, son?"

I pause behind the doorway to eavesdrop. I'm a little curious to hear how Merrick is going to explain his way out of this. For someone who hates lying, he's surprisingly good at it. If he tried, I think he'd be the best liar in town, second to me. Not that I'm proud of that. Maybe I'm lying to everyone every single dang day. But if even I can't remember what's in my truth basket…am I still lying? I don't want to think about it.

Watching the silhouettes of Merrick and Gammell, my stomach simmers with guilt. That's twice now I've gotten Merrick into hot water. Alongside me, he's always guilty by association. But Pruneface wants *me*. Me alone…

Let's keep it that way.

"Sorry, Merrick," I whisper, ducking behind a utility sink and slipping out the back door into an alley. Walking stiffly, I cut through the parade crowd. The marching band booms and blares, but I barely hear them.

She's me. Of course. No wonder all her gestures and movements seemed so familiar…

I dip my head low as I pinball through the jostling costumed crowd. Keeping my axe low and flat against the back of my thigh, I rake my free hand through my hair. This shouldn't have my guts so rattled. After all, I've dealt with Kyle clones before. But Pruneface isn't just a clone. She's got my scar. What does that mean?

And if she's a part of me...

Which part?

Whatever. My objective remains the same. Bury my axe in her tonight before one o'clock. Or before she can bury her claws in me first. And for either of those to happen, I need to get off this crowded street.

I spot Shepper's rusty old Ford truck idling by the curb, keys in the ignition. Unmanned, it rumbles sleepily, spewing diesel exhaust into the night air. I know Shepper won't be back for a few minutes. Right about now, he's dropped a quarter down the sewer and is hell-bent on retrieving it.

Glancing back over my shoulder, I open the passenger side door and climb into the truck cabin, sliding discreetly over into the driver's seat.

"Promise I'll return it tomorrow," I mumble dryly. Cranking the old gear shift into drive, I wait for the group of costumed zombie football players to move aside, then I drive away. I don't stay on Main Street, though, quickly steering the truck down the narrow, dimly lit back streets.

I plunk my Icemaker atop the steering wheel so I can see the screen while I drive. My axe is in my right hand, keeping it just low enough to be out of view to anyone outside the truck. I've got the rear-view mirror twisted around backwards. Maybe I can't shoot my Icemaker, but if Pruneface pops out of that mirror and so much as shakes a claw at me, I'll chop her arms off.

But there's no sign of her. My Icemaker screen remains strangely blank.

I make my third pass onto Main Street, rolling past the diner. The neon sign buzzes in the window. I steer the truck up Bishop Street and roll through the residential block. Jack-o-lanterns glow from porch doorsteps. Windows flash by, illuminating various living room scenes: Flickering TVs and popcorn, family dinners in progress; mirth, and meatloaf, and mashed potatoes. I shove a turkey jerky between my teeth and glue my eyes straight ahead.

Who needs homemade meatloaf when you've got monster hunting and a cold axe?

Yeah. It doesn't sound very convincing in my head, either.

Gravel crunches under the truck tires as I pull up to the water treatment plant. I shut off the ignition, but leave the headlights for extra visibility. Leaning across the metal railing, I stare over the row of sewage treatment tanks. A ghostly mist hangs over the gleaming, glassy green water. The bright moon is reflected in three pools. Three copies of itself.

I shiver.

Having a copy of yourself isn't all it's cracked up to be. I should know.

Drawing a deep breath, I flip my Icemaker open and walk toward the platform, axe gripped tightly in my left hand. My boots thud dully on the concrete as I walk around the perimeter of the nearest tank. No sign of Pruneface.

"You want me?" My husky voice is startlingly loud in the silence. "Okay...well, here I am!"

Nothing. My screen remains blank.

Somewhere in the trees, an owl hoots.

Licking my lips, I ease closer to the edge of the pool. My eyes dart across the dark, motionless water.

"You don't want to play with me anymore? I'm insulted."

I'm getting nervous. What if she doesn't show up? She certainly isn't obligated to appear.

Looping my axe arm around the cold metal railing, I slowly lean my body out across the misty water. My reflection slides into view, distorted and murky. Water soon to be mixed with blood, not yet loosed. Her blood, or mine... Remains to be seen.

"Come on," I mutter. "It's just you and me, Fish Stick. *You and me!*"

There's a soft sloshing sound, nearly imperceptible over the chilly breeze that just rattled the trees overhead. A ripple that takes the shape of an eyeless skull face, just beneath the water's surface.

She's here.

But she's not dumb. She sees the weapons in my hands, so she doesn't dare poke so much as a finger above that water.

We remain there in our respective safety nets, each refusing to budge. A silent game of double-dog-dare, only she has nothing to lose by letting the clock tick away. And she knows it.

Beneath the water, I swear I see her grin.

A particularly chilly breeze creaks the trees above, like masts of ghost ships. Another shudder runs through me, my flimsy polyester miniskirt doing little to keep my bare legs warm. Gritting my teeth, I unzip my jacket.

"Alright, fine. Let's get this over with."

Kicking off my boots and socks, I toss my jacket in a heap while Pruneface swirls back and forth, beckoning me with two bony fingers. I hold out my Icemaker, hesitating. This space-age shotgun doesn't appear to use gunpowder, but I still don't want to risk getting it wet. I gently lay the shotgun on top of my jacket, unable to shake the feeling that I'm crawling into my grave.

It'll be blade versus blade tonight.

Shivering, I walk to the edge of the pool. Moonlight glints off the axe in my hand, my bare feet freezing on the concrete. The murky water sloshes and swirls excitedly. I hesitate.

The instant I hit that water, I'll be on *her* turf. With my limited blood supply, and without a heart to circulate, hypothermia is going to hit me faster than you can say 'Frosty the Snowgirl.' That water will be cold. *Really* cold. Likely paralyze me for a few seconds... But if I can hang onto the ledge, she won't be able to drag me under. I think I can survive this.

Eliminate Pruneface, quickly as possible. Then get back into the truck and crank the heat.

Cold water.

Murderous corpse mermaid doppelganger.

What's not to love?

I inhale a deep breath. "Bottoms up." Gripping the ledge with my free hand, I hop off.

The icy water hits me like a full-body punch, like a thousand burning needles – shockingly cold – and I feel my arms and legs go dead. It's all I can do just to keep my numb fingers clutched onto both the ledge and my axe. I anticipated this.

But so did Pruneface.

She's all over me in an instant, grabbing and slicing, a dark onslaught that I can only feel, but can't see in the inky water.

So I just shut my eyes.

I kick my legs blindly, squeezing the ledge for dear life, my literal lifeline right now. I try to swing my axe in front of me, creating a slashing shield, but the weapon suddenly weighs a ton under the water. I might as well be swinging a telephone pole in slow-motion. And it doesn't matter, because the axe just slipped out of my hand. I hear it hit the pool floor with a muted clang. I think of my knife, still tucked in my boot – my boot sitting outside the pool, several feet out of reach. Pruneface's bony hands encircle my ankles, and with dread, I feel my fingers slip off the ledge.

Down she drags me. My frozen skin aches, my lungs scream for oxygen, scarlet fireworks blossoming behind my eyelids as I struggle in vain toward the surface. Several desperate gulps lead to nothing but swallowing mouthfuls of icy water. Wave after wave of freezing froth smacks over me.

This water is just another mirror, my panicked brain reminds me. My objective remains the same. Get her *OUT*.

But right now, I need to get *myself* out…or I'm about to become an eternal surf-and-turf.

Curling down, I land three solid punches to her skull face, blindly jamming my fingers into her eye sockets until I'm able to slide free of her claw-like grip. I burst to the water's surface, gasping lungfuls of sweet freezing air, and hurriedly I swim toward the ledge. I've just hoisted my upper body from the water when white-hot pain explodes through my lower leg. I don't need to look to know she just sunk her jagged glass-teeth into my calf. Frantically, I attempt to kick her off, but she's clamped down, attached to my leg like a giant leech.

Well, when life gives you lemons…

Still clinging to the ledge, I reach down into the water, wrapping my free arm around her skinny neck, pro wrestler style. With all my strength, I heave myself up onto the ledge, dragging Pruneface out of the water with me. Frantically, I scan the area. My Icemaker, boots, and knife are on the opposite side of the pool. Of course.

Resolute, I tighten my headlock around Pruneface and start crawling toward the weapons, dragging the thrashing mermaid with me. I'm trying my darndest to ignore the searing pain in my calf, and worse, the trail of precious blood that I'm smearing behind me.

Pruneface wriggles from my grasp and I roll over, grabbing desperately at her, grabbing nothing but air.

But I'm too late.

She's dragging herself toward the pool with alarming speed, like a big Komodo Dragon, her sandpaper underbelly hissing against the concrete.

She's about five seconds from a splash into Gone Forever.

"Kyle!"

The voice rings out behind me. I twist around and squint as the headlights of Merrick's Tahoe spill over me. I can just make out his silhouette as he jumps out the driver's side, tossing something toward me.

I catch my Icemaker in my outstretched hand, swinging it immediately toward Pruneface, who has just leaped into the pool, arcing through the air toward the water.

"Get outta my world," I growl.

I don't shoot her. I lower the gun's barrel a fraction, firing instead at the water below her, the blue flash impacting at the very moment that Pruneface smacks into the surface. A pulse flashes, like a beat of blue lightning deep inside the pool. The water solidifies instantly around the wretched creature, encasing her from the waist up like a mosquito in amber, muffling the unearthly screeching that mercifully subsides within seconds. The scaly husk fin stops twitching, slumping erect in the hardened pool.

"SHE'S DRAGGING HERSELF TO THE POOL..."

Panting on the wet concrete, I slide my Icemaker screen over with two fingers, just enough to see it. The red dot turns gray.

Gray. It's over.

"Woo!" Merrick punches the air, exhilarated. "'Get outta my world' – bam! That was *awesome*, Kyle!"

He grins at the steaming iced water for a moment, his breath exhaling in rhythmic clouds. When he turns, I'm gazing up at him. His smile drops.

"What's wrong?"

"Nothing," I blink, looking away. My voice sounds hoarse. "You just...always find me."

"Yeah, well, you sure don't make it easy."

"That was intentional. Wasn't it obvious I wanted you to stay away? I could've done this by myself."

"Yeah, probably. But why should you have to?" He extends a hand, then recoils. "Um, whoa."

He must have just noticed my oozing leg.

"That looks deep. You should probably see a doc."

Ugh. Thanks to Holliday, the word "doc" hurts worse than my hamburger leg.

"Probably," I agree.

Merrick smiles crookedly. "But I bet you won't go."

"Tell him what he's won, Bob." I wince, hoisting myself off the freezing concrete. Merrick offers me his arm, but I gently swat it away. Suddenly he stops, looking back over his shoulder at the pool. His eyes widen.

"Oh, shoot... What should we do about the body?"

"Leave it."

I narrow my eyes at the murky water. Nothing will be there to find tomorrow, anyway. Once that red dot turns gray, it's no longer real. It's as good as gone. I'm fine turning my back on the murky water as we limp back to Merrick's truck. Wordlessly, he offers me his arm again. This time I take it. Hopping on my not-mangled leg, I let him bear my weight, my arm slung across his shoulders.

"Sure, I get it," Merrick chuckles, lowering his voice to an enigmatic register. "Your black helicopter posse will swoop in and make it all disappear, right?"

My laugh is paper-thin. "Something like that."

Actually, I barely get the words out. My teeth are chattering so hard. The shivers have overtaken me like a jackhammer; my entire body quavers uncontrollably.

"Oh man, you're soaked," Merrick utters, his face knotted in concern. He rubs at my arms, trying to prompt my nonexistent circulation to resume. He suddenly goes motionless, presumably realizing he now has both arms wrapped around me. We both hold very still. His chest feels hot against my cheek, or maybe it's the strange flush that's filling the capillaries in my face.

Merrick hastily steps back. "Hold on. Here." He pulls off his hoodie and helps me fumble it over my head before we resume limping toward his Tahoe.

"And hey," Merrick says brightly. "At least you didn't have to sell your voice to an evil sea witch. You *poor unfortunate sooouuul!*"

I've always said his singing voice is way too good for a biochem student.

"Hey maestro," I grumble. "I don't think you've woken up the whole town yet. Want to sing a little louder?"

He obliges. I risk falling to poke him in the ear. He brushes me off and sings louder, watching me from the corner of his eye until I crack a smile.

"You want me to toss you into that pool, boy?"

"And smell like you? Nah." He grins. "Besides, I'm pretty sure I could outrun you right now."

I sigh. "Well, if we're looking for a bright side, at least we didn't die today while listening to Fat Bottomed Girls."

"Right?"

I look at Merrick. He looks at me, and we burst into unhinged, exhausted laughter. We laugh so hard we almost trip and fall. We laugh because it's the best way to deal with this flavor of crazy.

You have to laugh.

Merrick opens the passenger side door of his Tahoe, helping me climb up into the cab. I flump myself onto the seat. I'm shivering so hard my teeth rattle in my skull. Merrick cranks the heat, and within moments the cabin fills with that cozy, familiar burnt-plastic smell. Soul food to my nose; hot cocoa leather under my frozen butt cheeks. Ugh. Merrick is right, I stink like a sewer. And I'm bleeding all over his upholstery. I feel kind of bad.

Gingerly, I lean over and inspect my leg. A jagged, moon-shaped bite mark is oozing red down my calf. Looks like I got attacked by a lawnmower.

"It's not that bad," I lie, quickly pressing my leather jacket over the wound. Merrick shoots me a dubious look, but I don't have the energy to put up a song and dance tonight. All I want tonight is a gray dot, a face-meltingly hot bath, and my dry, warm bed.

One out of three ain't bad at all.

Merrick drapes the gorilla suit over my shoulders, and I finally stop shivering. Now I'm actually glad I made him buy that silly costume after all.

He hands me a granola bar.

"Hey, um." Merrick's tone grows serious. "Back at the pool... You said 'always.' I always find you." He's gazing at me curiously. "What did you mean?"

I sink my teeth into the granola bar. Oatmeal raisin.

*

Merrick parks the Tahoe in front of the Red Rooster. I get out and head for the door.

"Hey – Kyle!"

I turn. He smiles shyly. "You gonna be around town tomorrow?"

A hollow smile crosses my face, cracking the caked blood and grime. "Honey, I'm always here tomorrow."

*

Within minutes I've shed my soggy wet Joan of Arc costume, checked off a steamy soak in the claw-footed bathtub, and finished stitching up my calf. Now, splayed out on my bed, I've finished documenting today's entry in my pink kitten notebook.

It's written entirely in my special shorthand code, of course. Purely to annoy Holliday.

On my old record player, Ella Fitzgerald and Louis Armstrong are crooning a swoony duet of "They Can't Take That Away from Me." He's growling in his signature Kermit the Frog baritone, seductively recounting the miniscule memories of her that he's been stubbornly clinging to. Reminiscing about the way she sang off-key, changed his life, and how she held her dinner knife.

Reaching over, I grab my little utility blade and start absently flipping it in my hand.

I can't shake that image of Pruneface and her circular scar. Maybe she's some alternate future version of me. A "corpse me," the version of me that dies alone, heartless, angry, and...

A mermaid?

Okay, so maybe the wildcard oven just spit that little golden plum at me for bonus giggles.

Sighing hotly, I fling my knife across the room. The blade impales the wall, sticking there. Oops. Rolling off the bed, I wrench the knife from the drywall and run my fingers over the shredded paisley wallpaper. I feel like I should apologize to Mrs. Moffatt for putting a hole in the wall, but I decide to spare her. Anyway, that hole won't be there tomorrow. Just like the mummified mermaid corpse we left behind.

Gone. Wiped. Reset.

Just like everything.

Just like always.

Wow. You know what? It's getting harder to keep telling myself that I'm okay with this.

DAY 37: HENTOWN

It's quiet in this corner of the library. Well, quiet except for the preschool class singing "Hickory, Dickory, Doc" on the other side of the bookshelves. But I can barely hear them. I'm curled up in the glow of a computer station, completely absorbed in my gray time notes.

Gray time. That's what I call the restless waiting period when today's wildcard hasn't appeared yet. The quiet before the storm. I've used my gray time for a variety of extracurricular activities. Mostly prepping. Grab provisions from the General Store (knife, earplugs, floss…you know, the usual). Explore the sewer tunnels under town. Memorize the electrical grid. Do some spying, learn who keeps weapons in their homes; low-hanging fruit that I could grab in a full-sprint emergency.

But lately, I've started coming to this library every chance I get. Devoting all my gray time to solving the greatest mystery of all: Who I am, and why I'm here in Carnival Creeke.

Chewing my lip, I pick up my pencil and slowly write Holliday's last words to me on the paper.

Good luck, Doc. I'm bankin' on ye!

Maybe he'll literally win money if I don't croak?

Or am I stuck here in this 'game' for another reason?

When Holliday told me I had to find a way to stop time from skipping in Carnival Creeke, I detected an inkling of urgency in his twitchy, nonchalant voice. Like he *needs* me to do it…

I've got a new theory.

This *isn't* a game.

What if Holliday stuck me here in Carnival Creeke with another purpose in mind? Likely took my heart as morbid insurance, to pin me down, make dang sure I'd be a good girl and cooperate in whatever experiment or twisted test he's pulling the strings on. The wildcards…somehow, I suspect it's all secondary. I think there's something bigger beneath this picture, beneath this town. I just can't quite zoom out far enough to see it yet.

I've been digging for clues. Diving into the town's public records, searching for any shred of a tattered string that might connect back to the name 'C. Kyle'…or Rascal Holliday. A great-great-grandfather. Dental records. An overdue library book.

Something…stars almighty, *anything*.

I've even studied the topography, read who owned this land in the 1800s. But there's nothing about me. And there's no trace of Holliday, of course. As if he'd leave any.

He's a freaking ghost in a morgue of text.

I cross my foot over my knee, jabbing my pencil into the sole of my boot.

Oh, he's a tricky one, that Holliday. And maybe I haven't found any dirt on him, but I feel like I know him all the same.

Rascal Holliday has become the clearest and most ambient detail in my brain each night. His quiet, feathery Irish brogue is always the last thing I hear each night. Sometimes I imagine what I would do to him. The mighty whooping I would unleash on him. The things I'd say, those well-worn lines, rehearsed so many times in the safety of my dark room at the Red Rooster, polishing my script to a fine edge. I feel so ready, I'll actually find myself begging for him to show up. Right now. *Face me.*

Of course, he never does.

Then, inevitably, my confidence starts deflating and I'll just flop around on my mattress, punching my comfy pillow and cursing Holliday's gall for standing me up again.

I hate the guy.

I hate him so hard, I swear some nights I've almost managed to burn him into existence in my room, in those fading moments before I fall asleep. I'm so used to hating him, it's like a familiar old glove. It's part of my bedtime routine.

Calisthenics. Brush teeth. Hate Rascal Holliday.

So it's surprising when I discover little slivers of him creeping into my everyday life. Nibbling away at my sanity like a cookie. Just like the rat he is.

Nibble, nibble...

I've even started tying my boots like him. A reef knot, commonly used in sailing and surgery. It's more efficient anyway, Holliday's knot...as much as it irks me to admit it.

Yeah. Safe to say I'm a tad obsessed.

Overhead, the library clock tower strikes the hour with a deep, muffled clang.

Noon.

I glance down at my Icemaker. It's lunchtime, and the stupid screen is still clear and blank and frustratingly free of red dots. But sometimes that's just how it goes. Sometimes it can take hours for the wildcard to show up. You'd think this would be nice, like a mini vacation, but it's not. My stomach gets all twisty churny when the wildcard keeps me waiting. The later the wildcard appears, the more likely I'll find myself scrambling against the clock. Guzzle now so you don't have to sip later, that's my philosophy.

But who asked me?

Stuffing my scrawled notes into the pocket of my cargo pants, I erase my search history with a few keystrokes then unplug the computer.

Time to go recruit my partner.

*

Sometimes it's hard starting from square one each day with Merrick. By now, we should be best friends. Have our own little secret treehouse code language. But it doesn't matter how many tough scrapes we pull through together, or how often we bond crawling through monster guts. The day resets, and – bam! It always reverts back to that morning-after blush; that shy "now what" between two people who only experienced their first taste of thrill the night before. We should be seasoned veterans, but we never will be. We're perpetual honeymooners.

I mosey my way across the diner and take my place on the stool beside Merrick. When he sees me and chokes, I'm ready with a thump on his back.

"Hey there," I smile.

"Um, hey!" Merrick readjusts his glasses. He stares at me for a moment longer than usual. Probably because of the back-patting. I'm not usually this touchy-feelie right off the bat.

"So you're still alive," he remarks, raising an eyebrow.

"Yep! Still kicking."

"That's funny. Because when you ran after that gargoyle last night and never came back, I figured you were toast. What else was I supposed to think? You didn't call."

His smile fades. He's gazing at the sandwich in his hands. "But why would you? I mean, it's not like we were on a date or anything. Way to show a girl a good time, right?"

I blink.

He's never said that before.

A look of appall washes over Merrick's face. He goes beet-red. "Oh man, I am so, *so* sorry, Kyle. That, um…that came out totally wrong."

Yeah, no kidding. Very un-Merrick-like. He's never grumpy. If I didn't know better, I'd say Merrick woke up on the wrong side of his customarily good-natured bed. But I *do* know better.

I slide my folded-up Icemaker from my pocket just enough to get a peek at the screen.

Sure enough – a red dot.

Ha! I knew it. Merrick's been whammied.

So, am I looking at some kind of Jekyll and Hyde wildcard?

This could be fun…

A hand plunks my root beer float onto the counter. I look up. Instead of tall lumberjack Merle, a short, squat teapot of a woman stands behind the counter. Her thinning black and silver-streaked hair is jutting up through her hairnet in unruly angles. Her nametag says Margie.

Hello, Margie.

Nice to meet you, Margie.

You're not supposed to be here, Margie.

I narrow my eyes at her. My defenses prick on alert. Any moment now, she'll probably lunge over the counter and try to rip out my throat and fling it into the deep fryer. But we're surrounded by people. I need to avoid bloodshed as long as possible.

"Excuse me," I say to Margie Who Isn't Supposed to Be Here. "Is Merle on vacation or something?"

Margie looks at me with sagging eyes. "Beats me," she shrugs. "He just said he's takin' a sick day." She scoops a handful of empty plates from the counter, then waddles laboriously back to the kitchen.

"Wow," Merrick remarks through a mouthful of sandwich. "Merle's sick? That guy's never missed a day."

Yeah. Never.

"Excuse me!" I hop off my stool, grabbing a laminated menu from the napkin tin and waving it around until I snag Margie's attention again. "Do you happen to know where Merle lives? I want to...bring him a get-well card."

Margie sighs and shrugs, radiating all the sunshine of a deep-sea sponge. "No clue, hon."

Merrick is watching me with a bemused smile.

"A get-well card? I never knew you and Merle were so close."

"Oh," I shrug. "Yeah, well, he's my uncle."

Yikes. *That* lie is probably going to circle back and bite me.

I blink. "I never mentioned he's my uncle?"

"No," Merrick says. "But between bouncing off my car bumper and heroically chasing down a live gargoyle, it probably wasn't really info worth mentioning."

He takes another bite of his sandwich, chewing slowly.

"I..." He stops chewing. The sandwich drops on his plate. "I-I think I'm gonna throw up."

He bolts to the restroom so fast that I have to catch his stool with my toe to keep it from tipping over.

I jerk my head down to my Icemaker. The screen looks like it has chicken pox. Red dots, faint at first, popping up in a cluster. And continuing to multiply.

I slide my eyes around the diner. Now that I think about it, Jolly Phil has been uncharacteristically quiet on his stool beside me. He's busy chowing down on his fourth slice of pie. Usually, he stops at three. And Old Dapper Jack appears to have fallen asleep face-down in his dumplings.

Something is making these people sick.

Leaning close to Merrick's abandoned plate, I peer at his half-eaten sandwich. Looks innocent enough...

Wrapping my hand with a protective wad of napkins, I use a fork to slide off the top slice of bread. Turkey, mustard, tomato. The yummy, non-evil kind. No teeth, no alien worms. Nothing visibly out of the ordinary. I briefly consider Margie, poisoning all the hungry patrons in a fit of bitterness at having to work today. But then I watch her shuffle wearily from the kitchen, balancing six bowls of soup on her doughy arms, her drooping eyes laden with more bags than an airport luggage rack. A quick glimpse through the circular window on the silver swinging kitchen door reveals a near-empty kitchen. Looks like all the cook staff called out sick today, too. So I assume Margie is having to shoulder the burden of cooking all the food, as well as serving all the tables.

Guilt seeps through my stomach. Margie's not the villain.

She just really needs a nap.

No, whatever is making people sick must be coming from a different source.

After shouldering into the ladies' room and scrubbing my hands no less than five times (go ahead, call me paranoid; I'm just as susceptible to wildcard infections as the next guy), I frown at my Icemaker screen, which is now peppered with red dots.

Merrick finally emerges from the men's room, his face drained of all color. He blushingly explains that he's sick and needs to go home. I don't try and stop him.

*

I stalk down the sidewalk, hands in my pockets, Merrick's Douglas Adams book under my arm. He left the diner in such a hurry, guess he forgot it. Narrowing my eyes, I scan the surrounding area like a weirdness-seeking robot. Those velour-clad lovebirds aren't jogging today. Instead, both are parked on a bench, the wife laying a hand across her husband's forehead and clucking words of concern. Over at the library, the construction workers have abandoned their hammering and come down from the scaffolding, now reclining in the cemetery, looking like they just ran a marathon. A quick peek into the Auto Parts Shop window reveals Hank, slumped at his workstation. He uses his porkpie hat to mop his dark Jamaican face, popping two aspirin with a gulp of water.

Seeing the pattern, here?

Men. Only *men*...

So I'm dealing with a rampant wildcard virus – one that apparently favors males. I could really use some of Merrick's biochem expertise right about now. I don't want to bug him. But then again, I *do* have his book. And there's a payphone at the General Store.

On the plus side, at least I won't need my axe today.

Let's hope.

Cowbells clatter against the glass door as I enter the General Store. Sam is behind the cashier counter screwing lids onto jars of pickled eggs. He doesn't *look* sick...but the red dot on my screen tells a different story.

Sam straightens behind the counter, beaming at me with his customary grin of sunny Southern hospitality.

"Well, hello again, my dear! Forgot something on your list? Though I must say, you plumb cleaned me out of floss and medical tape earlier today. You into crafts?"

"Something like that."

"Oh!" He pipes brightly. "I forgot to ask you this morning! So...do we have a bun in the oven?"

He did forget to ask. He *always* asks. I noticed, but I chalked it up to the fuzzy brain of a middle-aged man with a freaky wildcard virus. If anything, I was grateful to not be bombarded with that embarrassing question today.

"Oh, mercy!" Sam pauses, gazing up at the ceiling with a dreamy smile. "I remember those baby days. Seems like only yesterday our Ellie was marchin' off to her first day of preschool." His hazel eyes mist over. "Askin' Julie to put her hair in pigtails. 'Gigtails,' she called 'em. Gigtails! How darling is that? Now she's all grown up, savin' the world over in Africa..."

He pulls out a handkerchief and honks loudly into it, causing it to flap around like a flag. Sighing wistfully, he continues to dab his creased eyes while I stare at him, flabbergasted.

First Merrick. Now Sam, going off-script, acting like a crazy bucket of emotions.

Bun in the oven...

And suddenly, all the pieces click into place. Realization tumbles over me like hot pudding dumped on my head.

Something is affecting these men, alright – but not a virus. It's something weirder. Something much more Carnival Creeke-ish.

"Can I use your phone?" I ask hurriedly.

"Be my guest!" Smiling, he sniffles and flaps the soggy handkerchief toward the back of the store. "It's in the back."

Stuffing the handkerchief back in his pocket, he resumes his lid-screwing, whistling a tune.

The pay phone is on the wall between the restrooms and the Styrofoam coolers that I stashed the frozen remnants of Mrs. Grubmueller's dog inside on Ice Day. I pick up the phone's receiver and stand there for a moment, twisting the metal cord. I really hate to bother Merrick. He looked pretty sick when he left the diner. Then again, I know Merrick, and I know he can't resist a mystery...

Plus, I have his book.

I shove a couple of quarters into the pay phone's slot and punch Merrick's number. I know it by heart.

He picks up after a few rings.

"Hello?"

Poor kid sounds gutted.

"Hey, Merrick. It's Kyle."

"Kyle? Hi!"

"I got your number from the phone book. How are you feeling?"

"Ugh. Been better, been worse."

He's quoting me. Cute.

"You left your book at the diner. But that's not the only reason I called you. Are you sitting down right now?"

"Uh, sort of. I'm on the bathroom floor hugging a toilet. Why?"

"I think I figured out what's wrong with you."

"Oh no. We're dying, aren't we?"

"Relax, you're not dying." I lick my lips, preparing my next words. I take a deep breath.

"I think you're pregnant."

6 COCOON

I tell Merrick to meet me at the General Store in ten minutes.

He's there in five.

I hear cowbells clatter as the door opens. I quickly straighten, a pink pregnancy test box in my hands.

Hoo-boy. He's going to hate this.

Box tucked behind my back, I step out from the aisle and immediately do a double take at him.

Merrick doesn't look sick. Actually, he looks great. Dare I say, glowing. Backlit against the glass door, he's haloed in gold; his skin looks flawless, his eyes greener than usual, his posture taller and broad-shouldered. I'm actually a little surprised I never noticed before.

When he sees me, he raises two fingers, his mouth open like he's about to say something. I give him a second.

"Okay," he begins. "If this town wasn't just pulverized by a living gargoyle yesterday, I would seriously be questioning either your sanity or my choice in acquaintances."

I nod. "I'd expect nothing less." Drawing a deep breath, I produce the pregnancy test box from behind my back. I hold it out to him.

"Here. I need you to…take the test."

Merrick takes the pink box from me, flipping it over. "Are you kidding me right now?"

"You need to pee on the stick."

"But these things measure HCG hormone levels. Which I don't have…because I'm a ***GUY***."

"Just humor me. Okay?"

He scowls at me, shutting the restroom door. The wooden heart-shaped sign swings on its string. *"How long a minute is depends on which side of the bathroom you're on."*

I tap the sign with my finger, swinging it like a pendulum.

It's awfully quiet in there…

"How's it going?" I ask after a minute.

"I can't go," comes his answer behind the door.

"You need me to bring you some water?"

"No… I can't *go*. Not with you standing right outside the door like that. It's giving me performance anxiety."

I try to suppress a smile.

"Right, okay, sorry." I mosey over to the magazine rack and call out, "Okay, Mozart, I'm out of earshot. Perform away."

"Your micro-aggression isn't helping!"

Ten minutes later, we're standing shoulder-to-shoulder, staring anxiously at the test stick. More specifically, at the crisp pink line displayed in the result window. I raise my eyebrows.

"Congratulations. You're pregnant."

"Okay…okay." Merrick paces back and forth, grabbing his hair with both hands. "Deep breath. This is fine. Male seahorses have babies. Seahorses are adorable. Did you know baby

seahorses are called fries? Not the kind of fries you eat–" He breaks into maniacal laughter. "*Who would eat a baby seahorse?*"

Uh-oh. His panic has kicked him into turbo-trivia mode.

Merrick reels himself in, taking a deep breath.

"Well, that explains how I could spend the last hour puking and still feel like I ate a humpback whale." He lays a hand on his stomach, shaking his head. "This shouldn't be possible."

"Pretty much Carnival Creeke's slogan," I smirk.

"No, I mean–" Merrick's face blanches. He opens his mouth, then shuts it again, clearly weighing what he's about to tell me.

"Um…there's something I need to show you, Kyle."

I have to jog to follow him around back by the soda fridges. I put my hands in my pockets, giving him a reassuring nod.

"Okay, Merrick. Let's see it."

He presses both hands together like he's praying. He seriously looks like he's about to pass out or puke again.

"Alright." He blows out a breath, and lifts up both his hoodie and shirt.

My eyes widen.

Merrick's typically flat stomach is visibly swollen. The bulge beneath his skin suggests that whatever is cozily gestating inside him right now is roughly the size of a softball. Still holding up his shirt, Merrick looks at me with a pleading expression.

"It wasn't like that when I left the diner!"

"Wow. This thing's growing like a weed," I remark.

"Yeah, a radioactive weed," Merrick groans, ripping into another granola bar.

Of course this thing is growing in fast-forward. With a deadline of one o'clock…

"I don't know if this will make you feel better or worse, but…" I slide out my Icemaker, showing him the two red dots on the screen. "It's not just you."

"Wait. *Sam* is…*pregnant, too?!*"

We look up. Sam is still over there behind the counter, blubbering to himself about his daughter and her gigtails. Merrick raises his eyebrows in mild amusement.

"Actually, now that you mention it..." He looks at me. "So, I'm assuming you've seen this kind of thing before in your X-files?"

I don't answer.

"Hoping?" he says.

I just look at him.

"Uh." I cringe apologetically. The color drains from his face.

"Seriously, what *do* you know about all this?" He presses in a hissed whisper. "We're government guinea pigs, right? Black helicopters, alien tests?"

"I'm as clueless as you, kiddo."

Turning wearily, he grabs a bag of chips off the rack, followed by one of each flavor granola bar. I follow behind him, trying to think of something reassuring to say.

"Okay, listen, I know this probably wasn't what you woke up today expecting to do–"

"Oh, you think?" he retorts.

I'm trying to stifle a smile. Merrick shifts his armload of snacks, using his free hand to grab a jar of peanut butter, then an apple from the basket by the checkout register. He spills everything onto the counter.

Sam whistles in awe, scanning the pile.

"Wowzers. Running a marathon, Merrick?"

Merrick rolls his eyes. "I wish." Then turning his head as though embarrassed, he waves his hand vaguely at the jar of pickled eggs. "Also…one of those, too."

Sam scoops an egg out of the briny soup. He hands it to Merrick, who devours it in one bite.

"I always thought these things were gross," he remarks thoughtfully.

Cowbells rattle and the door swings open. Randy and his band of teenage cronies saunter in, all swagger and rock star cologne body spray. I narrow my eyes at them.

I wonder…

"Hey," I step in front of them, blocking their path into the store. "Have you guys noticed anything…strange today? How are you feeling?"

For a second, they just stare at me through shaggy bangs, wearing glazed expressions. Their eyes dart at each other like a bunch of mice when the kitchen light turns on. Randy breaks into a sheepish grin, his shoulders bouncing in a nervous "*huh-huh-huh*" giggle.

"Ugh, never mind." I rub my eyes, waving them away with one hand. "Run along."

They skitter off into the aisles, howling like hyenas.

I should've known better. Those goofballs are probably still hungover from their UFO-watching party last night in Tannon's field. Sure as heck wouldn't recognize any pregnancy symptoms, even if they had any.

Behind me, Merrick pockets his change from the three more pickled eggs he just bought, popping the eggs one after another into his mouth with his free hand. I spot a roll of plastic trashcan bags sitting on the cashier counter. I tear off a bag and shake it open, holding the puke receptacle out to him preemptively. Merrick shakes his head, and I close the bag. He finishes chewing and swallows, pressing his fingers to his temples.

"Ugh. I think I should go check myself into the hospital."

The hospital.

I'm hardly jumping for joy to reenter that place, but I'm sure not letting Merrick out of my sight. He's my golden ticket to the wildcard, considering he's literally carrying one inside him. I don't know how these wildcard babies work. Tick-tocking away inside these people... But I don't know *how* they tick, and until I do, I'm sticking to Merrick like glue. Plus, I can't stand the thought of leaving him alone in this condition. Merrick is special. He's my responsibility. I guess I've developed a bit of a pathological need to look out for him.

"Good idea," I nod, heading toward the door. "I'll go with you."

Merrick waves me off. "That's okay, thanks. I don't want to drag you into all this. It's already weird enough with–"

Suddenly his face goes green. He freezes, his arm leaning against the door. I've already whipped open the plastic bag with time to spare as a fountain of vomit explodes from his mouth, the four pickled eggs making their unfortunate reappearance.

I wince sympathetically.

"Lord almighty, son!" Sam's voice exclaims from the counter. "Looks like somebody needs 'em some pajammers and chicken soup!" Voice cracking, he adds, "And grape soda. Oh, that always fixed Ellie right up. Whenever she was sick..." He dissolves into another fit of tears, spraying sloppy nostalgia into his handkerchief.

Merrick wipes his mouth with the back of his hand, shakily adjusting his glasses. "Ugh. Well, that was super embarrassing."

I jerk my head at the door with a sly smile. "Tell me you don't need me now, boy."

Merrick's shoulders sag in reluctant compliance.

"Okay fine," he mumbles. "Point made. Be my copilot, Supergirl."

We shoulder out the door into the warm sun, Sam calling out behind us, "Take care of him, young lady!"

I shoot him a zealous thumbs-up.

Probably see you later too, Sam.

We buckle into Merrick's Tahoe. As I hook the plastic bag over the plastic cup holder, I catch Merrick stealing a shy, sidelong smile at me.

He nods down at the bag. "You have crazy good reflexes, you know that?"

"I play a lot of whiffle ball."

"Clearly." Merrick chuckles. His gaze holds me, curiously, for just a moment longer than necessary. He must have realized it, because he quickly glues his eyes straight ahead over the steering wheel. "But I mean it. Thanks for coming with me, Kyle."

"Anytime, Merrick Cohen."

He doesn't know how deeply *I* mean that.

I lace both hands behind my head. "Besides, now you'll have someone to share the thrill of finding out if it's a boy or a girl."

"Ha-ha," Merrick rolls his eyes. "Anyway, I'll feel a lot better once I know more from a medical standpoint. Well, maybe 'better' isn't the right word..." Keeping one hand on the steering wheel, he gestures toward his stomach. "I mean, when I imagined having kids, this wasn't exactly the way I pictured it."

I regard him for a moment, watching the sun shine through his hair.

"You've thought about it?" I ask. "Having kids?"

"Well, yeah." He scratches the back of his head, suddenly bashful. "I mean, preferably not like *this*... But someday. Yeah. Definitely."

I gaze at Merrick, trying to picture him as a daddy.

He leans one elbow out the window, continuing.

"Carnival Creeke is even smaller than my hometown back in Idaho. But every time I come here to help my grandma, I notice things. Like the air is different. Sweeter...slower. Got me thinking, you know? This could be a great place to raise a family." He shrugs, tossing me a careless smile. "Could be home."

Something stirs inside me.

Merrick chuckles wryly. "Of course, I'm beginning to re-think this being a great town. Gargoyles coming to life, and now mass male pregnancies... Not exactly on the list of family-friendly activities."

I shrug, grinning. "Aw, I don't know. Depends what kind of kids you want to raise."

Merrick flashes a dimpled grin. "Gargoyle-slaying kids, eh? Does that pass as normal on your planet?"

We pull up to the stoplight, our attention drawn to a tall, muscular figure strolling along the curb. I immediately recognize Captain Epic. Surveying the passing cars through his wraparound sunglasses, he runs a hand through his beach-blonde hair, his pregnant belly on proud display underneath his t-shirt bearing the phrase, "There's no 'hood like fatherhood." He's carrying a stack of bright blue flyers under one arm.

Catching sight of the Tahoe, Epic breaks into a cool megawatt grin and saunters over. He leans into Merrick's open window.

"Howdy-howdy, bro! You guys coming to the big shindig tonight?"

He thrusts a flyer in front of our faces. We blink at it.

TOWN HALL MEETING

Carnival Creeke High School, 3:00 PM

Discussion and Q&A on the male pregnancy event.

Light refreshments will be served.

"Epic stuff, am I right?" Captain Epic jostles Merrick by the shoulder, interpreting his silence as enthusiasm. "Hey Merrick, your skin looks great, by the way. I noticed the same with mine. At first, I thought it was just the activated charcoal I've been taking. But turns out I have this little guy to thank!"

He pats his belly affectionately, continuing. "I've always wanted to be a dad. Have a few rugrats – nothing crazy, maybe just five or six. Share the genetic wealth, y'know?"

Merrick looks like he's getting ready to say something he'll regret, so I quickly reach across him and grab the flyer from Epic through the window.

"We are so happy for you!" I flash a mozzarella grin, waving the flyer. "And thanks for this. We'll check it out."

As soon as the light turns green and we round the corner, Merrick crumples the flyer and tosses it into the backseat.

"Yeah, nope. Pass."

I catch the paper in midair, uncrumpling it. "Could be helpful," I say.

"Helpful? It'll likely be a bunch of hormonal, uninformed shouting and general XY chromosomal chest-beating."

I gaze at the crumpled flyer in my hands. A collection of every wildcard in town, neatly assembled in one room… That's as close to a jackpot as I'll get.

"There'll be refreshments," I coax slyly.

"I don't need refreshments. Refreshments equal barfing."

But there's another flyer taped to the hospital's glass doors, with written instructions for everyone who's male, pregnant, and not actively bleeding or dying to please turn around and go attend the Town Hall. And since Merrick is all of the above, that's where we go.

*

We're early, but there are already quite a few cars in the parking lot when we arrive at the high school. Merrick unbuckles his seatbelt and I can't help but notice the bulge under his hoodie, which now appears to be the size of a medium pumpkin.

This thing inside him...it's growing like a marshmallow in a microwave.

"Feels like I'm smuggling a bowling ball," Merrick mutters in my ear as we cross the parking lot. I offer to carry him piggyback, but he doesn't see the humor in it.

The school's entrance double doors have been propped open. Across the lobby, a banner is stretched over the trophy display case reading, *"Welcome, new parents!"* Below it, a long table has been covered with a cloth, set with trays of pink and blue cupcakes adorned with adorable iced baby faces and candy pacifiers. I've always said, when Carnival Creeke does a thing, they do it with all their hearts.

Gladys, the Sheriff's old harpy of a secretary, stands behind the table, meticulously arranging carafes of ice water, coffee, and hot cider. We start across the lobby and Gladys looks up. She surveys us with a puckered scowl, her narrowed eyes oozing disapproval.

"You're *early*," she clucks. "The town hall meeting starts at three." Indignant, she flutters her eyes from us to the clock on the

wall. She repeats the action until we also turn and look at the clock, ensuring that we see the gravity of our offense.

"Yeah, sorry," I smile broadly, grabbing Merrick's arm. "My friend just needs to use the restroom. Because...well, you know."

I point at his pumpkin belly. We each grab a cupcake and slide around the corner, escaping Gladys' death glare.

"Um, not that I don't appreciate the advocacy," Merrick comments through a mouthful of cupcake. "But didn't we just pass the restrooms back there?"

"Yep." I nod firmly. "Wait, do you actually need to go?"

"Not really. But you look like you've got an idea."

"Bingo. We may not have an x-ray machine, but I think I know how we can get a peek at what's inside you."

I glance up the hall, handing him my cupcake. As adorably delicious as they look, the sugar would probably land my heartless body in a coma. Not helpful.

"You grew up in Idaho, right? Ever held an egg up to a light to see the chick inside?"

Merrick shrugs. "Uh, I grew up in a highly air-conditioned townhouse. But I follow the concept you're getting at. So, now we just need a really bright light."

A floodlight from the football field would work, but I'm not sure how to even begin sneaking Merrick up onto a goal post.

We stop at an intersecting hallway, deliberating. One direction is dark, the other a brightly lit hallway lined with orange lockers. A muffled buzz of voices and the clattering and scraping of metal chairs being set up drifts from the direction of the cafeteria.

"Science lab," Merrick says suddenly, popping my cupcake into his mouth. "This way."

I cock my head, smirking as I follow him down the dark hallway. I've rarely seen him in such assertive form.

"Hey Merrick, you know your pregnancy swagger is kinda hot?"

"So say we all," he says through a mouthful of cupcake, his ears growing red.

We flip on the lights in the science lab. Desks are arranged in a large square around the room. A row of computer workstations are set up along one wall, shelves packed with flasks and Bunsen burners. Colorful Styrofoam planets hang from the light fixtures. Merrick peers doubtfully into a drawer under a poster of the Periodic table.

"Not exactly cutting-edge equipment," he remarks.

We find an old video projector on top of a metal cabinet. Placing it on a desk, I press the button. The machine whirs to life, shining a dusty beam of light across the room. A four-foot-tall video of a human heart appears on the opposite wall, its lacy ventricles squeezing and contracting rhythmically.

A heart.

Of course it would be a *heart.*

If I didn't know better, I'd swear that creep Holliday somehow snuck in here and preemptively set this up just for me.

I grit my teeth, shaking off the heebie-jeebies and replacing it with a confident thumbs-up toward Merrick, signaling that we're ready.

"Okay, let's see what's cooking in there."

I point the projector toward Merrick and he dutifully angles himself sideways, so the beam shines directly on his belly. He stands there for a moment, preparing to lift up his hoodie. On the wall behind him, the film of the giant heart pumps and squishes, its distorted image swimming over Merrick's body.

But he looks anything but eager. He actually looks a little green.

"Um. I'm thinking maybe this isn't such a great idea..."

I pat his shoulder reassuringly. "As a scientist, then. Ready?"

"Ready or not..." He exhales through puffed cheeks. Then he lifts both his hoodie and his shirt.

Sometimes, you just know what to expect. You play this game this long, you become accustomed to certain surprises.

That's why I don't scream when I see the thing in Merrick's belly.

The long, thin, ropy body is about the width of my finger, and rolled into a tight, serpentine coil. It appears as a silhouetted shadow, surrounded by a warm, pink glow, laced with a network of blood vessels. In response to the light, the thing squirms, unfolding a spiral fan of legs – shrimp-like or insectoid, I can't quite tell – because that's when Merrick staggers backward out of the beam of light, colliding with a desk. I catch his airborne glasses.

"IN RESPONSE TO THE LIGHT, THE THING SQUIRMS."

"*WHAT THE FRAK IS THAT?!*" he screams.

"It's, uh, Baby Cohen."

"That's not human! That is *NOT* human…"

"Just try to stay calm."

"Humans don't have a bazillion arms!"

"Well, maybe it's a seahorse. With a bazillion arms."

His hands hover over his belly, like he's afraid to touch it.

"Ugh, I can't *believe* that thing is *inside* me. I'll never be able to un-see that!"

"Merrick, listen to me. If I can fix this–" I hesitate, my next words burning in my mouth. "If we play our cards right…you'll never even remember this."

Merrick stops. "Huh?"

I want to tell him.

The wildcards, the repeating day…I want to tell him everything. It's on the tip of my tongue…

But instead I feel myself plaster on a goofy grin, and say, "Well, you know that old saying? Mother Nature erases all the hard parts of pregnancy so you'll be ready to do it again!"

Merrick shoots me a withering glare, dropping onto a metal stool. "Wow, I feel better already."

The lights suddenly flicker on.

"What are you kids doing in here?"

Our heads snap around. Julie Dove is standing in the doorway, wearing a suspicious expression. I switch off the projector, trying to look casual.

"We just needed someplace private."

Julie narrows her eyes. "To do what?"

"Talk," I answer firmly, as Merrick blurts, "Hug." I shoot him an insane glare; he gives me a wide-eyed shrug.

Julie ushers us out like two chicks under her wings. The previously empty hallway is now brimming with people. The cafeteria is jam-packed. Beet-faced husbands with wives hooked proudly on their arms; men, sweating like a sauna, obviously and hilariously attempting to conceal their big bellies under winter coats, darting furtive glances around the room. The rows of plastic chairs are full and it's standing room only, people overflowing out the cafeteria doors into the hall. Kids scamper up and down along the outer edges of the room, weaving through the crowd, swatting the cranberry and orange balloons and trying to tear the homecoming streamers from the ceiling.

"Go ahead," I nod at the doorway. Merrick stops walking.

"You're not coming?"

"If I show my face, Gammell will assume I did this."

"*Did* you?"

"Yes. And you fell right into my dastardly scheme, you shmuck."

"I expect child support," he quips over his shoulder. I grin.

"I'll pay you in pickled eggs."

He makes a gag face but dons a weak grin, disappearing into the crowd of backs.

I've got to hand it to him, he's holding up admirably. He's visibly shaken since the science lab. Not that I can blame him, knowing now what's curled up inside him.

Inside *all* of them…

Sliding my Icemaker from my pocket, I steal a peek at the screen. A thick cluster of red dots is gathered in center screen. Exactly what I expected, but for some reason it turns my stomach. I quickly stuff it back into my pocket.

I glance across the room, noting all the attendees. I spot Big Kahuna, the hefty Hawaiian waiter from Lau Chow's, looking like he might be carrying twins. Randy and his buddies, indeed all pregnant, are pretending to battle like sumo wrestlers; they're quickly separated by Randy's father, Mr. Shepper, a dour-faced man with permanent grease stains under his eyes and cheekbones that could slice beef. He smacks his son upside the head, prompting Randy to slither back down into his chair with a sullen expression. In the far corner, Captain Epic and Julie Dove have set up a table with pamphlets. And there's Sam Dove, his long legs crossed contentedly in his chair, looking utterly unperturbed, thumbing cheerfully through a paperback copy of '*What to Expect When You're Expecting*.' Not that he'll find any answers in that.

After a few minutes, Deputy Scarecrow mounts the stage with long, dutiful strides. He's carrying so high that he's nearly managed to hike his belt up over his baby bump. Scrunching his chin, he taps the podium mic. It erupts in squealing feedback. After fumbling for a moment, he gives up and just gestures both hands toward the side of the stage, introducing Sheriff Gammell.

I fold my arms, leaning against the doorway.

Gammell raises his hands and the chattering room pipes down, taking their seats. Gammell adjusts the microphone.

"Thank you all for coming. I'll start by saying I don't know two pennies more than you about this whole thing. But we play the hand we're dealt, no matter how strange."

Murmurs break out across the room. Gammell raises a hand, shushing them back down.

"Now, we're in need of doctors. But don't worry. We got calls into Newburn."

I snort quietly. Newburn can't help. Gammell likely already knows that. It's impossible to make calls outside Carnival Creeke. Try it, and you get nothing but an earful of static on your phone. People can enter town – like the Pine Valley High School football team, the team we're supposed to play tonight – they arrived at noon, and are just as pregnant as the rest. But they can't leave. This town is a one-way, sealed-off magical roach motel.

You can check in. You can't check out.

Another uproar breaks out and Gammell's hand goes back up. He should just keep it there.

"And for those of you interested, we've got counseling available, and–" He presses two fingers to the bridge of his nose, clearly forcing his next words. "Prenatal yoga."

Behind their table, Julie beams proudly and Captain Epic curls both his hands into the shape of a heart, thumping himself on the chest and pointing out across the crowd.

"Alright, we're gonna open the floor for questions now."

I skulk around outside in the hall, pacing, but staying within earshot. A flurry of hands shoot into the air, a chorus of questions all thrown out at once.

"Will daycare be provided?"

"Will we be expanding the schools?"

"How's it gonna come out?" Randy chimes in, earning himself another slap upside the head from his dad.

"How'd this happen?!"

"Is it a virus?!"

"Well, the shape of biology is always changing, evolving." I recognize Merrick's voice from the back row of seats. Everyone turns toward him, and he shrugs. "There are too many factors. We don't have enough information to answer those questions yet."

"Darn straight!" chimes Jolly Phil, whose previously balding head now appears to be sporting fluffy brown hair in Partridge Family waves. I do a double-take. That shouldn't be as weird or as funny as it is.

"Yeah, but is this even possible?!"

Merrick folds his arms. "Physiologically speaking? No. But–"

Shepper jumps up from his chair so quickly it scrapes the floor. "I don't care about the mumbo-jumbo! Can't you just science us all back to normal?"

Merrick just stares at him agape, then rubs his eyes with both hands. "If you want to rephrase that into a question in actual English, I'll try my best to answer."

Gammell speaks over the mic. "Okay folks, let's just–"

The double doors in the back of the cafeteria suddenly bang open. Everyone spins around in unison.

Old Man Tannon stands in the doorway, a dead deer slung across his shoulders, his belly concealed under an ankle-length camouflage parka that looks like it hasn't been washed in decades. He glares smugly at the stunned audience through his wild, wide-set eyes, his feathery silver hair sticking up in defiant angles, and littered with leaves.

"Knock, knock, who's there? It's the voice of reason, kiddies!" Narrowing his eyes, he begins tromping slowly down the center of the gym, between the aisle of chairs. "How long I been warnin' ya? Big Brother served up a steaming plate'a experimental human rights violations, and ya'll gobbled it right up!"

He punctuates the sentiment by hurling the deer corpse to the floor with a thud, prompting several people to topple over backwards in their chairs. Sheriff Gammell grabs the podium mic.

"Alrighty there, Emmett, let's just–"

He abandons the sentence and jumps off the stage, using steady pats on the back to steer a wild-eyed Tannon out the far doors while Deputy Scarecrow and Captain Epic hurriedly drag the deer corpse back outside.

I'm sure the conversation only got more entertaining, but this is where my attention got diverted. You know that feeling when someone is watching you?

I spin around, one hand on my boot knife.

There stands Jemma, my favorite little four-year-old Twinkie lover (and apparently one of the only people who can sneak up on me. Man, she's stealthy in her sparkly ninja sneakers). She gazes curiously up at me, fiddling with the zipper of her purple jacket. Tucked under her arm is a plastic toy pony. The very one I secretly leave on her windowsill every morning.

The sight of her hugging that pony makes me feel like mini marshmallows melting in the warmest cup of cocoa.

Jemma stares at me, scratching the back of her neck.

"My daddy's gonna have a baby," she says matter-of-factly.

"So I've heard." I tilt my head and smile. Squatting down, I lean both elbows on my knees. "Think it'll be a little brother or a sister?"

"Nope."

I can't tell whether she's joking or not, but she isn't wrong.

"Ma'am. I don't believe we've been introduced."

I know that deep, gravelly voice. Leaping to my feet, I spin around to face Sheriff Gammell.

Ladies and gentlemen, I present the *other* person who somehow always manages to sneak up on me.

I quickly try to read him. His stony face may as well be made of granite. But there's Deputy Scarecrow behind him, his belt hiked to his armpits, his eyes darting around like he's expecting me to change into a werewolf and attack.

My arms go tense.

"Kyle," I extend my hand with a friendly smile. "Um, is there a problem, Sheriff?"

"Nice to meet you, Miss Kyle. You're under arrest."

7 BOOMTOWN

Fighting the sheriff right here would be a grave step in the wrong direction, so I grit my teeth and allow him to cuff my arms behind my back.

"Under what grounds?" I ask.

"Under whatever grounds I dang well feel like!" he barks.

Wow, he's super cranky. This is like Gammell at his grouchiest, plus one hundred extra grouchy points.

He marches me down the hall as people begin pouring from the cafeteria. Looks like the meeting just let out. I search for Merrick, but he's nowhere in sight.

*

Leaning against the jail cell bars, I recite my made-up story to Sheriff Gammell for the hundredth time.

"Listen to me. I'm with the CDC. We heard what's happening to your town. I'm here to help."

He won't believe me. He never does. Without Merrick here to vouch for me, Gammell won't care if I'm Miss America or America's Most Wanted.

At least that last part of what I said wasn't a lie.

I really *am* here to help.

"CDC, eh?" Gammell scratches his craggy salt-and-pepper chin. "I assume you've got some credentials?"

I grip the bars. "Must've left them in my other pants."

"And I must've left *my* sense of humor with my preconceived notions of *BIOLOGY*."

With each word his weary voice elevates, until he's full-on shouting at me, accentuating the word 'biology' by throwing open his jacket and gesturing wildly at his inflated abdomen. For a moment he just stands there, pointing a finger at me, as if preparing to chew me out further for making him lose his shitake. With effort, he dials himself back down.

"Now if you'll excuse me." He crams his hat on, jaw clenched. "Ma'am."

The station door slams shut behind him, and I'm left alone with Gladys, across the room pecking away on her computer keyboard.

I hate getting chewed out by Gammell. I don't know why we ruffle each other's feathers so much. He's not my father; I don't know why his reprimands feel so parental.

Mentally, I replay his same gravelly voice, the one that just ripped me a new one, praising me on those other alternate days.

"I won't forget what you did for this town."

I try to remind myself that Gammell doesn't actually hate my guts, even if he does right now. Present tense. Not permanent. Anyway, there's a worse predicament at hand.

I pace the jail cell confines, slapping each concrete wall.

I *can't* be stuck in here again. Not *now*, with that thing growing inside Merrick by each passing minute. All those ticking time bombs, growing inside everyone...

Tick, tock...

Grabbing the cold bars, I zero in on Gladys at her desk.

"Hey, excuse me? Gladys? I need to talk to Sheriff Gammell. Right now."

She scowls at me, like the sight of me smells bad.

"The sheriff is attending to important town business," she snips. "You will spend the night here. Then he will deal with you in the morning."

Morning? By that time, every male in town will be the proud, very-likely dead fathers to newborn alien prawn spawn.

"Gladys," I say steadily. "We don't have that kind of time. The men here...they're *infected*. And they're in serious danger."

Gladys keeps typing. She purses her thin lips, as though trying to create a mental barrier against the fact that I exist. I start banging my head against the bars. Gladys' lips tighten. Focus all energy on Kyle-deflector shields. Her keystrokes become one-finger punches.

I yell, "Ignore me, and you're going to have a royal mess on your hands!"

The phone on the desk jingles and Gladys looks nothing less than relieved to snatch it up and be distracted from me.

"Carnival Creeke sheriff's station–"

I hold my breath. Please be Merrick...

Gladys breaks into a girlish laugh. "Oh, Betty! Why, yes indeed, bingo is still on for seven tomorrow." She shoots me a look, her bony face briefly sagging into her customary harpy glare, before tossing back into another exaggerated giggle.

"Oh, who spilled the beans? Why, yes, I *am* Bingo Champion of eighty-seven!" She flutters her eyelids, twirling the phone cord.

I kick the bars. Of course Merrick won't call. He doesn't even know I'm here.

"Then could I at least get another pillow?" I holler, flopping down on the wooden slab that qualifies as a 'bed.'

But I'm not resting. My mind paces for me. Reviewing the dimensions of this cell. I glance up at the window grate. I could go for old faithful – pop my shoulder out of its socket and escape out the window. I've done it twice. The bone slides out pretty easily. But I don't have a tool to pry off the window's metal grate like I did last time. Even if I did, it would require at least thirty minutes of uninterrupted time to pull a Houdini, unscrew the grate, then squeeze myself out. I glance over at Gladys.

I could outrun her.

No, she'd probably fly through the bars and kebob my eyeballs with her keyboard-conditioned talons.

From the jail cell, my eyes drift to the clock on the wall.

Six o'clock. Normally, the homecoming parade would be firing up outside right now. But not tonight. Nobody has rah-rah school spirit on their mind tonight, I guarantee.

How do I fix this? Every wildcard has a solution. A big, red reset button.

So what is it?

It's so much easier when all I have to do is smashy-slashy my way to the win. But instead, I've got freaking alien centipede prawns in people's bellies… It's these Sloppy Joe multiple-choice brainy-brainfood puzzles that rub me raw. And worse, it drags innocent people into the muck. People I care about.

How do I fix this?

No, Kyle – don't focus on the blood red question mark. Focus on what you know.

Fact 1: However I fix this, I must *not* let them hatch. How will they be born? An image of those clawed prawn legs sends a fresh wave of dread thrumming through my body.

Fact 2: Merrick was the first red dot to show up. Which means Merrick is the farthest along with his gestation. Making Merrick first in line on a grisly train that I *cannot* allow to reach its destination. In other words…Merrick is in terrible danger.

Gladys hangs up the phone and resumes typing.

"Gladys," I press my body against the bars. "We need to get to the hospital. Are you listening?"

She flicks a glare in my direction, a nearly indiscernible movement, her lips pressed into a thin line.

A car passes outside, headlights flashing across the darkening window. Then another.

"Listen to me! Open that drawer and look at my machine! Look at the screen! See all those red dots? These aren't babies, they're ticking time bombs! And they're-"

The phone rings sharply, causing Gladys to startle.

"Sheriff's station-"

Suddenly her face drains, her eyes so wide I think they might drop from her head. Her mouth hangs open, quivering.

"Y-yes, I…I'll be there as soon as I can."

She drops the phone, twirling her sweater over her bony shoulders and stabbing an accusatory glare in my direction. I shout for her to wait, but she's already flitted out the door, keys jingling. I hear it lock behind her, the lights automatically shutting off.

I pace. I fume. I check my watch. This leaves me no choice. I need to bust out of here. On my tiptoes, I begin working to unscrew the window grate, working until my calves burn, working until my fingertips look like shredded pork. Sweat trickles down my nose. Nearly an hour later, I've accomplished nothing. This is hopeless. I can't pry off concrete nails, not with my bare hands. Kicking the wall, I sink down to the floor with my back against the cell bars.

I'm out of options.

Hours pass, my forehead against my knees.

And suddenly the wall explodes.

Concrete bricks blow apart and crumble like feta cheese, the window grate pops off the wall, accompanied by a shower of debris that rains down on the shiny black hood of the enormous

Hummer SUV that just drove through the wall into my jail cell. Through the thick cloud of drywall dust, I spot the license plate.

LUV-MNY.

Leaping to my feet, I cough a laugh in disbelief.

Just when I thought it wasn't possible for this dingdong to be a worse driver, he proves me gloriously wrong.

I fling the truck's door open and spring into the passenger seat, Mr. Luv Money going hysterical behind the wheel.

"I-I-I gotta get to the hospital!" he blabbers, flailing his hands.

"Yeah, you and everyone else," I remark, glancing down at his watermelon-sized belly under his Adidas jacket. He just shakes his head, hysterical, floundering for words.

"No, no, you don't understand, I–"

Then he slumps over against the window, passed out cold.

I don't have time for this.

Unbuckling his seatbelt, I drag him into the passenger seat like a sack of potatoes and take his place behind the steering wheel. Jamming the gear shift, I slam the massive Hummer into reverse, backing out of the gaping hole that was the police station wall and roaring down the street, spraying a trail of dusty debris behind us like Haley's Comet.

King Street is backed up with an unusual crowd of cars. We screech to a halt, the Hummer's headlights shining on the car bumper in front of us. Craning my neck, I peer out across the convoy of gridlocked traffic ahead of us. They're all heading the same direction. And I don't need two guesses to know where.

*

The hospital parking lot is jam-packed. Instead of driving around searching for a parking space, I just roar the mammoth Hummer up onto the curb outside the ER entrance and leave it there rumbling with keys in the ignition. Dang thing will run out of gas soon, anyway.

The emergency room lobby is utter chaos.

"Can someone take this guy?"

Several frazzled-looking nurses dash toward my shout as I tromp toward the check-in counter, dragging an unconscious Luv Money over my shoulder. As soon as he's off my back, I snatch the admittance clipboard and shuffle madly through the pages. I need to find Merrick. I don't even care if I run into Dr. Fairchild. Chances of that are slim anyway; he's likely pregnant on a bed somewhere like all the other men.

Cohen, Merrick – Room 42.

I shoulder through the swinging double doors and enter a madhouse. The ER hallway is clogged wall-to-wall with metal stretchers and gurneys, occupied by groaning men crying for water or pain meds or their mama. My brain is spinning. My throat feels stuffed with cotton.

So many wildcards. All waiting on me to fix them…

Here it is. Room 42.

I hear Captain Epic's tranquil California drawl before I even enter the room.

"You're doing great, my man! You *got* this!"

Merrick is sitting cross-legged on the bed nearest the door, panting, his teeth gritted. He's still wearing his t-shirt and jeans, but from the looks of it, he was probably already in too much pain to crawl into a hospital gown. Captain Epic on the other hand is dutifully clad in his papery blue gown, standing beside Merrick, thumping him cheerfully on the back.

"Deep breaths, bro! Stress is poison to the body. This is the miracle of life!"

Merrick cuts his eyes at him. "Ever seen the movie Alien?"

Captain Epic puts up both hands, nodding deeply. "Your pessimism is understandable, roomie. I'll give you some space. Gonna go get us some protein bars from the munchies machine, okie-doke?"

He breezes past me out into the hallway.

"Kyle?" Merrick spots me, his eyes lighting up.

I force a feeble smile. "I'm here, kiddo."

He doubles over suddenly, clutching his stomach. "*Ugh*, holy shneikies, I can't do this…" His face and shoulders are drenched in sweat. "*I can't do this!!*"

"Yes, you can!" Kneeling down, I grab his head with both my hands. "We'll find a solution. Listen, I know it hurts. But don't let the pain own you. Take charge."

Locking his gaze on me, he gives a tight nod. He takes a deep breath. Then he rolls over and snatches a pair of scissors off the bedside table, plunging them into his own stomach. The blade sinks about an inch into his skin before I can dive across the bed, grabbing his arms – then we both freeze. A shrill, muffled shriek erupts from his belly. I can only assume he gave his alien prawn a good jab. Right as I wrench the scissors from Merrick's hand, I swear I hear the same otherworldly shriek echoed a hundred times, all throughout the nearby rooms down the hall.

"Whoa, what do you think you're doing?!" I shout at Merrick, tossing the scissors aside.

"What's it look like?" he shouts back, his eyes blazing. "I'm taking charge! Being more like you! Smash first, ask questions later, right?"

My mouth drops. I press my fist to my face, shaking my head.

"No, no, listen to me. You don't want to be like me. Trust me."

"Y-you're strong," he gasps, almost pleading. "I *need* some of that, Kyle!"

"Just...hold on a little longer." I swallow hard. "I'll fix this. I'll find a way. Please just hold on, okay?"

I back away slowly as a flurry of nurses overtake Merrick's bed, strapping his arms and legs down as he thrashes.

"Kyle!" he screams. "You *know* what's inside us! Get it *out* and *kill it! KYLE!!*"

Grasping my hair in both hands, I take two steps backward then run out the door into the hall, Merrick's screams echoing behind me. I stumble past the stretchers and blankets in the hallway, checking my watch. Quarter past midnight.

I'm no surgeon. Sure, I've dug out claws, teeth, glass...but that was just me and rubbing alcohol and reckless confidence. I could never dig into Merrick like I dig into myself. And then do three hundred more people? Before one o'clock?

Forget it.

I've just stumbled into the next hallway when Sheriff Gammell appears in front of me, barring my way. His eyes are deep dark hollows, his mouth a thin white line.

"Miss Kyle," he growls solemnly. "I don't know who you are…but I know you're not with the CDC."

I nod tensely, letting my eyes fall. "You're right. I'm not."

"Well, I don't give a hoot or holler where you're from. I got good people in deep trouble tonight here." He exhales, rubbing a hand across his slick face. "There's…no surgeons coming."

"I know."

"And the way I see it…you're the last shot we've got. Blame the hormones, but something about you seems…aw, never mind."

He waves it off. Reaching into his pocket, he pulls out my compacted Icemaker. He hands it to me, his eyes tight with desperation.

"Tell me what to do, Miss Kyle. And I will do it."

My mouth goes dry. The swelling warmth in my empty chest is edged out by a twisting knot of dread.

What should I tell him to do? I don't *know* what to do…

You know what would be useful right now?

A tool.

A high-tech metal canister with the ability to perform cutting-edge organ-removal surgery and safe cauterization through vacuum suction. The canister that sucked out my heart. If only I had it now. I press my hands to my face.

Come on, Holliday. I need that canister.

*You jerk… Help us out…**please**…just this once…*

But why would he?

I glance through my fingers. Just before the double doors swing closed, all the way at the end of the hallway, stands a figure dressed all in black. A male figure...his back to me, hands in the pockets of his leather jacket, an unmoving eye in a hurricane of nurses in powder blue scrubs.

It can't be...

I explode through the double doors and hurtle down the swarming hallway, running after what was surely a mirage, running until I burst out a door into the chilled night air. It's the very same loading dock that I made my exodus on my first day here. An overhead floodlight illuminates the empty alcove and rusty green dumpster. There's no one here. Like I should be surprised. I shove my hands in my pockets and turn back inside.

Then I see it. There, sitting on the crusted lip of the dumpster. Gleaming metal in the cold light. My breath catches.

The canister.

This must be a trick. It can't be real...

I grab the canister, the realness of its weight and its cold steel surface rendering me momentarily stunned. My fingers brush against something. A piece of white paper, folded in half like a greeting card, is taped to the canister. With trembling fingers, I slowly unfold the paper. There's something typed here:

NOW YOU'RE THINKING LIKE A PRO.
GOOD GIRL.

I stare for a moment at the congratulatory message, my elation edged out by a dark thought. This message is typed. Not handwritten. Which means Holliday would have had to type this message ahead of time, then wait, watching me all day from the shadows, just waiting for me to arrive at *this exact conclusion*.

Quivering rage rises inside me.

He could have helped me at any point.

But how could he possibly have known…?

Gritting my teeth and shoving my tangled spaghetti of emotions aside, I jettison back through the hospital hallways. I skid to a stop by Merrick's bed, my boots squeaking on the prim floor, hugging the canister in both arms.

"Merrick," I gasp breathlessly. "This device can help. I'm going to use it to suck that thing right out of you. Okay?"

He swallows hard, his face ash white. "Like a solidarity scalpel or something?"

"Sure, uh. Something like that."

I yank up his shirt, trying to ignore the rippling and bulging going on under his skin. His belly is so distended the skin is practically paper-thing, nearly transparent.

Captain Epic appears in the doorway, holding a variety of protein bars in both hands.

"Yo, you like cashew or–" He sees us, dropping the snacks. "*WHOA!!*"

I start to remove the restraint straps from Merrick's arms and legs, but he firmly orders me to leave them. Nodding, I fumble with the little wires on the canister. They look like tiny jumper cables… I'm supposed to attach these, right? That's what Holliday did. I think, anyway. I wasn't really paying close attention. I was a little preoccupied, having just gone splat from the top of the water tower. Couldn't Jerkface have left me an instruction manual or something?

I *need* to get this right...

I position the canister over Merrick's swollen belly. The canister hisses, automatically attaching to his skin. He bucks, screaming into the pillow.

"Just *DO* it, Kyle!!"

"Okay." I swallow. "This might feel–" Grimacing, I rub the scar on my chest. "It might sting a little."

Merrick nods, his face bloodless. His fingers clench the sheets. I nod. "Ready? One...two..."

I don't count to three. Holliday didn't. And as much as I hate him for denying me the honor of including that last countdown digit, I survived, and so help me, I'm doing everything exactly like Holliday did it.

I press the button. There's a sharp, rising whoosh and then a dull *thunk* – and for the briefest millisecond, the canister is heavy in my hands, a thrashing, writhing pink thing inside, its segmented body coiling and uncoiling, its innumerable clawed centipede legs scritching and scratching against the canister's glass window. Then it vanishes. I blink. Merrick lifts his face from the pillow and gapes at the empty canister, then looks at his now-flat stomach, a sizzling circle imprinted on his abdomen like a tattoo. Bewildered, I yank my compacted Icemaker from my pocket, flipping open the screen.

One single gray dot.

Captain Epic punches both fists in the air and lets out a whoop. "*YES*, dude-man! *YES!!*"

My triumph is short-lived. Even if we managed to zap Merrick's wildcard, we still have hundreds left…and there's *no way* I'll have enough time to vacuum out each nasty little alien prawn, one by one.

Unless…

Suddenly I remember the way the other creatures all shrieked in pain when Merrick knifed his own belly. I jerk my head to my Icemaker screen.

And I can barely believe what I'm seeing.

Gray dots, popping up all over the screen. Little specks of hope, peppering the sea of red until the entire screen has turned a glorious gray.

"Did it work?!" Merrick croaks weakly from the bed. "It…was a hive mind, right?"

He's right. They were all linked. And since Merrick's was the first wildcard to appear, maybe his was the hive brain. The Queen Prawn. Zap it, and *all* the nasty buggers get zapped.

"Merrick, you beautiful genius!" I utter, clunking my back against the wall and expelling a laugh of unrivaled relief.

I run out into the hallway, where a chorus of similar relief erupts throughout the hospital. Crowds of disheveled men straighten upright, patting their normal-sized wildcard-free stomachs.

Sheriff Gammell makes his way through the crowd to me. He shuffles like his feet weigh a hundred pounds.

"Heck of a night," he grunts, rubbing his eyes. "Listen. If there's some Twilight Zone explanation for what just happened…I'm asking you to save it. I got people to tend to, and a whole lotta Advil to take. But I'll tell you one thing."

He clears his throat, gives me a terse nod. "I won't forget what you did for our town today."

There it is.

Whenever he says those words to me, it means I've knocked it out of the park. Won the day. Won his trust. Gold medal win.

So why does it feel like such a loss?

"Glad to help," I stammer, but he's already tromped off down the crowded hallway.

Back in Merrick's room, a pair of orderlies are bustling around. One of them removes a Velcro cuff from Merrick's arm, wheeling a cart away, dimming the lights on her way out. Stuffing my hands in my pockets, I lean in the doorway, lingering in the background. Merrick's eyes are closed. I probably should just slip out quietly. Let him sleep. He probably doesn't want to see me anyway, after everything I just put him through…

"Kyle!" Merrick points at me with a guileless grin, his green eyes unfocused. "Y'know what? You'll never be cinnamon, and I bet you'd never let anyone put you on a waffle!"

I stifle a laugh. He's as high as a kite. I glance at the middle-aged orderly; she gives me a weary smile and a shrug.

"We gave him a little something for the pain."

She places a stack of fresh folded sheets on the foot of the bed then shuffles out into the hallway. I turn back to Merrick, a lump welling up in my throat.

"Hey, superstar. How you feeling?"

"Well, my central nervous system has acquiesced to the analgesic. Aaaaand words taste like coconut."

"Ah," I force a smile. "Sounds like a win-win."

His glasses are folded on the bedside table. Dark circles ring his eyes, telltale echoes of the pain he's no longer feeling.

"Hey, Kyle? Would you...stay with me a while?"

"Got nowhere else I'd be," I reassure him quietly.

I pull up a chair beside his bed. The moon is shining through the window blinds, striping the room floor with bars of soft light.

"You want to watch TV or something?" I grab the remote and start clicking buttons. Merrick shakes his head emphatically.

"Nah. I wanna tell you something, Kyle."

I set down the remote.

"Sure. I'm here. I'm listening."

For a moment he just gazes at me, his expression unreadable.

"So, I know this is gonna sound crazy," he slurs. "But...I'm kinda glad you jumped in front of my car yesterday. Feels like ages ago," he laughs drowsily, his eyes sliding closed. "But if I'm honest with myself...ever since then...I..."

My cheeks flush hot. He started to tell me this very same thing once before, that night in the gymnasium, but Tannon's voice over the loudspeaker interrupted him. Never heard whatever he was fixing to say... Am I about to find out?

I swallow hard.

Eyes still closed, Merrick smiles and mumbles, "You know, you'd actually make a great mom."

I snort, rolling my eyes. Ideally speaking, I'd like that equation to include a guy. And there's only one guy I'm always thinking about, but definitely not in the romantic sense. Black eyes, Irish accent, a penchant for ripping out girls' hearts...

Or maybe I'm just special.

After a few more minutes, I'm pretty sure Merrick is asleep. I hold his hand a little longer. The bedside monitors beep steadily.

Maybe I've been putting up guards. I've tried not to let myself get too attached, but lately I've been slipping at that goal. Especially with Merrick. And each day, the more I *want* it to slip.

Reaching above his bed, I gently switch off the overhead fluorescents.

Want to know the worst part about a repeating day?

The ghosts.

People that were, then weren't. Progress that was, then wasn't. Every day I run around like a good little hamster, playing the right cards, hitting all the right marks. I meticulously build people up, get them to trust me, brick by brick, only to have it all collapse when that clock resets each day. And there isn't even a pile of rubble to show for it. Just a stack of untouched bricks. Like it never even happened. A thing like that, day after day...

It just wears you thin. Down to the fibers.

DAY 38: CAKEWALK

My boots thud on the sunny sidewalk, redbud trees flashing by. The red dot is just ahead, just around the corner.

I check myself. I've been running for three minutes.

With a reluctant growl, I drop to a jog, hands on my knees, walking in a tense little circle. Not because I want to. I've just learned my limits. Every three minutes and twenty-one seconds, I'm pushing the red. But if I stop running and take a quick breather, I found that I can avoid a crash, avoid that creepy-crawly I-can't-breathe-and-have-ants-under-my-skin feeling.

Four, three, two, one… Okay, that should suffice.

I plunge back down the sidewalk, letting the thud-thud rhythm of my running swallow my brain.

I check my Icemaker screen, even though I don't really need to. That red dot won't stray far. If I stop, it waits for me. Why? Because it's *horrible*. This is the cruelest and most evil wildcard I've faced yet.

Don't believe me?

There it is. The four-inch gingerbread man, scurrying in and out between people's feet. Look at its stubby little molasses arms. Gaze upon its soulless icing-dot eyes. A pint-sized terror.

"A PINT-SIZED TERROR."

True, it hasn't actually done anything that could be classified as dangerous...but it's made me chase it all day. *All* day.

How unspeakably annoying.

The cookie flips suddenly off the curb and skitters across the street, easily too nimble for my hopes of a car squashing it. Rolling my eyes, I hang a left and Bo Duke-slide across a honking Honda's hood, just in time to see the little demon slip between the bars of the wrought-iron gate and take off across the library lawn, unnoticed by the scattered picnickers smiling on their checkered blankets under the shade of the trees.

"Don't you dare," I mutter.

As if it heard me, the cookie turns, looking back at me with its beady frosting eyes. Then it scurries across the lawn, hopping into a family's picnic basket.

"Argh!" Vaulting the gate, I dart across the lawn and fling open the family's white wicker basket, prompting them to spill lemonade all over themselves.

The basket is empty.

I frown. Then which basket is it hiding in?

"Um, sorry." I hand their basket back, dashing to the next family, ripping open their basket and sending a shower of individually-packaged fruit snacks flying like missiles.

Where *is* that little snot?!

"Sorry, s'cuse me, sorry folks–" I plunge from one basket to another, terrorizing families, trying my best to avoid stepping on their sandwiches. "Sorry, picnic basket inspector! Just, uh, everything looks fine... Carry on! Sorry!"

This might be a whole lot funnier if I was wearing a giant bear costume, but I'm not, so it's not.

I'm rummaging through a cooler of Jell-O when I look up and spot the cookie scurrying away, already halfway down the street. I drop the cooler and take off after it.

Yesterday was an emotional steam roller. Not today. Today, there's only running. Kyle versus Cookie. Simple. Carnal. A sugar high. The bittersweet feeling of yesterday – *all* the yesterdays – I pound it under the pavement as I run, leaving it in my dust.

Today, I'm a fireball. Wild, untamable. An unstoppable, supersonic streak of light –

Ugh, hold on, my feet are going numb.

I slow to a walk, panting, soaked in perspiration. My shirt clings to my back. Pivoting, I stare at Merle's Diner. Through the window glass, I can see Merrick sitting at the counter. His back facing me, serenely absorbed in his book.

A lump wells up in my throat.

Merrick would help me chase that cookie in his Tahoe. He would come up with some bio-mechanical trap. He would make me laugh.

But I can't do it today.

What am I supposed to do? Prance into that diner like yesterday never happened? Well, I can't do it. Not today. I don't really want to see Merrick and Gammell's fresh pile of bricks, and their blank, cordial, unfamiliar stares.

Not today.

Phil can get his own stupid napkins today.

I turn on my heel, scanning the surrounding shops and passing cars for that obnoxious cookie. Across the street, the Carnival Creeke High School's cheerleading squad jogs by, pausing to tighten their ponytails and take swigs from their water bottles. I spot Candace, twirling a strand of her glossy golden hair and whispering to two equally-glossy friends, a poison sneer on her face. Back to her old queen bee self, I see. Forget the fact that I once watched her help deliver a woman's baby on the back of a homecoming float. Forget that I've never seen Candace happier. Forget it all.

She certainly has.

How am I supposed to feel about that? Watching people reach deep into themselves and unlock their potential, become a big fat butterfly only to completely revert back into a caterpillar, and just forget all about it the next day? It's like watching tulips start peeking up, only to be walloped by a big frost.

Am I expecting too much from them?

Do I really expect they'll choose the same path, once this day is kaput and all their new-and-improved slates get wiped clean?

Candace and her friends turn their eyes toward me.

"Ugh, is Salvation Army doing handouts today?" Candace snickers, eyeing my sweat-drenched cargo pants and muddy combat boots. She sniffs disdainfully.

"Oh, girl – and I use that term loosely – it's called *makeup*." She over-annunciates, as if speaking to a dumb cow. "Sorry you were born with that face, but if you weren't given any genetic favors, you really should at least...try. *Try*."

"*Try! Try! Try!*" they chant in unison, pumping their fists with mock bravado.

Whatever. I'm not in the mood today. That renegade cookie could be anywhere, and I'm not wasting my precious seconds on having my no-makeup face used as target practice for their mean-girl artilleries.

I turn. "Hey Candace, I think you've got a veneer falling off there," I point and cringe. Candace degenerates in horror, her hands jumping to her perfect white teeth as I run off.

Nothing I do matters. I don't make any difference. Why should I bother? Why am I even chasing this stupid cookie? Because Holliday told me to? Theoretically, I could just say no. Fill the bathtub to my ears, just binge old records, drown it all out. But then we'd be stuck on that day forever. And whatever wildcard sprang up would be crowned king. Why bother?

Because I *do* give a crap.

They're all counting on me. And they don't even know it.

Things in my head are getting all quantumed up again. Briefly I wonder if any 19-year-old has ever felt this way, and excruciating loneliness pools through my chest.

I chase the cookie all the way up King Street, into the park at the edge of the woods. It scampers across picnic tables and weaves through the playground with me hot on its heels, crashing and tumbling through the tube slides like some ridiculous Three Stooges routine. I'm right behind as it scurries across the clearing beyond the woods, to the old emergency lookout tower – and in a single leap, it springs up thirty feet to the top of the tower, like a big cricket, blatantly disregarding gravity. It halts on the railing, tauntingly peering down at me.

Lord help me. It's shaking its sugary little hiney at me.

"Do that again and see what happens!" I warn.

Of course it waits until I've run halfway up the stairs before it jumps off the tower, landing with a feather-soft *plunk*.

I scream, "*And quit defying the laws of physics!!*"

Says the girl yelling at a pastry.

Now we're hightailing back down King Street and I'm not even chasing this cookie anymore so much as bitterly savoring the feeling of my worries dissolving in the dust. When we fly past Gumby's Toy Shop, I can no longer hear Gammell's disapproving voice. By the time we reach the bakery, I've forgotten Candace's jeers. Only when we pass the thrift shop do I think of Merrick, scrambling my focus. I'm not watching and I slam into poor Mr. Nederson, splashing his potato soup across his cardigan sweater.

"Watch it!" I snap, instantly feeling guilty. Pausing, I shout, "Did you see a gingerbread man run by?"

He shakes his head so fast that his lips and jowls rattle around. But I've already spotted the elusive little fiend – waving its stubby arm at me, intentionally catching my eye before slipping into the open door of the hardware shop. I charge after it. Vaulting over a wood chipper display, I turn just in time to see the cookie scuttling up the leg of a mannequin wearing a lumberjack vest. It kicks off the mannequin's head, wriggling itself into the neck hole, disappearing into the plastic man.

You're about to get terminated, my little nemesis.

Clapping one hand over the hole in the mannequin's neck to seal off the exit, I fumble for the wood chipper plug and jam it into the outlet. The machine roars to life, and in one swift motion, I hoist the entire mannequin and stuff it neck-first into the spinning teeth. The wood chipper shudders and screeches. I shove harder until the plastic man is shredded into oblivion, my maniacal laughter echoing throughout the bargain lawn tools aisle. Flecks of plastic bounce off my sweaty face. I'm vaguely aware that a small crowd has gathered to observe my massacre, but I don't care. When all that's left of the mannequin is a foot, I plunge my hand into the foot's ankle hole and triumphantly yank out the troublesome little treat. It squirms in my hands. I stare at it. It stares at me. And then it sticks out a tiny icing tongue at me.

What would *you* do?

I take a big bite out of its head.

Mmm...not bad... Notes of ginger, molasses, warm vanilla...

It keeps on squirmin', so I keep on chompin'.

Yes, I realize that eating a wildcard is probably a terrible idea, and yes, it might turn me into a cookie monster or something, but it doesn't, and all this goes through my head while the crowd watches me devour a gingerbread man cross-legged on the trashed floor like a sweaty Neanderthal beast girl.

I stuff the last chunk into my mouth and lick my fingers. The red dot turns gray. Bada-bing, bada-boom.

Okay, I'm calling it now.

This was the dumbest wildcard ever.

DAY 39: SNOW WHITE & ROSE RED

Noon. Merle's Diner. Another day.

My waking nightmare continues.

I stand in the doorway for a moment longer. Exhaling deeply, I plunk down on the stool next to Merrick, spinning around in lazy circles. Merrick sees me and chokes on his sandwich. Right on cue.

I put on a smile as I spin round and round.

"Hey."

"Hey!" Merrick sputters. "Uh, so you're still alive, huh?"

"Still alive, yay!" I sigh, pumping my fist lackadaisically at the ceiling. Merrick watches me twirl around on my stool, attempting to hide a smile.

"Erm, are you drunk?"

"Nope," I yawn and stop spinning. "And the name's Kyle, by the way."

"Oh, um–" He wipes and awkwardly extends a hand. "Merrick Cohen."

Beside me, Jolly Phil is guffawing loudly. Most days, it's endearing. But today it's annoying the crap out of me. Next, he'll run out of napkins. I forgot to grab him some extras, like I usually do. I'm off my game today.

"Bless me, I'm out of napkins!" Phil chortles.

I whirl around. "And I suppose you expect me to fix that for you?!"

We hold each other's stare for a second, then I grab a handful of napkins. "Here," I mumble, thrusting them at him.

Ugh, what's my problem today?

Merle sets my root beer float on the counter with his warm smile and a wink, then ducks back under the orange-and-black Halloween garland and lumbers off to the fryer. Merrick watches with typical curiosity as I robotically scoop out the ice cream and plop it into a bowl, nudging it toward him.

"You like vanilla? Bon appetit."

Honestly, I'm just really wanting to move past my stupid outburst at poor Phil and his napkins.

Merrick looks at the bowl, then at me.

"I nearly made road hamburger out of you yesterday… And you want me to eat your ice cream?"

He deserves so much more. There's so much I wish I could say to him. So much. But I can't. I have to stay consistent. Have to act like the Kyle from Gargoyle Day, the one who called him "Tahoe" because I was too wrapped up in my own selfish, sticky, heart-removed problems that I didn't even bother to ask his name. But it's getting harder to act like *that* Kyle, all cold, distracted, and indifferent.

Because I'm not her anymore.

I'm tired. I'm lonely. I'm a zombie in a room of happy ghosts who will vanish by dawn. Oh, and I'm pretty sure my shirt is on backwards. All I want today is for somebody to just give me a hug.

Sighing, Merrick picks up the spoon. "Okay, fine. To your health–"

"And things that go grr in the night." I click my glass against his spoon and try not to let my gaze linger on him too fondly while he eats.

Ice cream.

That's as close as we'll ever get to a tomorrow together.

Grumbling, I swallow all the wishy-washy in a huge swig of root beer.

I hate you, Holliday.

"So what about you, Kyle?" Merrick broaches. "Or did you just grow up aspiring to vanquish gargoyles with decorative swords?"

I glance at my watch. Right about the time Merrick starts in with the personal questions about my cloaked past, Old Dapper Jack will finish his dumplings and mosey over and start giving us the scoop on his colon health. It's too marvelous for words.

Thankfully, that's when a red dot appears on my screen.

Gray time is over, baby.

I eagerly snatch the folded-up weapon from my pocket.

Merrick stops eating when he sees the chipped wooden device. Pushing up his glasses, he gazes keenly at the red dot on its fan-shaped screen.

"Pretty sweet tech," he remarks, like always.

"It's my big bad detector," I say, like always.

"So…it detects Big Bads?"

"Something like that," I chuckle, hurtling off my stool. "Enjoy the ice cream, Merrick Cohen. I'll see you around!"

Downing the rest of my root beer in a mega-chug, I bolt for the door. Merrick grabs his bag and sprints after me. I knew he would. Sure as the sun rises, Merrick will assume the role of my puppy and follow me into oblivion, because Merrick wants to see monsters. But just once…I kind of want him to tell me 'no.' I wish he would stand up to me. Defy me, bite me back.

There I go, expecting more of them again.

We skid to a halt outside by the umbrella-covered plastic benches. I scan the parking lot. Cars roll by. Carnival Creeke High School's cheerleading squad jogs past us in their maroon hoodies and leggings, all giggles, their ponytails swinging in the afternoon sun. Perfectly peaceful…

Well, color me confuzzled.

I frown at my Icemaker's screen.

There's the red dot. And according to this, the wildcard is right here. Practically in front of our noses…

"Um." Merrick coughs. "You think maybe it's an invisible gargoyle?" He's barely finished the word when the red dot does something completely new.

It splits into two.

Our heads jerk up in unison.

The cheerleaders have stopped jogging. A tizzy of commotion ripples through the group. Ten bucks says my wildcard is huddled inside them. My grip tightens on my Icemaker, ready to spring it open with a flick of my thumb. The cheerleaders jostle aside, revealing –

I frown.

It's just two girls arguing.

A petite, olive-skinned brunette and a tall, willowy gazelle with flame-red hair and freckles. I recognize them. It's those two that always hang around Candace. Right now they're trading rapid-fire insults, their voices rising to that shrill, high-pitched language reserved to teenage girls and screech owls.

Beside me, Merrick adjusts his glasses with a puzzled frown. He looks at my screen, then back at the girls.

"Wait. Danielle Shaw and Lisa Brinkley...are the *monsters?*" He tilts his head, squinting as though trying to see a giraffe in one of those abstract dot pictures. "Somehow I expected the Big Bad to look a little bigger...and badder."

"Expect the unexpected," I snort wryly.

More importantly – why the heck is my skin tingling?

I yank up my jacket sleeve and look at my arm. All the tiny, fine hairs are standing up. Similar to a buildup of static charge right before lightning strikes...

A lady exits the diner and stops, her necklace floating up on its chain. Acorns and dry leaves rise from the pavement like soda bubbles. Purple pansies rip from the diner's window boxes by their roots, spraying dirt particles that hover in mid-air. Only those two bickering cheerleaders seem unaffected. In fact, they've stopped yelling, now standing in the middle of the parking lot staring at each other, their flushed faces intense and blank, oddly oblivious to the hullabaloo around them.

Then I see their eyes.

At first, I think the brunette's eyes have rolled back in her head. But her eyeballs are stark white – like marbles, like two blazing white coals. The tall redhead's eyes have also taken on a similar supernatural glow, only instead of white, they're as red as atomic fireballs. Red and white. Both sets of eyes locked on each other, motionless.

No doubt about it. These two princesses are my wildcards.

Two wildcards standing *right in front of me.*

No running, no chasing, no death threats from my evil naked doppelganger.

So here's my dilemma. If we were looking at two drooling creatures, I could whip out my shotgun right now and just take them out – boom, boom, applause. Everyone would love me, and this day would be a glorious pile of win. But they're not monsters. They're cheerleaders. You can't just go off shooting cheerleaders.

It annoys the crappity crap out of me.

Why can't it ever be easy?

"Kyle…" Merrick utters. The air thickens; suddenly every car alarm in the parking lot goes off, a blaring cacophony of honks and whistles.

"THESE TWO PRINCESSES ARE MY WILDCARDS."

Well, I guess this is where I swoop in.

My eyes fall on the bench where Old Dapper Jack was sitting earlier. His black silk top hat and cane are lying on the seat, right where he forgets them every day.

"Pass me that, will you?"

Merrick hands me the top hat and cane with a quizzically intrigued expression. As I flip the hat, Old Joe's wallet falls out onto my lap. Seriously, who keeps their wallet in their hat? I stuff the wallet hurriedly in my pocket, making a mental note to drop it off at Gammell's office later.

"Okay Merrick," I say. "Time to break this party up. You try and get the redhead to follow you into the diner, okay? I'll create a diversion." I cram the hat onto my head. "Cover me, cowboy!"

"Sure thing, cow…girl," he stutters with wavering enthusiasm.

I watch him move cautiously across the parking lot toward the girls, leaves and napkins whirling all around. Then, taking Dapper Joe's cane in my hand, I hop up onto one of the plastic benches. I clear my throat ceremoniously.

"Can I have everyone's attention?" I bark over the car alarms. The two feuding cheerleaders swing their heads in my direction, momentarily breaking eye contact with each other.

Everything stops.

It's literally like flipping off a switch. All the car alarms instantly go silent. Napkins, flowers, and leaves flutter to the ground. Through the crowd, I see the two girls pass out cold, going limp as wet noodles; Merrick lunges forward, catching them both unconscious in his arms. He looks up at me, throwing me a 'what now' shrug. And Merrick isn't the only one.

Every eye is on me. It's like a parking lot full of owls.

I swallow.

"Um, you can unclench your hands now," I address the crowd, lowering my voice to an enigmatic register. "Because you've just been treated to our little trick! A good old-fashioned murder mystery, with a fun supernatural twist! Ooh, did it get you in the Halloween mood?"

I hook Old Joe's cane around my wrist and swing it around like a hula hoop, hamming it up. Everyone leans forward, intrigued. An amused grin pulls at Merrick's mouth.

"Hope you enjoyed act one," I belt dramatically. "Now keep your eyes peeled today for act two! Could be anytime…anywhere! Guess correctly what happens next, and win…uh…tickets to tonight's homecoming game!"

Scattered applause breaks out.

"That's all for now, folks!" I announce, leaping down from the bench and tap-dancing across the parking lot, hurrying to where Merrick is still clutching both comatose girls in his arms.

I grin deviously at him. "Can't keep the girls off of you these days, eh rockstar?"

"Hilarious," Merrick rolls his eyes, his face as red as the head cradled in his left arm. "Take one. *Please.*"

I hoist the brunette, all ninety pounds of her, tossing her limp body over my shoulder. We scurry off toward the diner like innocent little Sugarplum Fairies to a rowdy round of applause.

My lip twists in satisfaction.

It's barely past noon, and I've already got a dang wildcard slung over my shoulder.

In your face, Holliday.

*

I plow into the diner's restroom, locking the door then plunking the tiny brunette on a toilet as gently as I can. Her head lolls against the stall's wall. She looks so harmless...

I'm not fooled.

"Okay," I mutter, whipping out my Icemaker. "Let's get down to business."

Both red dots have vanished off my screen. Weird...

"Oh c'mon," I whack the screen with my hand. "Are you kidding me?"

Then I freeze.

Holy cats, did we just neutralize the wildcards?

If we did, then that was the most ridiculously easy wildcard smackdown in the history of...well, since I began smacking down wildcards.

But it doesn't make sense. A neutralized wildcard would still show up on my screen as a gray dot. And there's no gray dot.

Crouching on the floor, I narrow my eyes at the unconscious cheerleader slumped on the toilet. She doesn't sprout wings or erupt into scales.

I give her a little poke.

Her eyes pop open.

"Oh." I jerk upright. "Hello..."

"What just happened?" The girl exhales, her eyes darting around. "Why the eff am I on a toilet? And who are you?"

All excellent questions. Two of which I've got an answer for.

I quickly run my eyes over her. Whereas Candace is taller than me, Danielle is a pixie, only reaching up to my nose. She's so delicate that a stiff breeze would knock her over, but her maroon Carnival Creeke cheerleading hoodie and black leggings cling in all the right places. Her thick, dark chocolate hair is piled up into a messy ponytail, stray sweaty strands falling over her rounded, heart-shaped face, bulls-eyed with dimples, and drawn into a little upturned nose. The girl's huge almond eyes are meticulously dusted with shimmery white eyeshadow, and staring at me with a fierceness that defies her saccharine cuteness. Her tiny honeybee of a mouth presses firmly together.

She's waiting for an explanation.

Shakiness, dysphoria...

I lean down and pull up her eyelid, as though examining her eyes.

"Danielle, right?" I ask. She nods unsteadily. "Do you have a family history of hypoglycemia?"

"No. Well, maybe. Um, what's that mean?"

"It means..." I frown distractedly. "It means you might turn inside-out. Here, splash water on your face."

I usher Danielle to the sink and turn on the faucet, leaving her flapping around like a sea lion while I put my hands on my hips and start stalking around behind her.

Now what?

Turn her around facing the wall, tell her a story about rabbits, then cap her with my Icemaker? I may be heartless, but I'm not *that* heartless. Shooting cheerleaders is not a new low I'm ready to add to my resume.

And besides, according to my Icemaker, these girls aren't even wildcards anymore…

I crack open the bathroom door and peer out.

The diner is packed with people. Everyone is chattering excitedly about the end of the world, or whatever they just witnessed. Cheerleaders have filled the booths, crowding around a dazed-looking Lisa like she's a celebrity, while their frazzled coach buys Cokes and tries not to have a stroke.

"Merrick?" I hiss loudly through the door.

His face immediately pops into view. He must have been waiting for me right outside the door.

"A Halloween murder mystery?" he chuckles doubtfully. "That was total B.S., right?"

"Yup. Well, mostly."

"Because it sure didn't *look* like tricks and stunt wires."

"Why not?"

"Well, for one, this is *Danielle Shaw* and *Lisa Brinkley* we're talking about. Those two airheads couldn't act their way out of a paper bag. Didn't look like acting, anyway."

I grin, leaning my cheek against the doorframe. "So what did it look like to you?"

"Um, you want my honest opinion?"

"Let's have it."

He leans forward, pushing up his glasses.

"It looked to me…" Merrick's voice lowers. "Like a chemical reaction was taking place between those two girls at a sub-atomic level."

See, this is among the many reasons that I love Merrick. I don't know what kind of brain food he must read at night, but I hope he never, ever changes. Anyone who jumps to the 'atomic cheerleaders' theory is superbly awesome in my book. Someday, maybe I'll even get the words to tell him.

Alrighty. So if what Merrick is proposing is correct, these girls are still wildcards…but only when they're *together*. We just need to put them back together.

Right?

Only one way to find out.

"Stand back," I tell Merrick. "I'm going to take our theory for a test drive."

"You're joking, right?"

I point a warning finger at him. "Stand back."

Pulling Danielle away from the restroom sink, I hook the door open with my foot and lead her out like a human shield. The girl whips her head around in confusion.

"Pushy much?" she snaps. "What are you–"

Suddenly she goes rigid. Across the diner, Lisa rises upright in her booth, her gaze locked on us, her freckled face ghostlike, eyes glowing like flaming red coals. A loud rattle fills the diner as spoons, forks, and coffee cups begin to float up off the tables. My eyes jump to my Icemaker. Immediately, two gorgeous red dots blink onto the screen.

Bingo.

That's all the proof I need.

I seize Danielle and jerk her back into the restroom. Poor girl is glassy-eyed and bewildered; she staggers back toward the sink and resumes splashing water on her face. On my way out, I slap the "Out of Order" sign over the restroom door handle.

What kind of freaky pickle am I stuck with today?

Merrick skids over and leans his back against the restroom door beside me.

"Well, that was super fun." He exhales slowly. "So what are we gonna do with Carrie and the Phoenix?"

Another excellent question.

"We keep them apart, that's what." I frown. "I've got to – er, study this case a little deeper. I'll take Danielle with me." Zipping my jacket, I nod toward Lisa. "You stick with the Red Queen."

Merrick's expression crumbles in horror.

"You're kidding, right?" he whispers. "Please no. Those girls are so vapid, it makes my face hurt."

"Hey, you're a rockstar, remember?" I grin. "Just go talk to her. Maybe she's got a hidden passion for biochemistry."

"Yay. I'll try not to gouge my eyeballs out with a fork."

"Be nice, okay? Do something gentlemanly. Here, go take her a Coke."

"I dunno, she looks pretty well-hydrated already..."

"You said you'd be nice!"

"I *said* I'd try not to gouge out my eyeballs. Not the same thing!"

Slinging his messenger bag over one shoulder, he trudges slowly across the diner, Coke in hand, looking like a man going off to war. I'm heading back into the restroom when Merrick turns around and stops me.

"Um, Kyle, hold on." He reaches into his jeans pocket. "At least take this. So I can find you."

He's holding out his cell phone.

You always find me, I want to say.

I gaze at him. For all my hair-splitting efforts to protect Merrick, here he is, always looking out for *my* silly butt. Always consistent. Always caring about me. This boy is my constant.

Nodding gently, I take the phone from him.

"Good luck," Merrick hesitates, forcing a tentative smile. "Just, uh…don't blow up the world and die, okay?"

"Right." I nod confidently. "Blow up the world and die. Got it."

With a lopsided grin, I stuff his cell in my pocket and push into the restroom.

"Not super reassuring!" I hear him yell after me.

Danielle is standing at the sink, panting. She's soaked like a drowned rat, staring at me with eyes so wide I can see sclera around the iris. Mascara oozes down her dimpled cheeks in shimmery black streaks. I fold my arms.

She's not a monster. She's not a gargoyle…

Just a scared teenage girl.

A girl who doesn't seem to remember a shred of what just happened five minutes ago.

"Are you like a d-d-doc?" she hiccups.

What's up, Doc?

My jaw clenches involuntarily.

"Something like that," I mutter, forcing Holliday out of my head and the bile back down my throat. Danielle flaps her tiny hands, her delicate features scrunching into an unmistakable about-to-cry face.

"Am I gonna turn inside-out?!" she wails.

"No, just relax–"

I suddenly remember Old Dapper Jack's wallet. Digging it from my pocket with an official air, I flip it open like an ID badge, flashing it quickly in front of Danielle's face, then shoving it back into my pocket before she can actually see the name or picture on it.

"My name's Kyle," I say. "I'm a doctor. Don't worry. I'm going to stay with you until you feel better."

Or until that red dot appears again and we slaughter each other.

I ask Danielle if she wants to call her parents; with an eye roll, she informs me that her folks are in Vegas. But she has an appointment at the nail salon today – an appointment for two people – because apparently Danielle and Lisa were supposed to have a little girlie outing together.

So that's where we go.

Buttery afternoon sunlight streams through the Cloud 9 ½ Salon's cotton candy pink drapes. I've never been in here, not unless you count that time when Tannon smashed his Panhard through the wall.

Danielle and I are led over to the manicure stations and plopped into two boxy white pleather chairs piled with pink heart-shaped chenille pillows. A glass shelf displays assorted glitter nail polishes with badass candy-themed names like "Sourpuss Lemon Warrior Queen." There's a pink mat on the floor under our feet, also shaped like a heart. So many hearts. I'm sensing a theme here. I am not a fan of this theme.

Danielle is watching me like a hawk.

"I'm really good at making stuff," she declares fiercely. "I can actually do this myself, you know–" She spreads her fingers, examining her nails. "But I like to let the salon do it. I'm just so busy with cheerleading and school, and all. And I know they need the money. I'm, like, a humanitarian."

I drum my fingers on the chair.

Alright, how the flip am I supposed to fix these girls? Do a little dance around them? Sprinkle them with magic wildcard neutralizing powder, one with a pleasant orange scent? I'll bet Holliday is laughing his freako head off at me right now.

Unless...

Maybe the key lies in *why* these girls were arguing.

"So," I broach in a casual voice. "You and your friend. Looked like you were pretty mad at each other, back in the parking lot earlier."

"Lisa?" Danielle snorts. "Well, hel-*lo!* That slutty-poo bought the same exact dress that I'm wearing for the homecoming dance! Even though pink looks totally raunchy on her."

Okay, so much for that theory.

Maybe the solution is simple. Maybe I'm just supposed to keep Danielle and Lisa *apart.* Just keep these volatile little powder kegs from sparking each other, just until the day can reset at one o'clock. Maybe that's all.

But I hate putting all my eggs in the 'maybe' basket.

I clear my throat and try to concentrate on relaxing.

My attendant is named Ginger, a thirty-something gal with a flat-ironed, asymmetrical blond bob and eyelashes like tarantula legs. She takes my hand and chipperly starts assessing it. I watch her face degenerate in horror as she looks over my calloused mitts, her eyes lingering on my mangled nail stubs that got ripped off by the gargoyle.

I smile sweetly. "Oh, I do a lot of yard work. Pulling up trees and stuff. With my hands."

Her expression is pure gold.

"Well, okie-dokie!" Ginger quips brightly. "I suggest a complete silk resurfacing treatment. Then–" She glances again at my missing fingernails. "We can replace those, you know. A full set. You'll love them!"

"Whatever you think," I reply, slouching lazily back in the chair.

Several women in the corner are staring at me. I recognize them. It's those two women also staying at the Red Rooster, the ones always gabbing about Corgipoos during breakfast. Of course they're gawking at me. I stick out like a sore thumb here in Carnival Creeke, with my battered, touch-me-not red leather jacket, my utilitarian wardrobe and combat boots. I never bothered to get new clothes, gussy myself up. What's the point? It would all just disappear tomorrow.

Anyway, these dusty duds are all that's left of Cl. Kyle. Wearing these clothes, I know I can be myself without even trying. Just be Kyle. Whoever she was.

Danielle is still unabashedly staring at me.

"You know," she says. "You could be pretty. Maybe if you tried a little makeup..."

Really, the makeup thing again? Does Candace make them memorize a script or something?

I'm fully aware that the girl is assessing me, determining whether she thinks I'm worth impressing. Pretty sure I'm failing that test. I can tell by her pursed lips and contracted pupils that she thinks I'm weird. I haven't been bothering to act much like a doctor, but I can't seem to muster the oomph to care.

Whatever. I'm not here to entertain this girl.

I'm here to kill her.

Ginger returns a minute later with her arsenal box.

"We call this nail set our 'Shellac Attack'," she chirps proudly.

Hey, my kind of nails.

The next thirty minutes are spent buffing the epidermis off my rough monster hands, then slathering them with twelve different types of floral-smelling lotions. At first, I watch Ginger's face as she works. I can tell I'm making her nervous, so I stare at my cuticles instead. It's pleasantly nonviolent. Maybe even a little relaxing. A little. I can comprehend why people do this.

Fast-forward twenty minutes later: I take back everything I just said. *I am losing my ape-flipping mind.* I writhe around restlessly in the pleather chair. My butt is falling asleep. How on earth is Danielle still sitting there like that?!

I narrow my eyes longingly at the door.

Please, for the love of all that's good, let Deadhead Kyle tromp in and decapitate me with the battle axe. Then let her kick my head out into Main Street for Randy and his cronies to play soccer with. Let the other gargoyle spring to life and burst into this room. Let Rascal Holliday drop from the ceiling and rip out my heart again. Wait, no – put it back in my chest, just so he can rip it back out again.

Anything but this.

Agitated, I cross my legs and jig my foot, faster and faster, until everyone in the shop starts shooting me dirty looks.

The muffled Spiderman theme song suddenly pipes up in my pocket.

"Excuse me a sec!" I blurt, springing gratefully from the torture chair and slipping out the salon door. I fish Merrick's ringing phone from my pocket. I don't recognize the number.

"Hello?"

"Hey, it's me, Merrick. I'm calling from Lisa's cell. Uh... Houston, we have a problem."

"Is Lisa okay?"

"No, no, Lisa's fine. She's here with me at the bowling alley."

"So what's the problem?"

"Well...it's you." He hesitates. *"Apparently, someone at the diner saw your Big Bad detector and thought it was a bomb. They reported it. And now, well...Sheriff Gammell is sort of hunting you."*

Well, that's just super.

Why does my destiny always intersect with Frank Gammell? I gnaw at my annoyingly shiny nails, my brain gears cranking. My thoughts are interrupted sharply by Lisa's voice in the background on Merrick's phone.

"Guh-ross," she's bemoaning in a sing-song tone. *"Can we say suckiest cupcake e-ver? The 'molten' caramel was all hard and*

nasty. That's totally false advertising! If it's not molten, don't call it molten, right?"

"*Ah, First World problems,*" Merrick consoles through what sounds like a forced grin. Then he returns to me with a pleading whisper. "*Can we trade?*" he begs. "*This chick's a freak. I'm not kidding, either. When she thinks no one's looking, she pretends she's a fox priestess. You know she's trying to get me to go to the homecoming dance with her? Even though–*" He raises his voice, an obvious attempt to be overheard. "*I'm not a high-schooler!*"

"*Even better...*" I hear Lisa purr huskily.

"*See?*" he grumbles. "*What am I supposed to do with her?*"

"Whatever you want," I mutter, pacing up and down the sidewalk. "Just take her someplace away from people. Away from crowds. I'll do the same with Danielle. Just keep Lisa safe."

"*I know, I know,*" he sighs. "*Save the cheerleaders, save the world.*"

I've just slid the phone back into my pocket when Danielle comes breezing out the salon door. She pauses, tipping her chin back and sliding her eyes up me with a casual expression. After a moment she says, "So where are you from?"

Wow. This girl is actually broaching civil conversation with me? Maybe I misjudged her, thinking she was a walking mass of selfishness.

A swell of warmth wells up inside me.

"Well," I begin. "That's kind of a long story–"

"Oh sorry," she cuts me off, tossing her hair in my face. "I don't really care. I just wanted to say, do us all a favor and go back."

Zing. That actually stung.

*

My plan is to get Danielle back to the Red Rooster, safe and hidden, lickity-split. But she whines about having a headache, and I know she's not lying – from what I saw, those blow-ups really knock the stuffing from these girls. She's probably got a killer headache. So I give her five minutes at the General Store to grab some aspirin.

I haven't forgotten that Sheriff Gammell is on my tail, either.

As we approach the General Store's pumpkin-lined porch steps, I fondly recall a day when I was hiding in the bushes outside. I saw a bird fly straight into the glass doors – *thump*, just like that. The little creature was fine; it got up and flew off after a few minutes, so that was a relief. I definitely wasn't going to attempt bird mouth-to-mouth again. I've got a back track record with that stuff.

Danielle sulkily pushes past me, marching ahead. She's mad at me for spoiling her cuticle-buffing thingy back at the nail salon. Not that I can blame her. It wasn't my proudest moment.

Cowbells clatter as we enter. Sam Dove looks up from his cashier counter, screwing the lid onto an enormous jar of pickles.

"Danielle, Danielle!" He beams under his superstache. "Is that the sun, or has Hollywood's prettiest little starlet just graced my doorstep?"

He's referring to our little 'show' at the diner earlier. At first, I expect Danielle to ask what he's talking about – but to my relief, she's a sucker for compliments and decides to play along. Instantly, she transforms into a gushing volcano of sunshine.

"Oh my word!" she giggles coyly. "Well, I've had a few scouts approach me, you know. After cheerleading practice, asking me if I've ever done any modeling and stuff."

"My dear, your beauty just radiates. How's cheerleading?"

"Oh," Danielle tosses her dark hair, assuming a rehearsed distant gaze. "It's super stressful. I'm just so busy all the time, with my honors classes and all. They say I could be a real frontrunner for the new face of Bacon Blast salad dressing, but…I just don't know if it really makes my heart sing. But my future is bright. Sometimes I feel I'm about to burst, I have so many dreams!"

"And I betcha they're as cute as you!" Sam gushes.

I interrupt before he can start blowing raspberries on her tummy-tum.

"Can I get you anything?" I ask Danielle.

She shoots me a toxic glare and saunters off between the aisles.

"Hot dog?" I call. "Twinkie? Nothing?"

I sigh, laying an assortment of packaged munchies on the cashier counter. Sam scans my items one by one. After a moment, he pauses.

"Don't worry, my dear." Sam pats my hand. "Those tests are never one-hundred percent accurate."

I stare at him like a brain-dead cow. He points down at my pile of turkey jerky and snack cakes. "*Cravings*," he whispers covertly, tapping his nose with a wink.

Oh, for Pete's sake. Will that stupid pregnancy test *ever* quit haunting me?

I blow a long, slow breath out through my nose.

Anyway, how could *I* have a baby? *I'm barely even human,* I want to shout. Sure, I pretend I'm normal, pretend I'm one of them, all happy with a heartbeat, just shooting the breeze, but deep inside, my Icemaker is burning a hole in my pocket.

Imposter.

And Kindly Sam Dove isn't helping, standing there smiling at me because he has to, smiling because he's obligated to be all doggone congenial, smiling because I've been in his town just one day and I saved it from a rampaging gargoyle, and I'm not pregnant, and my shirt is still on backwards.

I want to scream.

Stuffing my receipt into my pocket with a gnarled smile, I trudge over and plant myself near the door to wait for Danielle. I spot her brown ponytail over the beef-a-roni aisle, which, when I last checked, is not where the aspirin is located.

Princess Bacon Blast better not try to skitter off, or I'll wring her skinny neck.

"How's it going?" I call.

"I'm looking!" snarls Danielle's voice. "Don't get your ovaries in a bunch!"

Wow, this day just keeps getting better and better.

Leaning back against the ice cream freezer chest, I open my bag of munchies. I stare at a Ho-Ho. The Ho-Ho stares back. All I want to do is comfort-eat the heck out of that thing. But with my delicate lactose-intolerant stomach, all that sugar and cream filling would probably rip me up from the inside.

Then again…death by Ho-Ho could only improve my day.

I peel open the wrapper and plunge the cylindrical, chocolately cake into my mouth. Ohh. It's obscenely good.

I unwrap another.

I'm unwrapping my fourth Ho-Ho when I look up and see Danielle suddenly standing in front me. Her glittery pink cell phone is in her hand, an ominously venomous look simmering in her narrowed eyes.

"I looked up hypoglycemia," she says icily.

"Oh yeah?"

"Yeah. It's like some sugar disease that fat people get," Danielle tosses a distasteful glance at the Ho-Ho in my hands. "But Wikipedia didn't say anything about hypoglycemia turning people all gross and inside-out."

"Is that right?" I smile. "Huh."

"That's right. I'm not a retard. I read the whole article. Looks like you're a liar."

A lady and a scholar, I see.

Danielle sashays slowly toward me, one hip at a time, narrowing her eyes and bringing her pixie face right up to mine, inches away. I suppress the instinct to flip her over my head.

"You're not really a doctor, are you?"

"Okay, fine." I sigh, raising my hands. "You got me. Truth is, I believe something is happening to you, Danielle. Something off the record, and outside the books. You're in danger. And like it or not, I'm here to protect you."

"Whatevs. I bet you're just some crazy old freak who gets their kicks by creeping people out. Or maybe…"

Pausing, the girl circles around me, her babydoll eyes taking on a vicious glimmer.

"I bet you ran away from home." She fakes a pout. "Or maybe they chased you off, because you're so ugly and no one loves you. Boo-hoo, and you just couldn't bear it anymore. Unless–"

Her glossy lips curl upward into a delighted smirk. "Oh, gag! Is there something going on between you and Cohen? Well, no big shocker, he's the only person who's an even bigger freak than you."

Sam's mustached grin pops around the corner of the aisle.

"Help you gals with anything?"

"No!" we both bark in unison. Sam withers and recesses back behind the shelf.

I turn back to Danielle. "Merrick is a good person; leave him out of this. And believe whatever you want. But I'm not going anywhere."

"I should call the cops right now." She waves her cell in my face like a cobra. I bat the phone out of her hand.

"Knock it off, Danielle."

"Or what? Screw you! Y'know what?"

She inhales a deep breath, essentially broadcasting that she's about to scream. I've swung her into a headlock exactly one second after my hand clamps over her mouth – a tricky feat, because I'm still holding my half-eaten Ho-Ho.

"Now listen here," I hiss into her ear. "There's one vital flaw in your mean-girl voodoo. It only works if the other person cares. I understand this has been a crazy day for you. But quit trying to bite the only person here helping you, or I swear, I will take you over my knee and tan your fannycakes like your daddy should've done a long time ago."

Why does this scene feel familiar?

Suddenly, all I can think of is Holliday's warm breath as he purred into my ear, that first day in the alley, *my* head clamped under his arm...

"I'm going to let go," I tell Danielle. "Behave, alright?"

At first, I think she's going to cry.

Then her hand flies at me, missing my cheek by a millimeter. I catch her wrist. Did she just try to slap me?

Wait, this is good.

Let her get mad.

If I can get Danielle ruffled enough, maybe she'll turn into the wildcard again. Maybe we don't need Lisa at all...

I roll around on my heel.

"What do you want, Danielle? Want to punch my face? Would that make you feel better?"

I catch her by surprise. She reddens, averting her eyes from me and pretending to be interested in some sunglasses on a rack.

"Stop saying that," she mutters under her breath. "Gah, why are you so creepy?"

Want the long or short version?

"C'mon," I press. "Here's my face. Punch me. My offer stands. Going once, going twice–"

Without waiting she reels back, catapulting her free arm at me. Plenty of spitfire, but there's no real speed on this swing.

"Pretty hopeless," I grin, ducking.

I wish she'd give me more. *Really* lay into me.

There I go again, expecting more from these people.

I open my arms and make a kissy-face at her. Danielle screeches, her delicate nostrils flaring with rage.

Now we're talking.

Sam's kindly mustache reappears over the chip rack.

"Ah, act two continues!" he declares with delight. "And in my little shop, no less!"

I deflect Danielle like a gnat; she screams and barrels past.

"Come on!" I bark. As I kick her in the tush and send her spinning off into the chip rack, it occurs to me that I'm acting just like Holliday. A naughty thrill runs through me.

No...

I *am* Holliday.

"Y'know," Sam waggles his bushy eyebrows mischievously. "I used to dabble in a bit of drama club, myself." He clears his throat dramatically, placing a hand over his chest. "Hold my brain, be still my beating heart!"

My head suddenly goes foggy.

My eyes zone out– and not just because my stomach is feeling a little weird. Because Sam's comment just prompted an awful thought to pop into my head. My beating heart…

What if I'm still ***connected*** *to my heart?*

Wherever it is, lying in a jar somewhere…like a battery to a remote-controlled airplane…

Is it still beating?

And if that's true…what happens if it stops? Will I drop dead? Like a puppet with my strings sliced off? On the sidewalk, on the toilet, face-down in a plate of spaghetti…?

My stomach rolls over.

I am *literally* in Holliday's fingerless gloved hands.

I hate that so much.

It's only when I catch sight of Sam, smiling by his gourmet lollipop stand, that I'm jolted back to my senses. I look down at my Icemaker. No red dot.

This isn't accomplishing anything.

Everything we do is a choice. A chance to either make the world a better place, or a worse one. Make the people around us nobler, more pleasant…or make them cynical buttholes.

With a sigh, I lower my hands and let Danielle hit me.

I really sell it. Tumbling backwards with way more enthusiasm than necessary, my back collides with the cardboard Halloween candy display, demolishing it spectacularly as I hit the floor. My arms flop open, spread-eagle on a bed of fun-size Butterfingers. I lay still. Just for kicks, I keep my eyes closed.

"Kyle…?" I hear Danielle whisper in a tiny voice.

I lay there motionless, playing possum. Because screw this day. Maybe I'll lay here all afternoon, amidst these Butterfingers. Who's going to stop me? Sheriff Gammell? Rascal Holliday?

Please. Come try.

Motivate me.

There's a scuffling of feet, then I hear Danielle's breathing up close. Fingers press against my neck.

Oh crap. She's checking my pulse.

"Oh, no...Kyle?" she squeaks. "*Oh...my...gawww...*"

I wait just a moment longer, until I'm sure she's close enough to lick a grasshopper. Then I pop my eyes open.

"Boo."

I'm a terrible person.

But her scream is hilarious.

We're heading for the door when Randy and his buddies come swaggering up the General Store's porch steps. Behind them, parked at the curb, is Randy's fancy new street bike – a Ducati Streetfighter 848. A sleek little beast, its gleaming Italian curves are painted a sexy yellow and black. I don't even want to guess how many toes Randy's father must have had to sell to buy that thing.

"Wh'sup, ladies?" Randy assumes a smug grin. "Heading somewhere?"

My stomach gurgles, churning around like a cement mixer.

Uh-oh.

Feels like those Ho-Hos are about to make a reappearance...

Over their shoulders I see Sheriff Gammell's brown police car pull up to the curb behind Randy's bike, letting out two quick, electronic whoops.

Seriously. I don't have time for this.

"Hey Randy," I say impatiently, glancing at my watch. "I'll bet you five bucks a bird hits that door."

"Huh?"

A loud '*plunk*' causes them all to jump out of their sneakers.

"Holy shneikies!!" Randy yelps, as they all run outside to crowd around the kamikaze starling that just bounced off the glass. I grab Danielle's arm and we slip out the door, around the side of the store, to freedom. Then I barf all over her.

*

We catch a trolley bus to the Red Rooster. Danielle calls me a freak, a zombie, and a bunch of other stuff I deserve. Then she clams up completely, glowering out the window in nasty silence.

I feel horrible.

At least my stomach feels better. Wish I could get rid of Holliday the same way. Just puke him up like a Ho-Ho. Purge my body of his superior, smirking face.

That sharky grin… Those pitch-black eyes, gleaming in his perfectly sculpted, sickly-pale face… Shoot, the guy looked deader than me, and *I'm* the one without a heart.

We trudge up to my room at the bed-and-breakfast. My prisoner immediately goes into the bathroom and slams the door.

Ah, just like a teenager.

Did I ever act like that? Bet I did.

Fine, let her do whatever she wants. I notch the record player needle over an old vinyl disc and flop onto my four-poster bed, stretching my feet out as my belly slowly unknots itself.

At least Merrick is keeping Lisa out of trouble. Alone, away from people... Just the two of them...all cozy, together...

My eye twitches. I practically sent them on a date. Whatever. Fox Priestess had better keep her paws off Merrick, that's all I'll say. Not that he's mine, or anything. Why should I care? Merrick is a big boy. He can do what he wants. I'm just trying to protect him, that's all.

On the scratchy record player, a muted jazz piano tinkles jauntily as Billie Holiday sings an aching plea to her lover. The jerk took her heart, left her incomplete, so now she's rationalizing that he should just come collect the rest of her.

I squirm uncomfortably on the bed.

"*You took the part that once was my heart,*

So why not take all of me?"

Gritting my teeth, I realize I'm absentmindedly tracing the circular scar on my chest with my fingertips.

My face flushes hot.

I quickly jerk my hand away from my scar, as if Holliday has some kind of alarm that alerts him every time I touch his gruesome handiwork. Stupid, I know... But so is walking around without a heart.

I roll upright and sit on my hands. No good. My music usually settles me, strokes my zinging nerves until they lie smooth again. I flip through the stack of records.

'My Man Don't Love Me'… 'Something's Gotten Hold of My Heart'… 'Take Another Piece of My Heart'…

Is that all they sang about back then? Losing their stupid hearts? What kind of twisted people wrote these songs? It occurs to me that maybe literal organ thievery might not have been on their minds…but it's still irritating.

"Buck up, girl," I growl at the record player. "Quit whining! He didn't create you, and he can't un-create you!"

Maybe she can't find the jerk. Maybe he just vaporized, along with her heart. Gone like a dream. Like fog in the morning. Fine. Sit and cry about it some more. See if I care.

Sliding abruptly off my bed, I yank the record off the turntable and wrench the window open, flinging the vinyl outside like a Frisbee. It bounces off a tree, shattering into modern art.

The bathroom door opens. Danielle stands there in the doorway, her eyes flickering from me, to the empty hissing record player, then to the open window.

Shrugging, I slide another record from its sleeve and hold it out for Danielle.

"Here, give it a try. It's therapeutic."

Danielle pauses. She bites her bottom lip, then daintily tosses the record out the window. It lands in the tea garden below us. Her next toss is better. We take turns pitching the sad ballads of yesteryear out that window – Lady Day, Ella Fitzgerald, Mildred Bailey – the shiny vinyl discs go sailing into the sky, some bonking off silvery trees, others landing in the grass behind the Quik-Pump gas station next door.

I chuckle, raising my eyebrows at Danielle.

"Hey, don't ever let anyone tell you that records can't be broken nowadays."

In spite of herself, my prisoner smiles.

*

We hang around the room for a while, until the sun goes down and Danielle starts getting bored. She wants to go to tonight's homecoming football game. I tell her to forget it, but she whines a bunch and eventually I cave. Not because I couldn't easily shoot down all her flimsy arguments for why I should let her go. But another rationale comes to mind.

Merrick is keeping Lisa *away* from crowds.

By every standard of logic, a packed stadium is quite possibly the safest place for us on earth tonight.

What could go wrong?

*

Carnival Creeke High School is pulsing with pre-game energy. The night air is filled with the deep, oily-saccharine smell of funnel cake and cold air as Danielle and I weave our way through the chain-link fence and into the jam-packed football stadium. My eyes rove constantly through the milling crowd. This must be what the president's escort feels like. Danielle put on lip gloss, and braided her thick, dark hair into pigtails. She breaks

character here and there, spotting someone she knows, sporadically switching into a volcanic-cutesy smile and waving at them with hysterical enthusiasm, bouncing on her toes, then immediately falls back into a gloomy slouch beside me. At one point we run into Randy and his cronies, all painted up in Carnival Creeke's colors. The teen's maroon-and-orange face lights up when he sees me.

"Dude!" he jabs both hands in my direction. "Do it again!"

I blink. "What?"

"That bird, man – *BAM!*" Randy punches the air with a wolfish grin. "That was majorly sick!"

"Ugh." I shake my head. "Kid, *you're* majorly sick." We skim aside them and walk a few steps. Then I twist around again, hollering back at Randy, "Oh, and get rid of that firecracker you've got in your pocket!"

Danielle and I bumble our way up the metal steps and take our seats on the bleachers as the marching band starts to play.

It's weird, the normalcy of it all. Allowing myself to get lost in the crowd. Nobody screaming, nobody turning inside-out. I've gotten accustomed to always racing around, moving like a shark. Even when sitting still, never truly at rest.

Exhaling, I lean back and melt down onto my bleacher a little.

I could get used to this.

Grinning cheerleaders in long-sleeved maroon and orange take the field, their hair up in ribbons, silver pompoms glittering under the bright stadium floodlights as the marching band pounds out a silly, syncopated rendition of "Hungry like the Wolf."

Beside me, Danielle huffs a sigh and fidgets on the bleacher.

I watch her in the corner of my eye.

Can't blame her. She should be down there with her friends tonight. By all rights, in another reality, she'd be a normal kid – doing normal stuff, flashing her teeth and high-kicking with her fellow cheerleaders under those Friday night lights. Danielle didn't ask for this. But the wildcard hijacked her. Burned its freaky stamp on her, whether she agreed to it or not. Lucky her.

I know the feeling.

"For what it's worth," I say. "I'm sorry you're here, and not down there."

Danielle snorts testily and rolls her eyes. After a moment she shrugs.

"Cheerleading is..." She pauses, wrenching her mouth. "I dunno. They expect me to smile and all, but...I'm not really always having a good time."

"That's not surprising."

"What's that supposed to mean?"

"It just makes sense," I reply gently. "That's all. You don't always have to be what everyone expects you to be."

"Yeah, whatever."

"Listen." I sigh. "You'll reach an age when you finally start to see through it all. See the big picture. Beyond yourself, beyond all their eyes and their flimsy opinions and expectations of you. You get happier in your own skin. Then you finally start to relax.

Make choices for yourself. Mess up, try again… But it's yours. *Your* story."

She doesn't respond. The girl hasn't eaten all day. Bet she's starving. I reach into my cargo pants pocket and pull out my last Ho-Ho (the one that's not squashed from my earlier dramatic fall into the candy display). I peel the wrapper and hand it to her.

"Here. My last hypoglycemia bomb."

Danielle stares at my offering with wide eyes, like it's a poisonous snake. Then, very delicately, she takes the Ho-Ho from my hand with two fingers, casting a quick glance around, as if someone might catch her in the act. She starts to nibble at the cake's corner.

"Sorry I called you ugly," she mumbles quietly.

I pat her knee. "Sorry I made you think I was a zombie."

The marching band finishes up their tune with a thunderous and slightly-out-of-sync stomp. Beside the risers, off to the far-right corner of the field, an archway of cranberry and orange balloons is illuminated in a spotlight. The homecoming court begins parading through – a cavalcade of flashing white teeth and glitter, each girl handed a red rose as they pass under the balloon arch. Candace Cole strides out last, looking luminous in a sweeping, strapless feathery-silver gown. A pair of cute, sweaty quarterback boys present her with a football signed by the team, then awkwardly place a tiara on her head. She looks so happy. I stick two fingers in my mouth and whistle loud as I can muster.

Is this what it feels like to be normal?

I let my gaze wander happily across the field, to the crowded bleachers facing us opposite the football field.

Suddenly my eye catches on something.

Amidst the roaring audience of cranberry and orange, a splash of bright red hair.

You've got to be kidding…

I squint. The guy beside me has binoculars.

"Can I borrow these for a sec?"

He unhooks the binoculars from his neck, upsetting his nachos. I press the binoculars to my eyes.

It's Merrick and Lisa.

"IT'S MERRICK AND LISA."

COLLISION COURSE

"Danielle, we have to leave right now–"

I spin around in my seat to look at Danielle. The girl's back is rigid, her body pitched slightly forward. Her face is ghastly. Lips drawn so tightly I can almost see the outline of her teeth, hands clenched, still clutching the Ho-Ho, her white eyes blazing in her skull.

"No, no, *not here*, c'mon honey," I plead. "*Not here!*"

I snap my fingers in front of her glazed white eyeballs, but she's gone. Vacant.

We're toast.

There's a deep, metallic rumble and the bleachers suddenly vibrate beneath us, causing people to glance around in confusion. Down on the field, all the football players halt in their tracks, and I know they felt the tremor, too. I jump to my feet.

"Everyone get out of here!" I yell at the top of my lungs. "Get up, get to the exit!" Then, when everyone turns to me with amused smiles, I bellow, "This is *NOT* a show, people!! *Move your butts!!*"

I go to grab Danielle by the shoulders, but I have to yank my hand back. The girl is hot to the touch, zapping me like a live wire. I examine my blistered fingertips.

"So there's a forcefield now?" I mutter.

I throw my head around until I spot Merrick on the bleachers across the field, through the fleeing crowd. He's on his feet next to Lisa, her red eyes burning, fixed straight across the field at us. Merrick is holding an umbrella in the air like a baseball bat, frozen and uncertain whether to swing. No doubt he also tried to shake Lisa out of her stupor and received the same zap that I got when I touched Danielle. He looks over at me, and across the field we make eye contact. I nod my head furiously –

Do it, Merrick.

He drops the umbrella to his side and shakes his head, torn and apologetic.

Fine, looks like I'm on my own.

Leaving Danielle stewing, I leap the rail and clank down the bleachers, nearly bowling over Binoculars Guy, who's trying to run and finish eating his nachos simultaneously. At the bottom of the steps, just over the chain-link fence by the track, there's a coiled length of chain hanging off two football training tackle dummies. That might work as a lasso…

Yee-haw, baby.

I grab the chain and turn. The stadium has transformed into a massive, nightmarish snow globe.

Objects are whirling through the air over our heads – soda cups, people's hats, foam #1 fingers, red roses – they're all swirling around the stadium like it's one gigantic whirlpool drain. The chain flops in my hand like a live snake. Under my boots, the bleachers start to rattle; the metal groans as the structure gives an almighty lurch.

I've got to put a stop to this now.

I'm plunging back up the bleachers, plowing furiously against the stream of people bolting down, but it's obvious I'll never get up fast enough to lasso Danielle.

Not before this whole place goes kaboom.

Eyes on Danielle, I shove my hand into my pocket and run my finger hesitantly over the activation button on my Icemaker.

Just shoot her. All that matters is the wildcard.

Can't always come out smelling like a rose…

Wind whips at my face, debris swirls faster. With a deafening squeal, all the loudspeakers feedback at once, then every floodlight explodes, showering sparks over the screaming heads. I whip out my Icemaker decisively, springing it open into a shotgun. In the brief flash of falling sparks before the filament goes dark, my eye catches on something glinting silver –

A tiara. Candace's homecoming queen tiara, flying through the air over our heads.

I take aim.

Sorry Danielle. This might hurt…

I shoot the tiara, a big, fat calculated shot in the dark. The blue blast from my shotgun ricochets off the metal circlet, sending it spiraling in a new trajectory downward, clonking Danielle squarely in the head.

She instantly goes limp, her body pitching forward.

I bolt up the bleachers, a rain of hats and purses thudding all around me – but I can't make it in time to catch her. Someone else does. Through the panicked crowd, I see the tall man in the suede lumberjack coat stoop over with a collapsed Danielle in his arms. When he turns around, his enormous kindly mustache fills me with relief. It's Sam from the General Store.

"Good night a'livin'!" Sam exclaims, plucking French fries from his hair. "Can Carnival Creeke put on a halftime show, or what?"

His wife, Principal Julie Dove, hovers over them, as if trying to shield them with her scarf.

Suddenly I remember Merrick and Lisa. I search the bleachers, but everyone is gone. Something vibrates against my hip. Stuffing my hand into my pocket, I yank out Merrick's cell phone. There's a new text on the screen:

"Got out. Hope you're ok.
Took Lisa to my house
107 Bishop St."

My eyebrows raise.

I leave Danielle in Sam and Julie's care, with explicit instructions to apply ice to the knot on her head, get her inside, and lock the doors. They're good folk. Danielle will be fine.

Now to deal with Merrick.

*

I stomp down the dark residential sidewalk, my ears ringing from the stadium's exploding speakers. I can't believe Merrick brought Lisa to that football game. Merrick is a smart guy. Didn't he consider what might happen?

How could he outright defy me like that? Were my instructions not clear? Is today Opposite Day?

I replay my instructions in my head: *'Keep Lisa away from crowds.'* Nope, there's no earthly way he could have misinterpreted that.

I storm along the sidewalk faster and faster, my temperature rising. By the time I'm standing on the stone front porch, I'm shaking like a rabid hummingbird. Reaching for the doorbell, my hand hesitates.

The yellow stucco house is surrounded by a low picket fence. I glance up at a decorative Halloween flag, flapping in the metal holder above the porch. The flag depicts a calico kitten peeking up from a smiling jack-o-lantern. Countless bunny statues stare at me from the shadows beneath neatly trimmed azalea bushes. A pair of cherubs recline on the rim of the bird bath, their plaster lips pressed together in a kiss.

This looks like some old lady's house.

Frowning, I check Merrick's text again.

Yep, 107 Bishop Street…

I reach again for the doorbell, then decide to knock instead. Shave-and-a-haircut. There's a muffled click of locks inside, then Merrick pulls the door open.

I immediately launch into him.

"I said *AWAY* from crowds, Merrick! What part of that didn't compute?!" I spot Lisa, passed out on the living room couch, and switch my voice to a harsh whisper. "Someone could have been killed, do you understand?"

He backs away from my onslaught until his back hits the living room wall, causing a framed painting of ducks to bounce on its hook. On the couch, Lisa lets out a little snort and snuggles deeper into the cushions. The slim teen's long red hair is wet. Guess Merrick let her use his shower. For some reason, that infuriates me.

"I said I'm sorry, okay?" he snaps defensively. "Anyway, you said you were staying away from crowds, too!"

"Change of plans."

"Well, thanks for *telling* me!"

"It was a bad call, Merrick, and you know it." I pause, looking around. "You...live here?"

"Me and my grandma, yeah." He points at my face. "What's with the shiner?"

I touch my face, cheeks hot.

"Danielle punched me. Long story." My hands suddenly feel awkward; I shove them into my pockets. I pull out Merrick's cell phone, slapping it on the coffee table. "Look, don't try to change the subject!"

Rolling his eyes, he crosses into the kitchen and pulls a bag of frozen peas from the freezer.

"Well, here's an idea," he says flatly. "Maybe we should just let them talk?"

"About *what?*"

"Y'know, their...friction. Their female issues." He tosses the bag of peas to me. "Express their feelings."

"Are you loony?" I snarl, pressing the cold peas to my bruised cheek. "You *saw* what happened when they see each other. I'm not watching this town explode in a massive mushroom cloud just so Miss Bacon Blast and the Fox Priestess can have a therapy session."

I already blew up Carnival Creeke once, thanks so much.

Merrick shrugs. "I'm just saying, sometimes two people need to work out their poison."

"Not your best idea."

"I never said it was a good one!" He follows me when I whirl out of the kitchen. "Anyway, are you yelling at me or yourself here, Kyle? You made the same call, soldier. Get off your high horse!"

I stalk out of the house, slamming the door behind me.

Maybe I'm out of line. Maybe I shouldn't have flown off the handle at Merrick like that. He's right. He's not a soldier.

Am I upset at him because he didn't follow orders?

Or because he let Lisa into his shower...?

I walk faster. My boiling blood won't cool down, not even when I stop a few houses down and pump out twenty pull-ups on the swing set in their front yard.

I need to blow off some steam.

I half expect Merrick to ignore my knock and leave my butt outside on the porch. But he doesn't. Opening the door, he clenches his jaw and looks the other way, but swings his hand in a come-on-in gesture.

"Look," he says. "I'm sorry I brought Lisa to the game. But do me a favor, if you came to yell at me some more, write it down or something because my ears are still killing me from the speakers–"

"Quit talking for a minute."

I mash my lips into his and I kiss him.

If he hesitates, it's only for a stunned fraction of a beat. In one swift motion he grabs the back of my head tightly, kissing me back. His free arm is no longer free, seizing my waist hungrily, almost frantic, as if given a second, this might cease to be our reality.

And it does.

It's the muffled Spiderman song coming from his pocket.

I mumble against his mouth, "Your phone's ringing..."

"Can't hear anything."

Granted, I'm not exactly making any moves to disentangle myself from him either, even though I'm pretty sure we've just knocked over a lamp.

"Merrick, hold your horses a sec."

"Hold them for me?"

Reaching around him, I pull his cell phone out of his jeans' back pocket and look at the screen.

"It's Sheriff Gammell." I break away and hold it up. "You'd better take this."

Merrick gives me a pleading look. I tap the sleek blue cell to his forehead. With a delirious grin, he takes the little nuisance and brings it obediently to his mouth.

"Sorry, Merrick is gone right now but if you'd like to leave a message–"

I yoink the phone back from him.

Through the tiny speaker, Sheriff Gammell's gravelly voice sounds muffled and tinny.

"*Merrick?*" he's growling severely. "*You listen, son, and you listen good now. I don't know what this Kyle character has told you...but she's dangerous.*" I raise my eyebrows. "*Just tell me where she is, Merrick.*"

Dangerous, huh? Never knew Gammell thought so highly of me. Makes me feel all warm and fuzzy. Or maybe it would, if I hadn't just glanced over at the magnets on Merrick's fridge and realized something.

I think I know what needs to happen.

I know how this day ends.

Looking Merrick in the eye, I slowly bring the phone up to my mouth.

"You want me, Gammell?" I challenge. "Come and get me!"

Then I press the button and cut the call.

"Kyle, what the flying monkeys did you do that for?!" Merrick catches his cell as I toss it. "You know Sheriff Gammell's on his way here–"

"You're right."

"Huh?" Merrick stares at me.

"What you said earlier." I nod gently at Lisa's feet, slung over the arm of the couch. "Maybe we just need to let them blast each other. Work out their poison."

"Sure. Okay. I'll go make popcorn and get our hazmat suits."

"I'm not talking to Merrick the Humanitarian, I'm speaking to Merrick the Biochemist."

His expression changes suddenly.

"Equal and opposite forces!" he exclaims in a loud whisper, dragging his hands over his face in elation, obviously forgetting he's wearing glasses as he knocks them right off his nose. "These girls could cancel each other out! Well, theoretically. Heavy on the 'theoretical' part."

"Fingers crossed." I start hoisting Lisa up by the armpits. "Now, what's the biggest open space you know?"

*

We flip off the porch light so nobody will see us hauling Lisa down to the Tahoe. On our way out the door, I pause, digging Old Dapper Jack's wallet from my pocket, and hanging it on the brass door knocker. Then I slap a sticky note onto the wallet, scribbling a cryptic little message:

Where can a guy get a taco this time of night?

There. Have fun chasing *that*, Gammell.

The all-night taco joint is on the opposite side of town. Better if I know exactly where the good Sheriff is going than to have him charging around and randomly running into him on our way.

I *refuse* to end up in his jail cell tonight.

We speed along the dark streets, Lisa slumped unconscious in the Tahoe's backseat. We've got her belted in, her bright red hair flopping like a pompom each time Merrick turns a corner. I just called Sam and Julie, told them to bring Danielle, and meet us in twenty minutes at the abandoned McKenzie farm on the edge of town. It's the perfect isolated location for two nuclear cheerleaders to explode. But I didn't tell Sam and Julie that. I told them it was a matter of life and death, that the fate of the universe depended on it, and for the love of hominy, they just have to trust me on this.

I hope they do.

We roar around the corner and pull onto Main Street. The library's clock tower illuminates the graveyard passing to our left. It's 9:27.

Wait. This time of night...this street...

The Tahoe's headlights fall across a shiny black Hummer SUV stopped in the middle of the street. My stomach sinks.

LUV-MNY.

Merrick screeches on the brakes.

"Don't stop," I say quietly.

That doofus in the Adidas sports jacket is standing in the street beside his big dead car, hood propped up, his posture slumped and hopeless. He looks up at us, squinting in Merrick's headlights.

"Hey, that's Graham Sutherbee." Merrick frowns. "Looks like he ran out of gas."

Of course he did.

Merrick puts his Tahoe in park, and I start to panic. How can I make him realize this doesn't matter, that this caviar-munching moron and his abysmal ability to keep tabs on his gas gauge aren't going to matter tomorrow? Sam and Julie are on their way to the McKenzie farm right now. And need I mention Sheriff Gammell is still out for my blood...

We need to move.

"Please," I grab Merrick's arm and he freezes, midway out of the car. I shake my head. "Don't go out there. Just please get back in the car and let's go."

"Graham's wife is supposed to be having their baby tonight," he says. "I mean, Graham wasn't even supposed to be here for it. He was on some business trip in Aspen. Must've driven all night to make it back..."

My hand slides off his arm.

So *that's* why he was bawling the other night about needing to get to the hospital. Not for himself, but for his wife...

And the Scum of the Earth Award goes to Kyle.

At that moment, another truck comes swerving around the corner. The sky-blue Ford F150 rolls to a halt in front of us, nose-to-nose with Merrick's Tahoe. Behind the glare of the truck's headlights, three figures take shape – Sam's emperor mustache at the wheel, Julie on the passenger side. Danielle's petite form is sitting on the bench seat between them. Her white-hot eyes are shining like a second set of headlights from within the truck.

Merrick draws in a sharp breath at the sight of her.

"Well, at least Lisa's still asleep–"

We both whip our heads around. Lisa is sitting erect in the backseat.

Of course she is.

And her eyes are doing that dang glowy thing.

Of course they are.

Merrick tosses his hands, exasperated; I bang my head on the dashboard. Because we're not in a big, safe, empty farm field.

We're in the freaking public Main Street square.

We couldn't have picked a worse spot for these girls to blow, aside from possibly an orphanage on free puppy day. Twisting in his seat, Merrick tries to grab Lisa's arm. He gets zapped.

"Oh, forget it, Romeo!" I snap. "There's nothing we can do now!"

We eject from the Tahoe like a couple of greased cannonballs. The pavement rumbles under our feet. Our skin prickles and a blistering wind gusts up, wind like a vacuum trying to suck the skin off our faces. Mr. Luv-Money is standing in the street, pivoting in circles, jabbering away in confusion. I grab the panicked man by his jacket collar and haul him with us over to the sidewalk, where we join Sam and Julie clinging to the wrought-iron fence surrounding the library lawn. Merrick and I both lean over at the same time to grab the fence bars, bonking our heads together.

"Romeo?" he shouts at me over the screaming wind. "I think that was a little unnecessary!"

"Tell me more about your feelings!" I retort at the top of my lungs.

Huddled there together, we cling to those cold metal bars, flying papers and dirt exfoliating us, the gale-force windstorm peeling our mouths back and threatening to flick our teeth from our skulls. I don't have a clue why it suddenly pops into my head, but I think of something Danielle said earlier.

She was right. Carnival Creeke *isn't* my home.

I'm no closer to untangling my stringy past than I was the first day I woke up in this hellish hamster wheel. Even if I win this game – if I *do* stop time from skipping – what then? Where would I go?

Danielle and Lisa rage on inside their respective vehicles, the metal chassis surrounding them not doing jack to dampen their destructive powers. Red beams of light streak from the Tahoe's windows as Sam's truck is engulfed in white lasers that dance off the dark shop windows around us. Metal trashcans rise into the air and swirl overhead, the blue Post Office mailbox tugs and groans at the cement screws in its feet. Atop the library, the builder's scaffolding wobbles and tips over into the graveyard with a crash.

Hooking one arm between the iron bars, I fumble my compacted Icemaker out of my pocket and jam the button to spring it open.

Two red dots.

This plan isn't working.

And for the second time today, I aim my shotgun at Danielle. Then I shift it to Lisa. My jaw tightens and I swallow hard.

Land sakes, I don't want to hurt anybody.

What's left to slice me with, huh, Holliday?

Let's go. ***You*** *and* ***me****, freak.*

Leave these people alone. Let's have our final showdown right here. This street. Right now.

I'm screaming inside my head, sending out burst after burst of fiery, mental homing flares into the sky, praying that Holliday hears me, senses me, latches onto just one of my messages.

Come on, Holliday. If you can read my mind...come and get me...

I shut my eyes tight and breathe faster.

The streetlamp bulbs pop all at once, and every window bursts in a magnificent shower of glass. Our three vehicles hop about a foot off the pavement, spinning in the air, then bounce down again, facing the opposite direction.

And then it's over.

The wind dies. A swirling snow of papers drifts slowly to the pavement around us.

We're okay.

Especially now that I'm smiling at two gray dots on my Icemaker's screen. Relief washes over me. The girls neutralized each other. Nobody blew up, nobody died. Merrick was right.

It worked.

Merrick fumbles his glasses back on, leaping to his feet when he sees those gray dots, his triumphant whoop echoing down the street.

The only thing missing is Holliday.

That creep stood me up again.

Sam is staring at the futuristic shotgun still outstretched in my hand. His jaw drops.

"Just what the bleepity-blip are you doing, girl? Hunting elephants?"

With a sigh, I spin the shotgun by the cocking loop and press the button. Their eyes bulge, wide as cereal bowls when the weapon folds itself up into my palm. I smile wearily.

"Mr. Dove, there's a few things you need to know about me."

Merrick snickers. Sam just rolls his eyes.

"Do I look *like* I just fell off the turnip truck? I know you're an alien, Miss Kyle. But I also know you're here in our little town for a reason."

He grabs his wife's hand. Julie presses her lips together, her pale gold hair shifting in the night breeze, shooting her husband a look that clearly says she's not-so-much on the alien bandwagon, but it's a look warm with affection as they wade hurriedly through a sea of papers to catch Danielle in a big group huggy-hug.

Dogs have started howling in the distance. Looks like the power is knocked out all along King Street and Main. Merrick valiantly ignores a huge gash down the driver's side of his Tahoe, going instead to help Lisa from the backseat. He offers her a hand and she tumbles out onto him, her eyelids fluttering daintily.

Irony punches me upside the head. We're in nearly the same spot that Merrick and I faced down Deadhead Kyle. Same streetlamps, same stars. Different people.

Different me.

I step over a bent-up bicycle and approach Sam and Julie's truck. Danielle pushes their hands aside when she sees me. Her thick chocolate hair is wavy and tousled, all the makeup rinsed from her pixie face. She looks nine years old.

"Kyle?" she croaks. Her huge eyes are glassy. "What you said earlier…something was happening to us…"

"Off the record, beyond the books."

She gives me a tiny, strangled nod. "Are we…fixed?"

I give her hand a squeeze, smiling faintly.

"Cross my heart."

It's not a lie. When that clock tips over and today is erased, Danielle will pass by me on the street, indifferent, and sneer at me again. Sam and Julie will top off their evening at home together, icing their tennis elbows and doing their crossword puzzle. And Lisa will rather stick fishhooks through her eyelids than be caught dead fondling Merrick's arm like she's doing right now. Our little adventure team here will scatter their separate ways, and I'll be left standing alone, like a kid in the lunchroom.

Again.

As Sam scoops Danielle up in his arms, I pause.

"Hey Danielle, check out your hair." I hold a strand out for her to see. The dark tangle is now streaked with a snow-white stripe.

Danielle rolls her eyes.

"Oh *gag*," she yawns weakly. I feel a smile melt my cold face.

"Don't worry," I assure her. "Got a feeling it's not permanent."

*

Sam gives Mr. Luv-Money a quart of lawnmower gas from the bed of his truck. It's just enough to get him to the hospital, where his wife awaits with a new title for him: Daddy. After he's gone, we drive our little ex-wildcards back down Lincoln Street to the residential block. Since Danielle's parents are in Vegas, she'll be spending the night with Lisa. I let Sam do the talking, and by the time we pull up to Lisa's house, I think he's got them convinced we're all victims of my wacky alien mothership. We watch the two girls shuffle up the stone steps to Lisa's rose-latticed porch. Tomorrow, they'll wake up to a new world – or, if they're lucky, an old one.

I guess my story of today should've ended there. But it didn't.

"Gracious me!" Sam exclaims suddenly from his truck. "It's nearly ten o'clock! Well, that pot roast isn't gonna eat itself. You kids hungry?"

*

Tossing their keys into a basket, they welcome me and Merrick and take our jackets. The Dove's home is cozy, with blue embroidered gingham throw pillows and lots of wooden shelves filled with little elephant statues. Framed photos on the wall show a tall, smiling young woman, her thick, curly hair pulled back into a French braid. Merrick identifies her as Sam and Julie's daughter, now serving on a medical team in Africa with Doctors without Borders. Then we all sat down in their dining room for dinner.

Never, in all my "choose-your-own-adventures," did I picture this. Never in any combination of rational scenarios did I ever end up invited to dinner at somebody's home. This is new. Uncharted territory. I don't have a script for this.

While they all talked and laughed around the table, I just sat there dumbly and soaked in the details of that moment. Congealed gravy around the edges of our plates as it cooled, the puddle of hot wax pooling at the center of the cinnamon candle, spicy and sweet. And I couldn't help but think how if time had been moving normally, it would be near Thanksgiving now. Something in my chest ached. A hole filling with warmth. It felt sweet, and so did the little glances that Merrick kept stealing at me from across the mashed potatoes. At one point, Julie emerged from the kitchen and tugged at the arm of Sam's suede lumberjack coat, which he'd been wearing all night.

"Honestly Samuel," she laughed. "Take your coat off and stay a while, why don't you?"

Sam craned back in his chair to watch her breeze around the foyer corner. Then he leaned toward me and Merrick.

"Now, listen here." Sam whispered to us, chewing at a green bean. "I don't care what planet you're from. Love takes work. It takes elbow grease. Take it from us oldie-weds. Marriage is a delicate balance. It's teamwork. She does all the chores, and I appreciate it!"

He snickered mischievously as Julie tossed a hand towel at him. Merrick and I quickly opened our mouths to dismiss his idea of us being a couple, but my eye roll did little to deny our flushed faces and darting smiles at each other. With a knowing wink, Sam rose and gathered the rest of the dishes to meet his wife in the

kitchen. From my chair, I watched them. Smiling at each other, her arms around his neck. His hand on her cheek.

The embrace of two people with a lifetime of yesterdays.

For some reason, I thought of Gargoyle Day. And for one very bizarre flash-in-the-pan moment, I wished my pregnancy test had been positive.

*

Merrick pulls his Tahoe up to the Red Rooster. He turns the key and shuts off the ignition. We sit there for a moment, a single porch lantern shining on the striped flower boxes outside the bed-and-breakfast's bay window. We're holding juice boxes. Apple-cranberry. Julie made us take them.

Merrick clears his throat.

"Um, about what happened earlier. At my house."

I knew this conversation was coming.

I don't know what possessed me to go off and kiss Merrick. It was extracurricular stupidness. An incidental hiccup in reason. Anyway, who cares? Soon Merrick won't even remember it.

That comforting reminder makes my fingers clench around my juice box.

"Yeah, sorry." I mutter awkwardly. "That was my mistake, Merrick."

"Okay, that's cool. But I don't think it was a mistake. And I want you to know that I'll never cross any lines too early with you. I'm just saying... Maybe we should get to know each other a little first?"

I drop my juice box on the floor. I quickly retrieve it, praying for my red face to cool down.

"I mean," Merrick continues. "All I know about you, beyond you hitting my windshield – and, well, maybe your freakishly impressive emergency med skills–"

"I know you're a good person, Merrick."

"Huh? No offense, but you don't know anything about me."

I can't keep counting the stripes on the porch flower box, so I turn in the passenger seat. And I look Merrick straight in the eye.

"I know you hate lying. You play guitar and you sing really well. You're a brilliant biochem student, but you only have a B-plus average because your grandma just had surgery and you take care of her. You wear glasses, even though you can see fine without them. Roller coasters and consumerism make you nauseas…"

My throat goes dry. I jam the straw into my juice box and suck a sip.

"And," I continue quietly. "I know you'll never let someone you care about be alone. Even if they fight you tooth and nail and say they don't want your help. You'll do it anyway. I know you, Merrick. And I know this all sounds weird. But I also know that in twenty-eight minutes, everything I'm telling you won't matter anyway. Because you won't remember a freaking word of it."

There's a thick, hot silence. I drain my juice box, chugging down its contents. Merrick is staring hard at me.

I exhale, raking both hands through my hair.

Finally he speaks.

"Why'd you say 'in twenty-eight minutes'?"

Slowly, I take a deep breath.

Then I spill my guts to Merrick. I tell him everything. How I woke up in the hospital. How this day resets at one o'clock every night. How each day is a nightmarish roulette game, with a fun new wildcard, with big fun fangs to obliterate our existence, and how I'm the lucky winner who gets to fix it every day. Stories of days and wildcards passed – the good, the gory, and the ridiculously unforgettable – which isn't *really* unforgettable, because everyone forgets, every single stinking time. It all comes tumbling out of me, bubbling to the surface like shrimp in a pot. I'm not one-hundred percent sure which words I'm even stringing together to tell him all this, but for once, it's all one-hundred percent true.

It's liberating. Therapeutic. Like burping, or having a good cry.

Of course, I omit the little detail about me being a heartless zombie. If Merrick found out I'm a sideshow-class super-freak, he would undoubtedly look at me differently. And I just don't think I could handle that right now. I can't lose Merrick, even for our remaining eighteen minutes. So I keep going. I tell him everything I know about myself, how my past is a blank, whitewashed slate. I talk and talk.

Then I'm done talking.

Merrick sits silent, digesting everything I just dumped on him. I wish he would say something. My juice box is empty. Finally, he reclines in his seat.

"So you seriously do this kung fu every day, Kyle?"

"Yep," I laugh grimly. "Every day."

"Like that Bill Murray movie with the groundhog, only with us all turning, uh...inside-out?" He looks a little pale.

I blush at the floor. "You never turned inside-out. That was just an example."

So now I'm using the same examples as Holliday. Great.

When Merrick finally sits up, he's gazing at me with a familiar kind of awe.

"Wait–" He suddenly looks at the dashboard clock. "One o'clock? That's when you said it resets, right?"

"Yeah." I reply bleakly. "One o'clock."

"Okay, wow. Nine minutes. So...should we get to a basement or something?"

"It's not like a tornado," I chuckle.

"Okay. So how would you describe it, smarty-pants?"

"More like..." I chew my lip. "Well, it's gentle. Hard to describe. Understated...like anesthesia. Like falling asleep."

Merrick considers this, but I can tell it really doesn't matter. He keeps stealing cautious glances in my direction. Looking at me differently.

Exactly what I didn't want to happen.

Merrick mumbles at the floor. "You seem so calm."

"I've been on this ride a few times."

"Yeah, but...doesn't it ever get to you?"

My answer might have been different, if he had hit me with that question on the first day. Or even the tenth. But it's true. It *doesn't* ruffle me so much anymore. Try to look at things objectively. This weirdness, the concept of just how impossible my life and my very existence are – it rolled off me, like rain off an oiled tent. If anything trickled through the cracks, started making me shiver, I quickly filed it and sealed it off.

How else would a person deal with this?

But lately I couldn't stop the shivers. Water, loneliness, pouring in the cracks. Too many cracks. I've been drowning.

Tonight, for the first time, I'm not alone.

"Got to me bad," I confess softly. "But telling you all this…it makes me feel human again."

Wordlessly, he reaches over and grabs me in a hug. How is this exactly what I needed? My solar flare loneliness, my silent rage at the injustice of my trials – it slides right over me like I'm a cool, smooth glass ball. I don't even care that my shirt is still on backwards.

"And honestly," I lean back against his chest and grin. "It's not all terrible. A new challenge every day. I may not remember my past, but I've always liked mysteries. At least, I think I did. Like that children's game 'Guess Who?'"

"Okay, fair." Merrick twitches a smile. "Still, chasing monsters and curing inside-out people isn't quite like asking if you have a red mustache and an egg-shaped head."

"Bill."

"Ah, poor Bill. Ask the egghead question, and it always narrows it down to Bill."

We laugh a bit, then Merrick goes quiet and gazes demurely at me. “Hey.” He says after a minute. “Have I ever died?”

“What? Pfff...”

“Seriously. Kyle, did I ever die?”

He repeats the question and I look over. He’s weighing my expression carefully.

He’s not ‘Grinning TRON-patch’ Merrick. He’s ‘Deciding Whether to Shake My Hand’ Merrick.

Finally I mumble, “No.” Then I add, “But you almost did.”

Merrick raises his eyebrows in interest.

“What happened?”

“I saved your sorry butt, that’s what happened!”

“No, I mean, what happened? What almost killed me?”

“You really want to know?”

“Yup. I really do.”

“Well, tough luck, because I can’t remember them all... But one time you almost turned into a cow.”

“Ugh. Seriously?! Okay, that’s just freaky.”

“Well, it’s not exactly a near-death experience.”

“Depends on who you ask! But I’ll bet you’re lying.”

“About what?”

He wears a thin smile. “I bet you remember *everything*.”

Yeah. Without even trying.

When Merrick suddenly speaks again, there’s a change in his voice. That urgent clarity, that rarely-seen authority that I’ve recognized and held fast to and tucked away like a rolled-up note, reminding me to remind the world that Merrick Cohen is something to be respected.

"So in just a few minutes," he says slowly. "I'll get wiped and won't remember any of this…right?"

I nod miserably.

He swallows. Rubs his fingers into his temples.

"Okay, listen. I know I won't remember this conversation. I know I'll be wiped. But…come find me anyway, okay?"

I say, "I always do."

"I'll still be me, right? So I know I'll help you."

"You always do."

"Now it's your turn, Kyle. I want you to promise me something. Okay?"

With nothing to say, I just stare at him. Merrick holds my gaze hard, his green eyes sparking.

"Promise me you'll fix it. Find a way to save our town. Stop time from skipping. Do whatever it takes. Just *promise* you'll find a way. Promise me, Kyle!"

I've made so many promises. To this town…to scared kids with round eyes glued to me like I'm Superman. To scared grown-ups, pleading at me with that same silent look. With a confident grin, I started making promises left and right, handing them out like free balloons. Don't worry, I'll slay the dragon. I'll turn you right-side-out, I'll put the world back on its hinges and dust you off. Here's a snow cone and a pat on the head. I've got this. I promise.

I promise, I promise, I promise.

Does it even matter?

I've seen some of these people die a dozen times, dozens of different ways. Who cares whether I came through or not? They won't know the difference. Come tomorrow, they don't remember.

But *I* do.

I wear all those promises, strung heavy around my neck, like chain links. I'm Jacob Marley, rattling my invisible promise chains. And somehow, by grace and the skin of my teeth, I haven't broken a single promise yet. It's not always pretty, not always clean – but I've somehow managed to come through.

Until the day I don't.

Right?

Inevitably, I'll break a promise. My foot will slip. I'll sneeze. My reaction will be half a second late, and some wildcard will get the better of me. And then Carnival Creeke will be unprotected. Fish in a bloody barrel. So for a while, I just stuck with the promises I knew I could keep. Then I quit making promises altogether.

But this is Merrick.

Merrick, who I owe my life more times over than he'll ever know. Merrick, who hates lying… So I won't lie to Merrick. I can't.

I owe him more than that.

I open my mouth and whisper, "I promise."

*

I'm lying on my four-poster bed, the pink kitten journal draped across my chest, listening to the seconds tick down on the little tin clock on my bedside table. Head back, I've got my fingers pressed to my neck. Feeling that familiar empty silence where my pulse should be.

His quiet, feathery brogue is the last thing I hear as I lay down at night.

Sometimes, two people just need to work out their poison.

Holliday...

Our day is coming.

I promise.

12

DAY 40: STAGECOACH

The note was there when I woke up this morning.

An ordinary sheet of paper, folded in half, lying on the floor where someone must have slid it under my door.

That's not supposed to happen.

Every day is the same. Beginning with that blasting car alarm outside my window, it's the same predictable sequence of events, every day, playing out like little clockwork dolls. The only ripple in the pond is the wildcard. For forty days, I have never gotten a note slid under this door. A note under the door is wrong.

Dynamically wrong.

I slide out of bed and creep toward the offending object. I circle it like a shark. Give it a poke with my toe. Finally, squatting, I slowly unfold the piece of lined notebook paper. In beautiful, meticulous handwriting, someone has written a single sentence:

Careful. Someone in town is not who you think they are.

Well, that's disturbing.

I stare at the words. The perforated edge along the left side tells me this paper was torn from a notebook. Then I realize something truly unnerving about this note.

The slight rosy tint of the paper…I *recognize* it…

My face on fire, guts churning, I throw myself under my bed and rip aside the mattress. My pink kitten notebook is gone.

My impossible journal.

Gone.

My eyes dart around the room. It's not ransacked. Not a wrinkle in the towels, not a doily out of place. Yet clearly, someone came into my room. Someone who knew exactly where to look.

Someone in town isn't who you think they are...

There's a knock on my door.

I freeze.

That's the second thing today that's not supposed to happen.

My skin prickles, all my senses firing on high alert. Grabbing the porcelain rooster and shattering it into a stab-worthy weapon, I edge slowly toward the door. Flattening against the wall and angling my body, I crane up on tiptoes to peer through the peephole.

There stands Merrick. Fidgeting in the hallway, he's wearing his Tuscany Mill waiter uniform, white button-down shirt and black dress pants. He's holding a large white pastry bag in his hands.

This is wrong.

When did I tell Merrick where I was staying?

Sure, there was that one night, way back at the beginning, when I dragged him up here to my room when he was in mid-cow transformation... But he shouldn't remember that.

To him, it never happened.

I pull on my pants and slowly open the door.

"Hey!" Merrick blurts when he sees me. "Sorry, hope I didn't wake you. Um, how's the shoulder?"

"Been better, been worse." I lean on the doorway. "What are you doing here?"

"Oh, um. I was just on my way to work and thought I'd drop this by for you."

He lifts the white bag. I eye it warily.

"What's that?"

"Just some get-well stuff." His face reddens behind his glasses. "No biggie. I mean, it's the least I could do, after almost making road hamburger out of you yesterday."

Leaning over, I peer into the bag.

Turkey jerky, a pack of Ho-Hos, and some sort of board game. I peer closer. It's 'Guess Who.'

I blink. "Who told you I liked this stuff?"

"You did." He suddenly looks puzzled. "Wait…didn't you? Ugh, sorry. Feels like my memory hasn't been so great lately." Laughing sheepishly, he gestures at the bag. "Anyway, hope I got it right."

"Yeah," I frown. "You got it exactly right."

Which is exactly the problem. Because I never *told* him I liked any of this stuff. Not *today*, anyway.

Keeping one eye on Merrick – or this thing claiming to be Merrick – I back across my room and peer out the curtains.

"What day is it?"

"Huh? It's Friday," he answers, looking legitimately concerned for my sanity. "October twentieth. Homecoming game is tonight."

I shake my head a couple times. The alarm bells in my brain won't stop ringing.

Someone in town isn't who you think they are…

I lunge forward out into the hallway, slamming Merrick back against the wall, my right elbow pinned against his throat.

"Who the heck are you?!" I demand, pressing the jagged broken rooster to his jugular.

"Merrick, Merrick, holy crap!" He gasps under my arm. "My name's Merrick – we met yesterday, remember? Gargoyle, library books, dislocated shoulder?"

Mrs. Moffatt passes by the opposite end of the hall, holding a stack of fresh towels. She stops, staring at us.

My face grows hot. I let go of Merrick, forcing a laugh.

"Ah, geez. You know what?" I slap my palm to my forehead. "I'm so sorry. I get a little crazy when I haven't had breakfast."

"Uh, sure." He winces. "Fiber is…vitally important to my sanity, too."

I nod. "So vital."

Awkwardness. Definite awkwardness.

The events of this morning have already turned me into a major stress-monster, and worst of all, I unloaded all my psycho on Merrick. But the fact remains: Merrick diverged from the script. *Nobody* pulls a surprise on me like that. I need to know what on earth is going on. I need to know if Merrick has somehow been affected by the wildcard.

Or if he *is* my wildcard.

I need my Icemaker from the bank vault. As soon as possible.

*

Merrick offers me a ride into town. Ever the chivalrous prince, even when the princess just put you in a chokehold. To fill the guilt-a-riffic awkward silence, I ask Merrick who was a better Star Trek captain – Kirk or Picard. Thankfully he obliges, launches into a lengthy and passionate dissertation on human leadership qualities versus cowboy diplomacy in space. From the passenger seat, I sit quietly and watch Merrick's mouth move.

Remembering how I kissed that same mouth just yesterday…

Remembering last night, how that same mouth formed the words that hogtied me into a promise.

"Find a way to save our town. Stop time from skipping. Promise me, Kyle!"

I watch him laugh easily, sliding his hand around the edge of the steering wheel. There's no trace of urgency in his voice. He's not the assertive leader that he was in the Tahoe last night, the leader I've seen Merrick become – and un-become – again and again. My Boomstick Merrick.

This Merrick doesn't remember the promise I made to him. It's okay. He's safer that way. But I won't let him down. I'll deliver.

I *will* stop time from skipping.

After all, that was my original primary objective, dumped into my lap by Holliday himself.

It's been only a few hours since I made that promise to Merrick last night. And since then, I've sunk my teeth into my mission with renewed vigor. It's a tricky tough bite of gristle, for sure. There are just so many variables. What's causing time to skip?

Possibility #1: Someone is causing it.

I've done a deep background dig on all the good citizens of Carnival Creeke, hoping I might sniff out some suspicious association. Exotic travels, occult dealings... A time traveler who stopped for a burger and accidentally caused a rift in the space-time continuum. Don't laugh. You've got to narrow down all possibilities.

Possibility #2: The cause isn't a person. It's an object.

When my record player skips, it's due to an imperfection in the record. When a wheel gets stuck, there's usually something wedged into it, jamming the mechanism. Maybe that's what I'm dealing with here. So what would this evil time-jamming artifact look like? Small as a marble? Bigger than a bus? Animal, vegetable, or mineral? How can you be expected to find a snake if you don't know what a snake looks like?

It frustrates the spit out of me.

Especially since Holliday *could* tell me what I'm supposed to be looking for. But I know he won't.

Anyway, I have a more pressing current problem – and he's sitting in the driver's seat.

Someone in town isn't who you think they are.

I've kept my eyes discreetly locked onto Merrick since we left the Red Rooster, assessing his body language for any further odd behavior. Nothing out of the norm. Relaxed hands, insecure shoulders; the typical, wide-open posture of a college kid untrained in the art of self-defense. Here and there he's cast a few wary glances in my direction – not that I blame him, after my lovely spaz-out back at the bed-and-breakfast. But otherwise, he just seems like Merrick. Plain, sweet Merrick Cohen.

My Merrick.

A possessive surge flares up inside me, and I want to punch something. I clench my fists.

Why the frick did Holliday have to drag Merrick into this? Merrick, of all people... Is it because I kissed him last night? Am I being punished or something?

Is Holliday...*jealous?*

My fists unclench abruptly. A stifled cough catches in my throat. The notion that I could make Rascal Holliday jealous sends a tingle through me, one that any decent person with half a brain knows better than to indulge.

Okay, moving on. Even if Merrick isn't the 'someone' that my creepy warning note was referring to, that still leaves the lingering question of how he knew where to find me this morning. No, that's easily explainable. There are no hotels in Carnival Creeke. If you're a stranger, and you're moseying through town, then logically, there's only one place you would stay: The Red Rooster. Merrick probably just asked Mrs. Moffatt which room I was in. No mystery there.

But Merrick also knew I like turkey jerky and 'Guess Who.' Nobody else knows that stuff. Nobody could have told him.

I freeze, shifting my gaze to look at him out of the corner of my eye. Holy mackerel…

*Did he…**remember?***

Residual memories that should be wiped from his brain, days that never happened, somehow clinging to his subconscious?

There's only one way to find out.

"Hey, Merrick." I say casually. "Ever seen one of these before?" Leaning back, I extract the plastic 8-ball keychain from my pocket, watching him scrupulously for a reaction.

"Uh, it's a keychain?" He shrugs. No hint of recognition in his eyes as he glances at it.

"Not your garden variety keychain, kiddo. Check this out."

Raising an eyebrow, I lift the tiny 8-ball to my lips, and in a clear voice, I ask, "Will today be the best day of our lives?" (Which yields the always-hilarious answer, "*Ask again later.*") Merrick cocks his head, watching me. Then he nearly drives off the road when the 8-ball reacts to my voice, cracking open in my hand.

"Whoa!" he exclaims in alarm, veering the Tahoe back onto the road in a cloud of gravel. "How did you–?"

"Coded to my voice." I fish out the tiny silver key, shaking the liquid off my hand. "You like it?"

"Like it?" Merrick runs his hand through his hair. "It's amazing! I mean, bio-recognition is one of the most fascinating phenomena of life! That keychain would be an impossible piece of work. The research alone would require a junction of all life sciences."

I grin. "Wanna hold it?"

"Uh. No thanks. Sorry, flashbacks of you nearly decapitating me for bringing you a board game this morning."

Immense guilt burns my cheeks and neck.

"Yeah, hey, about that…" My mouth goes dry. So much I want to tell him… Every fiber of my absent heart, all that I poured out to him last night…those words pound inside my skull, begging me to tell him. *Just tell him…*

"I'm really sorry about that, Merrick. Really."

"Look, Kyle." Merrick pulls over to the curb, turning off the ignition. "Don't pretend I don't know what's really going on."

My breath freezes.

"Going on?"

"Yeah." He inhales slowly. "I mean, I ran you over yesterday. Dislocated your shoulder. Just last night, you vanquished a corporeal gargoyle with a discount katana. It's pretty obvious you've had training." He grimaces a smile. "Self-defense combat training, even. Whatever you've been through…must be pretty heavy stuff. I may not be the smartest guy in the world. But the way you act, always looking over your shoulder…it's like you feel you're being watched. And I didn't help, springing in on you this morning. Also," he pauses, rubbing his throat with a sheepish grin. "That dislocated shoulder of yours did seem…pretty strong."

"Ah," I cough. "I'm a fast healer. I eat eggs."

But he's right.

He's bang-on right about me. He's right about my squirmy paranoia, no matter how cool I try to carry myself. And it's also occurred to me how my knee-jerk reflexes do suggest that Cl. Kyle underwent some sort of combat training. Merrick is right about everything. Well, except for one thing –

He *is* the smartest guy in the world.

We crunch through the leaves together up the sidewalk to the bank. Merrick accompanies me into the honeycomb hallway while I retrieve my Icemaker from the safety deposit vault, watching in wide-eyed wonder as I pop open the screen. There's a red dot, sure enough. But it looks like the wildcard is somewhere outside the bank.

So it's *not* Merrick.

I blow out a breath in relief. Merrick as my Big Bad? That would punch some serious holes in my sanity.

"Hey Merrick." He looks over; I pause, chewing my lip. "Sorry again about this morning. For assaulting you in the hallway."

He waves it off. "Nah, forget it. It was presumptuous and uncouth. Couth is important."

"It was a sweet gesture," I correct him.

"I don't blame you, Kyle. But…well, earlier, you were ready to rip my lungs out. And then you're asking if I want to hold your clandestine X-file biotech keychain? You obviously didn't trust me this morning. Why trust me now?"

Let me think about that. Because of all the crazytown shenanigans that we've been through together. Because Merrick is the most genuine person I know. And, somewhere deep in the recesses of my unplugged brain, I still can't shake the feeling that he reminds me of someone. Really wish I could remember who... That bugs me. Add it to the list.

"Well," I smile, spinning the keychain on my finger. "You were the one who figured out how to open this little thing."

"Huh? Me? When?"

I draw a deep breath, then exhale. "A day that never happened."

I drop the keychain into his hand, then shut the drawer and cross out into the honeycomb hallway. Merrick darts after me and once I'm out of range of security cameras, I tell him everything.

If it felt liberating opening up to Merrick last night, today is pure bliss. Feels like a lead weight has been airlifted from my shoulders. Bringing Merrick into my lonely, secret world feels like a warm hug, like lemon zest air bubbles in my soul.

"One time," I jabber brightly as we push through the bank doors out into the crisp sunshine. "I had to break into this bank when the whole town was covered in ice. And another time, we hid behind that desk over there. You helped me detonate a bomb – your cell phone, actually – so we could escape an evil clone of myself."

Merrick hangs on my every word, nodding, making an obvious effort to appear cool and collected, despite his hand clapping over his back pocket at the mention of his phone becoming a bomb. I stifle a laugh, my gaze resting fondly on him.

Man, this feels good. To have a partner. To have a friend.

Why didn't I do this sooner?

He swallows. "Wait, so what happened to your evil clone?"

"Oh. You shot her. With this."

Once I've turned the corner into an alley, I hold my Icemaker up over my head, springing it open into a shotgun.

"Smile for my boomstick, baby!" With a sly grin, I spin it once by the trigger loop then press the button again, snapping it back into my hand. Like always, his green eyes go wide. The look on his face is everything I want in my life.

"I-I shot…I…with *that?!*" he blurts.

"Yup. You hungry? I'm starved. C'mon, I'll spot you a turkey sandwich after I go slay this monster."

But Merrick isn't deterred by my lunch offer. A gleeful grin spreading across his face, he hops from my left side to my right.

"I *shot* your *evil clone?!* Let's back up to that part again. And you just said 'this monster.' So there's *another* monster? Right *now?* Where?"

We exit the alley, and there's no missing it. There, sitting in the center of the intersection of Main and King Street, is a stagecoach. Yes, *that* kind of stagecoach. Like a snapshot straight out of some Old West movie.

The body of the carriage is burnished scarlet, a flamboyant red and gold leaf scroll design painted on the door panels and the starburst wooden hub wagon wheels. The carriage rests on thick leather shock-absorbing straps along its underside, a luggage roof surrounded by low railing up top. Affixed high at the front of the coach is a lazy-back spring seat, its empty leather cushion indicating where a stage driver would sit to hold the horses' reins and guide the vehicle. I admit I'm relieved that there's no monstrous driver occupying that seat - and maybe more relieved when I crane up on tiptoes and see that the carriage is empty. No ghoulish passengers huddled inside, waiting inside to munch on my intestines.

In fact, there's nothing menacing about this stagecoach at all.

It's...just...*sitting* there. Like a non-lethal bump on a log.

Cars are beginning to back up in the street behind it, although the stoplight continues to cycle merrily from green, to yellow, to red, then back to green again, oblivious to the anachronistic hairball parked in the intersection. A small crowd has already gathered on the curb to goggle. If there's one thing these folk do better than smile, it's goggle. Hank stands on the doorstep of his auto parts shop, leaning on a broom and squinting at the spectacle, his deep coffee complexion shining in the sun. Sheriff Gammell and Deputy Scarecrow are crossing back and forth at a fast jog, setting up orange cones and directing traffic from King to Lee Street.

I discreetly open my pocket and glance down at my Icemaker screen. Big fat red dot. This stagecoach is the wildcard, for sure.

I frown.

I'll admit it. Every now and then, the wildcard takes a proverbial pee in the bed. And unless this clunker starts belching fireballs or birthing bloodthirsty monkeys, this is shaping up to be one of those wet puddles on the sheets.

I cock my head at Merrick. "Care to get a closer look?"

"Lead the way, cowgirl," he grins. He's practically radiating eagerness. It's contagious, and I can't help but feel giddy as we saunter across the intersection toward Gammell and the gleaming red stagecoach.

"Yee-haw," Merrick remarks innocently. "What time does the saloon open?"

The Sheriff shoots him a look.

"Not in the mood, son. We've got the homecoming parade coming through here tonight." Gammell squints at the crowd lining the sidewalk through his mirrored sunglasses, then casts a hateful look at the stagecoach. "Halloween pranks aren't supposed to happen for another week. Why are these kids always so determined to speed up my gray hairs?"

Deputy Scarecrow appears in much brighter spirits.

"Gee Frank, reminds me of being a boy!" He pats one of the wheel spokes. "Cowboys an' Indians, y'know?"

Grimacing, Sheriff Gammell just shakes his head.

Turning, Gammell lowers his sunglasses a fraction of an inch. He's looking straight at me. And he's wearing his usual distrust.

"Who's your lady friend, Merrick?"

"Oh, uh, this is Kyle. She's my sister's friend from–"

"Never mind, son." Gammell waves a hand. "Got to get this street cleared before the parade tonight. And if Miss Kyle's got two hands and a pulse, she can help us push."

Ouch.

That's okay, I didn't need my soul.

Plastering an indifferent smile on my face, I take my place behind the stagecoach, and we start trying to push it out of the street. We're joined by Captain Epic, passing by on his morning jog. We push, we strain, we all sweat off six pounds – but the stagecoach refuses to budge. Not even when Captain Epic rips off his t-shirt, making everyone feel inadequate. More townspeople join in the pushing party. Shepper slaps his tow hitch onto the coach's rear luggage boot, but all that accomplishes is spinning his truck tires, spewing a whole lot of smoke and a whole lot of bad words. The stagecoach won't move.

Let me show you my shocked face.

Deputy Scarecrow throws up his hands, his boyish glee of earlier gone. "Aw man, Frank, they got some kinda juju voodoo on this thing!" he wails.

I take a step backward. I slide my hands in my pockets.

A little inkling just wiggled its way into my brain.

My job is to neutralize the wildcard, or else this day sticks for good. That's how it works. Righty-o. That's the rule.

But what if I *intentionally* don't fix it?

Cool my heels, just let it ride…

This stagecoach isn't all that bad. Evil menace that it is, clogging up traffic on Main Street… It's not like anyone would be in mortal peril because a big stupid Old West relic is permanently planted in the middle of the intersection.

So what if I just left it alone?

Let one o'clock come and go?

But then it would stick. Time would never start spinning, days would never resume, and the good people of Carnival Creeke would never turn their calendars over to Saturday, October 21st. I would be stuck on this day forever. But would that really be so bad? Merrick by my side, knowing these people will never be in any real flavor of danger again…albeit maybe bored out of their minds… It's a bizarro, sutured-up kind of happily ever after, but…

No. I made a promise to Merrick.

Promise me, Kyle! Promise me you'll find a way, stop time from skipping!

I pull Merrick's turkey jerky from my pocket and start gnawing resolutely at the leathery smoked meat.

No. I'll make good on that promise. I don't care how long it takes me. The solution to this Game…I'm getting close. I feel it.

But then what?

Buy an apartment here? I admit, it sounds nice. But would these people really accept me? Blood-spattered Kyle, black sheep in a sparkling white town… Am I such a delusional dreamsicle to think that I could still maintain a role here? Hang up my shotgun, trade my battle axe for baseball bats and hot dogs?

Am I really ready for that?

For life beyond the only day I've ever known…?

"Disassemble it!" Sheriff Gammell finally bellows. "I want this thing *off* my street. I don't care if we have to rip it apart piece by piece–"

"Excuse me…Sheriff?" The voice calls out suddenly, meekly. "Um, a little help, please?"

We all turn.

There, sitting inside the stagecoach, is Phil the jolly businessman. He's crouched in the doorway of the carriage, peering sheepishly out at us, his tie rumpled and gray suit unbuttoned. He sips a can of diet soda.

Gammell sighs and rests both hands on his hips. He makes a half-hearted beckoning gesture at Phil. "Come on out of there, friend."

Phil doesn't move.

"Would if I could, Sheriff. But…well, *look*–" Extending his hand, he slowly reaches outside the carriage's doorframe. Immediately he receives a sharp, static shock.

"See?!" Phil protests, his voice raising an octave.

I narrow my eyes.

Sure enough, a faint, bluish vapor shimmers over the stagecoach, as though the entire carriage has been enveloped in a liquescent pane of glass. It would be easy to miss, discernible only by the way it's causing Phil's pasty face to shift and distort behind it. This chowderhead has activated some kind of electric barrier. And now he's trapped inside.

"AND NOW HE'S TRAPPED INSIDE."

I let my head fall back, releasing an audible moan.

Phil, oh, Phil.

So eager to screw up my retirement plans.

Hands on my hips, I begin pacing slowly behind the crowd, my eyes trained on the motionless stagecoach.

"I only climbed in for a quick peek," Phil squeaks. "Seems I've gotten myself into a bit of a pickle, eh?" He laughs nervously, taking a sip of soda. "So sorry for the trouble."

"Oh crud," Merrick mumbles, throwing a sidelong look at me.

Phil clears his throat. "So gentlemen, if you'll just kindly instruct me how to turn off the electricity?"

"We don't know," Gammell replies brusquely.

"Pardon?" Phil blinks. "You don't *know?*" Beads of sweat have begun to pop out on his forehead. "Can't you ask the owner? Tootle them on their cell phone?"

Sheriff Gammell ignores him, turning to us in a huddle. His voice lowers to a gruff whisper.

"Now, we've got no idea how this thing got here." Gammell jabs his thumb toward the stagecoach. "The earth could have farted it up from the pavement, for all I know. I don't rightly care. I just want this street cleared. Joe, get everyone out of here. Now."

Deputy Scarecrow rattles a nod and hurriedly lopes off on his gangly legs. Sheriff Gammell rubs a hand across his face. He turns back to Phil.

"Alright friend, I want you to take a look around in there. Do you see anything? A lever, or release switch?"

I pace faster. Phil rummages around the carriage.

"Nothing," he moans. "Nothing! Shouldn't you people have the owner's manual, or something?

A shot from my Icemaker probably wouldn't deactivate the forcefield. My weapon solidifies liquids. It doesn't magically abracadabra all problems away. Even if I could fire off a shot at the stagecoach without throwing the whole town into anarchy, I'd probably just congeal Jolly Phil in the process, making him trapped *and* dead.

"Wait – I found something!" Phil announces in a shrill voice. "There's something under the seat here! It's…a notebook. A pink notebook. With kittens on it."

My toe catches the pavement.

My notebook.

My journal, stolen from under my bed, is sitting in that stagecoach. My fingerprints are all over that notebook. There's nothing to prevent Phil, Gammell, and everyone and their mother from reading every word I wrote about them. Bizarre tales depicting them all by name, grisly accounts of monsters and mayhem, poor kind Merle going nutso with a knife… Luckily, I wrote it in shorthand code.

But every code is crackable.

"*Don't touch it!!*" I bark, then I quickly add, "Just don't touch anything, you hear? Sit tight. The Sheriff is going to get you out of there."

Oh, how I wish that were true.

*

The crowd along the curb has grown thicker as the sun moves across the sky. Randy and his buddies are taking turns snapping pictures of each other by the stagecoach, striking poses in front of it, waggling their tongues. Deputy Scarecrow shoos them away for the umpteenth time then strides back over and rejoins us, gripping his belt and sighing. A good lawman's work is never done.

And the blue forcefield is still shimmering strong. It zaps Phil's hand again and again, until we all tell him to quit poking at it and just sit on his hands while we think.

Captain Epic crosses his sculpted arms. "Okay," he says slowly. "So you can climb *in*...but not *out*. Right?"

"Yep," I nod. "It's a one-way ticket. A roach motel."

Sheriff Gammell rubs his temples wearily.

"C'mon, people!" Captain Epic hollers. "We're getting a 'C' for chatty, let's go for that 'A' for action! Oh, screw this–" He rips off his shirt again with a flourish. "I'll do it myself."

Merrick looks up from the curb. "Uh. Forcefield, remember?"

"Then I'll just run up and drag Dude-Man out quick. What's the worst that could happen?"

"Your skin fries off your bones," I say.

Captain Epic mulls this possibility over for a moment.

"Well played," he finally says, solemnly pulling his shirt back on and seating himself beside Merrick on the curb. We mull it over for another moment.

"It's okay," Phil bleats ruefully. "You can leave me here. I don't matter to anyone."

"Shut it, Pie Man!" I bark, pointing at him. "You matter to me."

Suddenly Merrick snaps his fingers.

"Maybe it's a balance system!" he exclaims triumphantly. "An object of equal size–"

Pushing up his glasses, he holds up one finger and jogs over to the sidewalk. He reaches through the wrought-iron fence and selects a pinecone from the grass on the library lawn.

"Here." Merrick holds up the pinecone. "It's about the same size as a soda can, right? Check this out–"

Walking out into the street, he tosses the pinecone underhand toward the stagecoach. There's a loud *zap* as it bounces off the forcefield – but this time, both the pinecone and Phil's diet soda can are sent spiraling through the air in opposite directions, away from the carriage. The pinecone goes tumbling end-over-end down the street, the soda can clattering across the pavement and coming to a rolling halt at the curb.

We stare, our jaws on the ground.

Merrick crouches over the pinecone. Curls of smoke rise lazily from its crispy, blackened spines.

"Wow," he remarks, picking up the burnt pinecone between two fingers. "This thing's seen better days…"

Inside the stagecoach, Phil looks like he's two seconds from peeing himself. He presses himself eagerly against the doorframe.

"Did it work?" he calls out in a loud voice.

"Hold tight!" we all holler in unison.

"Hot dang," I say as Merrick rejoins my side. "Merrick, you're a genius. So we just need to trade. Replace the object inside with an object of equal size. That's the gist of it?"

They all nod in agreement.

"So now we just need Phil's replacement."

Gammell and Captain Epic find a café table and drag it out into the street. They try heave-hoeing it into the stagecoach – but the table just bounces off the forcefield, nearly taking off Captain Epic's arm.

"Dude, I don't get it," he scratches his beach-blond head. "We got the size right... Right?"

"Yeah." Merrick sighs. "But Phil is a person. I don't think inorganic objects work for organic life forms."

"You mean it's gotta be *alive?* That's kinda sick."

"An even trade," Merrick shrugs.

"Merrick's right," I mutter, waving a hand in disgust. "That's just…how it works."

"How 'bout a cow?"

"I resent that," Phil mewls from inside the coach.

"Or maybe a whole bunch of hams?"

"Not helpful," Phil pouts.

"So it's gotta be a person?"

"Well, any volunteers?"

"I was kidding! Did you see that pinecone?!"

Everybody starts jabbering at the same time. Nobody can really hear what anyone is saying, so Sheriff Gammell raises his arms and tries in vain to quell the chaos. That's when I feel an idea creeping into my head.

An idea that I am *really* not looking forward to.

I pat myself down, slapping my chest through my leather jacket, over my circular scar.

No heart...

I have no heart to stop. And I'm a fast-healing superfreak. I could stand a little electric jolt. If anyone can get into that coach, it's me. I'll be fine. Or I end up fried like an onion ring.

Hands still on my chest, I blow out a hard slow breath.

I should consult Merrick. Get his biochemist vote. But he'll just try to stop me, and he doesn't know about my missing heart. Besides...that's *my* pink kitten notebook in there. If anyone should risk their life climbing into that coach, it had dang well better be me.

I clear my throat.

"There's another option."

Everyone clams up and looks at me with hope in their eyes.

Good. Just what I'm counting on.

I put my hands on my hips and rattle off some kind of plan involving jumper cables and a homemade lightning rod. I tell them it needs to be attached to the stagecoach in order to reroute the electric current of the forcefield harmlessly into the telephone wires above, and then Phil is free, we all go eat cake, and live happily ever after.

It's a lie, of course. A total baloney sandwich. But they're lapping it up. All except Merrick, who's listening to me with his eyes gently narrowed.

Rats.

Merrick can *always* tell when I'm lying. Merrick and Sheriff Gammell. They just see right through me. It's like their superpower.

I turn my head away so Merrick can't see my face.

"So this'll knock out the electric barrier?" Gammell rubs a hand across his face and glares wearily at me. "You're sure?"

"Dang skippy," I lie.

Then Merrick speaks up.

"How thick does the copper wire need to be?"

"Oh. It doesn't really matter," I cough into my shoulder.

"Scientifically speaking, it *should* matter."

"It doesn't, okay? Just trust me. Go," I flap my hands. "Captain Epic needs help with his rod, and my shoulder's acting up."

Merrick's green eyes are still narrowed, his concern for me burning like a candle. He takes me by the elbow, gently pulling me aside.

"Kyle. What's going on?"

"We're saving Phil, right?" I force a confident smile. "Just trust me. This will work." Laying my hands on his shoulders, I whisper, "I promise."

My stomach churns. I hate lying to Merrick like this. Whether he actually believes me is for the birds – I've always said his poker face is even better than mine – but his expression relaxes.

He starts walking back toward the group. Then he hesitates, throwing me a dubious grin over his shoulder.

"Hey, did I really say that? 'Smile for my boomstick, baby?'"

"You bet your butt you did!"

Merrick raises his eyebrows. I point at him. "Now go help Captain Epic before he electrocutes himself."

I wait until I've watched him rejoin the huddle. That should be sufficient to keep everyone distracted. Can't have anyone interrupting me right now.

Don't watch, guys. This might not be pretty.

I begin stalking in a slow circle around the stagecoach, pretending to be doing something important. But in my head I'm calculating. I'm 5'3. Phil is about 5'5, but his suit buttons are working extra hard because he's got a bit of a doughy spare tire around his middle. Blame the pie. If I'm going to be Phil's replacement, I'll need to strap on some extra bulk. My eyes scan past the crowd, down the row of shops.

Let's see, extra bulk…

My gaze stops on the General Store. Specifically, on the pumpkins on the wooden porch. Slinking across the street at a fast trot, I crouch down and select a nice hefty pumpkin, testing its weight in my hands. The wooden chief statue scowls down at me disapprovingly.

"Don't look at me like that," I mutter at him.

Let's get this over with.

Hugging the pumpkin to my chest, I take a deep breath, and hop down off the porch. The instant my feet touch the pavement,

I take off at a dead sprint toward the stagecoach. I'm praying that I can do this before anyone notices me.

But I don't.

Merrick just looked over.

He shouts something – my name, I think – but I know if I look at him my focus will unravel. So I just keep running, purposely keeping my eyes locked straight ahead.

And that's why I don't see him coming.

Merrick hammers into me. Totally blindsides me, shoving me hard with both hands. The pumpkin slips from my grip; I catch a jerky glimpse of it bouncing down the pavement as I land sprawling on my shoulder. I roll quickly up to my knees, turning just in time to see Merrick look back at me over his shoulder as he streaks toward the stagecoach. Shielding his head with his hands, he ducks slightly then leaps toward the carriage's shimmering door.

There's a loud snapping sound, followed by a blinding flash. Merrick is jolted backward the instant he touches the forcefield, and Phil is simultaneously catapulted out of the opposite side of the stagecoach. Merrick hits the street pavement at a rolling tumble, Phil goes sailing over the library's iron fence, windmilling his arms and landing in the grass. He lets out a long groan, flopping around like a fish. Merrick lies motionless in the street.

Merrick won't flop around like a sissy.

Merrick won't complain, or go all pale-faced, or ask for gratitude for what he just did. Because even before I can run across the street to him, it's already sickeningly obvious.

Merrick is dead.

When CPR is performed correctly, the odds of resuscitating a person are in the single digits. So don't be afraid to try.

Never let that stop you from trying.

Merrick's lips are white as chalk, cold as lifeless clay when I close my mouth over his. It seems somehow wildly inappropriate, thinking of how we kissed just the other night. Circumstances drastically spun…

What a difference a day makes.

His chest lifts obediently each time I force my breath into him. Each time I pound his ribcage, his head jerks gently in response. But it's just me moving him. Under his white button-down shirt, small wisps of smoke rise lazily from his skin. His fingertips are blackened. The image of that charred pinecone burns into my head.

"Come on, kiddo…please…*please*…"

His glasses are gone. Probably fell off when he hit the ground. For some reason, I find that unbearably heartbreaking.

"*Merrick Cohen, you get up off this road! You quit screwing around, you hear me?!*"

I don't actually scream those words. I want to, but I don't. My body just plunges along, mechanically slamming him with CPR chest thrusts. I've gone so far into auto-pilot mode, I don't think I could even chew an apple if someone shoved it into my mouth. My breath comes in jagged gasps. The crowd watches me in stunned silence.

Red lights strobe behind us as the ambulance throws its rear doors open. I wasn't aware that I was clutching Merrick's hand, but I must have been because they had to pull it from my grasp when the EMT workers lifted him onto a stretcher. The ambulance doors swing shut behind them. All the air is suddenly drained from the street. I just stand there, blinking. Unable to process. Unable to panic.

This just feels unreal.

A supersaturated scene under a neon orange afternoon sun.

Merrick doesn't die. Merrick doesn't die in my story.

Because I won't *let* him.

I rise to my feet, my face blank as a bone.

None of this matters. Not their frantic efforts in that ambulance, their silly oxygen masks and defibrillators. It's all stale. Inconsequential background noise. They keep trying to drape a blanket over Phil's shoulders, even though he keeps insisting he's fine. He looks fine. I kind of despise him for how fine he looks, but then I don't. Phil and his blanket don't matter.

All that matters in the world is one red dot.

Pivoting numbly, I turn my back to the crowd. I stare straight at the stagecoach. They've already got it wrapped off in yellow police tape and orange cones. The forcefield is gone. When I get a little closer, I spot Merrick's glasses lying under one of the coach's big wooden wheels. Stooping down, I gently pick them up off the pavement. A dull ache squeezes my throat. I forcefully swallow it down.

Can't think about the insignificant stuff. Not now.

'Now' only equals a singular task.

This horrible day…it never happened. Not if I make it all okay. Play the right chords. Connect all the right dots…

Slipping Merrick's glasses into my pocket, I duck under the crime scene tape and climb into the stagecoach. The moment I enter, the wicked wagon reacts to my presence. A low hum rises up around me, the open space between the window and the doorframes enclosed in a faint blue shimmer. I tap my hand to the shimmer and get a sharp zap.

Thy forcefield hath returned.

Only now, *I'm* the chowderhead trapped in here.

Retracting my hand, I calmly examine my singed knuckles.

Not for long.

The first thing I do is grab my stupid pink notebook off the floor. Briefly, I fan through the pages to check if anything is missing. My hand halts. Nothing is missing, but there's something new here. On the last page, written in beautiful, meticulous handwriting:

Hickory, Dickory, Doc.

I stare at the three words.

Now what the heck is *that* supposed to mean?

Well, I know who calls me 'Doc.' And this is *definitely* the same handwriting from the psycho love note left under my door this morning. Now it's clear. Holliday wrote both notes.

Whatever. I'll figure out his freaky riddle later.

Rolling up the notebook and shoving it into my cargo pants, I drop onto the black silk seat and examine my surroundings. Feels like an old-timey photo booth. The carriage interior is draped with black satin, with small pockets embroidered along the inside of both doors. In the old days, passengers would use these pockets to stash their wallets, pocket watches, and snuff tins.

I look straight ahead and see that the black silk is split down the center and drawn back, like theater curtains. Behind them, a softly glowing computer screen is mounted at eye-level for whoever happens to be sitting in this unlucky passenger seat. I'm pretty sure the coaches of the Old West didn't come with *that* special feature.

The blue screen bears a single command, presented in blocky white letters:

ENTER ABORT SEQUENCE CODE

4011: _____

"Okay," I growl tensely. "What am I supposed to do now?"

As if in response, a small keyboard slides out from under the screen.

"I don't know your stupid riddle!" I shout at the keyboard. Snarling, I whip out my Icemaker and squeeze the throttle, firing off a blast point-blank at the screen. The blue flash simply dissipates, shimmering harmlessly, absorbing into the console. Well, it was worth a try. But mindless rage won't work here. I need an *answer*.

4011.

What does that mean? Merrick would know...

My throat constricts sharply and pain stabs through my chest. I swallow hard.

I need help.

"It wants a code," I call loudly, and everyone outside listens. "4011... Anyone have any idea what that means?"

There's a brief buzz through the crowd. Then someone shouts out, "I think...it might mean...bananas!"

Leaning forward, I peer out the doorframe of the coach and scan the crowd for the wise-guy who just dared to offer that ridiculous suggestion. It was Randy. Face perked, the teen takes a hesitant step forward, slinging his shaggy bangs from his eyes.

"No, wait!" he yells. "Dude, I'm serious! 4011...I used to work at the grocery. 4011 is the price code for bananas!"

I deliberate this long and hard. I wrestle with the idea until smoke comes from my ears. Folk outside start whispering and shifting anxiously. Randy genuinely might be trying to help. Well, what the heck. If I'm wrong, and I blow my face off for *this*...

With sweaty fingers, I type each letter slowly.

B-A-N-A-N-A

The screen blinks once. Then the word is replaced by something new:

ENTER ABORT SEQUENCE CODE

4045: _____

It worked.

"*Gotcha, you crap-faced snot bucket!!*" I scream victoriously at the screen, causing everyone outside to murmur. I clear my throat. "I mean…okay, good job, Randy. How about 4045?"

"Uh, that's cherries!"

"4048?"

"Limes!"

"4450?"

"Uh…uhh…oranges! No wait, Clementine oranges!"

And then it's over. The accursed screen flashes "*Abort Code Accepted*," and the red dot on my Icemaker goes gray. The faint blue shimmer around the coach dissipates with a shivering hiss.

I clunk back in the seat in relief, tossing Randy a weary thumbs-up through the doorway. The teen is immediately engulfed in cheers and congratulatory slaps on the back. And by the look of it, he's loving every bit. I'm glad he can relish his hero moment. Because I can't.

Victory never tasted so hollow.

*

Sheriff Gammell is hanging up the phone as I slouch into the doorway of his office, my hands deep in my pockets.

He grumbles, "That was the hospital."

"And Merrick…?"

Gammell doesn't answer me. He just exhales long and hard and massages his fingers into the bridge of his nose. Then he looks up at me. His jaw is locked, a muscle twitching, and for a very long minute he just stares straight at me, his expression unreadable. Finally I can't take the silence, so I fill the gap.

"Sheriff Gammell, I know–" My throat goes bone-dry. I swallow, but my voice still cracks. "I know this has been a difficult day for you."

"A difficult day?"

We stare at each other.

"*NO!!*" Gammell's sudden bark makes my bones jump. He slams his fist on the desk, then regains his typical composure.

"No," he growls quietly. "Not just a difficult day. Not just because I've known Merrick Cohen since he was a toddler. Or because now I gotta make a call that boy's parents in Idaho. Today, you are responsible for the death of a soul in my town."

My eyes are burning. My face is burning. Everything is burning.

It was better when he wasn't talking.

But he's not done yet.

"I know them *all*." Gammell's deep voice is thinly controlled. "Because the people in this town, they are family to me. Every single last one of them."

A horrid, sickening tug wrenches at my insides.

"I'm so sorry," I whisper. "Merrick was–"

"Merrick was family. Now get out of this room before I break your legs."

I've never been completely at a loss.

I am now.

Numbly, I rotate and stagger out of the police station, raking my hands through my hair. I guess I'm walking, but I can't feel the pavement under my feet. Can't feel the chilled air, can't hear any of the muted voices whirling around in my head, or the milling crowd on the sidewalk. It feels like they're all watching me, though in reality, all I can see are people's backs clustered around the curb. They aren't looking at me. They're still gawking at the stagecoach sitting in the middle of the street. Guess they're not sure if the show is over yet.

Reaching into my pocket, I pull my folded-up Icemaker just enough to glimpse the screen. Gray dot. Show's over, folks.

I slide the weapon back into my pocket and my fingers brush Merrick's glasses.

My stomach drops. I hiccup.

Hank's Auto Shop is the nearest, so that's the toilet I end up at. I hit the bathroom floor on my knees, vomiting so forcefully I think my stomach turns inside-out. It all hits me at once. Every smile from these people that I returned with a taciturn glare, every lonely night that I lay on my bed, stewing in my own selfishness instead of taking Merrick up on his offer for all-night tacos. The feeling of his warm arms around me… The feeling of his cold body under my hands on the street… Every regret, everything I've ever shoved down into my brain files – it all gushes back up in one sour cocktail. I must have stuffed down more than I realized, because there's too much to count.

Just too much.

I'm bent over the toilet as wave after burning wave pours out from my throat. Heaven help me, I can't stop coughing into the porcelain basin. The acoustics in here are impressive.

"Git your hands where I can see dem!" barks a deep Jamaican voice.

My Icemaker is in my hand and sprung open before he even finishes the sentence. Hank stands there in the bathroom doorway in his grease-stained jumpsuit, a lug wrench poised defensively over his head. I keep my Icemaker fixed on him, even though I make no move to get off the dirty floor. I probably don't look very threatening.

Actually, I think I'm about to cry.

"Okay, um, how 'bout dis." Hank clears his throat. "I put down dis here wrench…and you put down your, er, Jedi blaster there. Yeah?"

I lower my shotgun into my lap. Hank shakes his head and returns to his desk. The small shop is crammed floor-to-ceiling with metal shelves, the only light wafting dimly through a periscope crafted from an old hubcap on a top shelf, and the soft caramel glow from the lamp on the cluttered work desk.

"I seen you around," Hank remarks. "You're that gargoyle slayer girl, aren't ya?" He frowns, rummaging through a toolbox. "Listen. Pretty clear you're on the run. Don't gotta tell me why. I'm new in dis town, too. But got me a new life here, though."

I notice a small, black velvet box on his desk. The kind of box that usually holds a ring.

"What's her name?" I ask quietly.

Hank grabs the little box and stuffs it protectively into his pocket.

"Lilly. Dis weekend, gonna ask her to marry me. Lilly… She's the only one dat ever seen me for the man I *could* be, not the man I was. She knows who I was. She don't care. Man can't change, they say. But you got someone who believes in you…well. You can make each new choice a better one." Hank glances at me, pointing with the rag. "Looks like *you* could use a friend right now."

"I'm fine," I mutter hoarsely. "I don't need anything. But thanks."

He puts his hands up and shrugs, then turns back to the cluttered desk. Merrick's signature gesture. Hank picks up a pair of pliers and a soldering iron. I remain slumped on the floor. He glances at me, frowning.

"Uh, you want a cup of water?"

Heck yeah, I do.

"No," I snap.

Hank shrugs again. "Okay. Just thought you might. Rinse the pukey taste outta your mouth."

I don't deserve Hank's water, or his kindness. I'm a brainless, heartless zombie. I'm the Tin Man and the Scarecrow, all wrapped in one anomalous package. I'm empty. Lacking even the courage to get up off this bathroom floor.

Great…so I'm the Cowardly Lion, too. How special.

Hank looks up from his soldering and lifts an eyebrow at me.

"*Ouch*. Aww, man." He abruptly drops the soldering tool, sucking on his finger. "Burned my finger."

I watch him cross the room to a mini fridge and crack a little ice tray.

"Rub your hair on it," I mumble.

Hank pauses. "Say what?"

Hauling myself up off the floor tiles, I slide my Icemaker into my pants.

"Your hair. It's good for the burn," I say.

With a shrug, Hank pulls off his porkpie cap, revealing a balding head. I start to cross the room; he shoots me a big warning eye and points at the soldering iron at me. I tamely raise both my hands where Hank can see them. He nods slowly; I resume my way over to him. Bending my head down, I take his finger and start rubbing a handful of my hair against it.

"Helps prevent a blister," I tell him. "Something about the oils in hair."

Hank observes me incredulously. "What are you, a doc?"

"Hardly." I chuckle grimly through my hair.

I'm just full of useless surprises.

All my featherheaded fantasies about what I would do with a free day…the books I'd read, the pie I'd scarf… Now here I am. Nothing but a heap of time in my lap, and I don't feel like doing a dang thing.

So when I leave Hank's shop, I just start walking.

Nowhere in particular. Just plodding forward, one foot in front of the other. Somewhere between the covered bridge and the cornfields, Mr. Luv-Money pops into my head. Tonight, that rich dork's wife is going to give birth to their first child while he runs out of gas and strands himself. Probably misses the birth…

Well, that's *one* thing I can change.

I trudge past the Red Rooster and head next door to the Quik-Pump gas station. I lean my forehead against the gas pump, listening to the hose whir as gas dispenses into a red plastic canister. I slide my Icemaker from my pocket and flip it open. My eyes drift over the battered Winchester 92. The crisscross patchwork of deep grooves, scratched into the beautiful walnut forestock. Sometimes I think about how similar we are, me and this old shotgun. Scuffed up. Empty chambers. We run dry. We recharge.

But I'd like to believe, when I'm firing on all cylinders, I too occasionally light up the sky.

A mangy black dog trots past the gas pump, carrying something in its mouth. I gaze vacantly at it. Then I see what the dog is carrying.

It's a human arm.

I let go of the gas nozzle and the handle clicks off abruptly.

I must be hallucinating.

Replacing the pump nozzle, I grab my full canister and follow the dog around the corner of the gas station into a muddy backyard, littered with rolls of chicken wire and stacks of old tires. Over by the rear service garage, a powder blue Toyota Tercel sits up on concrete blocks. Ah. So that must be the pain-in-the-tush that blasts its alarm at 6:11 every morning.

I'm about to give the old clunker a vindictive kick when I spot the dog again. The animal is digging joyfully in the dirt beside a peeling doghouse; turning, it drops the arm into the shallow hole and trots away, its body low to the ground. Creeping around the doghouse, I peer into the hole. Inside is a pile of body parts. *Plastic* body parts. A couple of arms, a few painted plastic bones, all heaped in the dirt alongside a grinning plastic zombie head.

Just silly Halloween decorations.

My countenance relaxes a little.

Then my eye catches on something else. Behind the doghouse, something black in the grass – a shard, gleaming in the setting sun. I draw closer, sinking slowly to a crouch.

The vinyl record is scattered in pieces all over the grass.

"You're joking..." I utter. I pick up a jagged piece, turning it to read the label. 'All of Me,' by Billie Holiday.

I drop the record in the grass.

This can't be...

I take two steps backward, my head spinning like a blender. Unless the gas station attendant enjoys playing Frisbee with classic vinyl, I am unmistakably looking at one of the records that Danielle and I flung out the window from my room.

Yesterday.

A day that never happened.

This record should be sitting in its sleeve up in my room. I squint up at the Red Rooster next door, then back at the shattered record in the grass.

First, Merrick remembered those details about me this morning. Now, this record showing up here…

Backing away, I turn sharply and start walking back down the road, one hand tensely on my Icemaker. The blood-red sun is low by the time I reach town. I plunk the gas canister down by a streetlamp, nudging the heavy jug behind a Post Office mailbox with my toe, right where I'm sure Mr. Luv-Money's headlights will shine on it, and he'll be sure to see it later tonight. Then I plop down on the curb. Maybe I'll just wait here for him.

Heck, I've got nowhere to be.

I fish Merrick's last strip of turkey jerky from my pocket and sit there chewing dully on a mouthful. The distant sound of popping snare drums drifts by. I raise my head. It's six o'clock. The homecoming parade is starting.

My jaw clenches. After what just happened to Merrick? This hardly seems an appropriate night for celebrating…

Hopping up, I jog along the sidewalk until I run into a wall of people lining the curb outside the bank across from the library. Floats appear at the far end of Main Street, cranberry and orange balloons fluttering. I notice that the intersection is now clear. The stagecoach is gone.

Then I see why.

The stagecoach is *in* the parade.

And it's moving.

Rolling down the street, the unearthly wagon is a chilling sight, its eerie empty driver's bench swaying gently back and forth. The stagecoach rumbles along behind the float with the giant Grim Reaper, keeping perfect pace with it, as though the ghoulish carriage is actually *part* of the parade. And even from a distance, I notice the stagecoach is boasting a new feature. A display screen is now mounted on the roof of the carriage. A row of tiny theater spotlights illuminate the screen's scratchy image, displaying the number '20.' Like an old film countdown, the screen promptly wipes the number '20' away in a circular motion, replaced now by '19.'

A countdown.

Counting down to *what*... Well, I guarantee it's not glitter and sunshine. My Icemaker confirms my sickening dread.

The gray dot has turned bright red again.

A horrific heat wells up inside me with dizzying ferocity. I've had enough. I've had it up to my chin with this wildcard. I want this hell-on-wheels *out* of my town.

I swear I will chop that thing into firewood myself.

Hank looks absolutely horrified to see me on his doorstep again, and this time I'm carrying a battle axe to boot. I feel genuinely sorry that I'm not out of his life yet. He grasps his porkpie hat with both hands.

"Aw man, whatcha doin' here, Jedi girl?!"

"I'm here to kick butt and eat Ho-Hos," I reply flatly. "And I'm...all out of Ho-Hos. I need your help, Hank. Please."

Gritting my jaw resolutely, I add, "For Merrick."

A deep frown creases the lines on Hank's face. Then he nods.

"Okay, 'den. ...For Merrick."

Hank swears he can knock down the barrier surrounding the stagecoach, but not for long. Just long enough for me to get inside. When I ask him to spill his plan, he just shakes his head. He starts chucking tools into a canvas bag.

"It's electric, right? Dis forcefield? Well, there's our lucky break. Even alien tech got its weak spot." Hank points at me, giving me a staunch nod. "Be ready to kick some butt!"

He gallops up the sidewalk and disappears around the corner. I stand at the curb, battle axe in my hand, looking over the crowd and scanning the street. It's packed with parade floats. Drums pound out a rhythm and marching snares echo snappily. The gleaming scarlet stagecoach comes rattling around the corner into view, still rolling right in step between the Grim Reaper float and the giant paper mâché wolverine.

Taking a deep breath, I dig my hand into my jacket pocket and pull out Merrick's glasses. I slide them onto my face. Holy cow. I can actually *see* better. Maybe it's just my imagination, but everything looks sharper, crisper. My perspective is clear.

Through Merrick's glasses, I can now make out the faint shimmer over the coach. A nearly imperceptible ripple, but it's definitely still there. Whatever Hank is fixing to do, he hasn't done it yet. I need to be ready. The instant that barrier disappears, I'll need to jump.

I should get closer.

I've just taken a step when the gravelly voice rings out behind me.

"Drop the weapon, Miss Kyle."

Behind me, Gammell and Deputy Scarecrow have drawn their guns. Gritting my teeth, I rotate slowly, crouching, laying my battle axe on the sidewalk. I glance over my shoulder. The stagecoach is about two blocks away.

Rolling steadily toward my location…

I raise both hands in the air.

"Please, Sheriff Gammell. You've got no reason in this universe to believe me. But you have to listen to me. I'm no super hero…but right now, I'm the only one who can prevent that stagecoach from unleashing a big fat can of horrible on this town. I know you're a good man. At the end of the day–" I dart my eyes to the side. The coach is approaching fast.

"At the end of the day, I know you'll do what's right. *Please*, Gammell. Look into your heart. You'll know you can trust me."

Without wavering, Gammell unhooks his Taser from his belt.

Well, so much for candor.

Suddenly, everyone down the street flattens and yelps as fireworks explode. We all turn. A power cable has snapped from its telephone pole like a rubber band, and as the stagecoach rolls by, its carriage is showered in white sparks. It seems unaffected, and keeps rattling right along. My stomach sinks when I see the coach is still wrapped in a blue shimmer. Then I spot it.

There, on the carriage roof, a clear spot right where the electricity touched it. No shimmer.

An opening.

Hank! That son-of-a-gun pulled it off.

I can't see him, but somewhere up the street amidst the shrieking crowd, I hear Hank's unmistakable shout.

"Fly like you got wings, girl! *Go, go!*"

Gammell could have stopped me. Shot me, Tasered me – and that's exactly what he's telling me with his frosty lingering glare. But he spins on his heel with Deputy Scarecrow and runs off down the street, toward the source of the downed power line. Snatching my axe from the ground, I spring open my Icemaker and sprint up the sidewalk until I'm running alongside the stagecoach.

Looks like the top of the carriage is still electricity-free. Somehow I'll have to go through the roof. But I'll fry myself if I touch that shimmering coach by climbing up there.

I'll have to drop from above.

Yippee.

Stuffing my heavy axe under one arm, I fling myself onto the nearest telephone post and shimmy to the top, using the little wooden birdhouses as footholds. The homecoming banner is attached to this telephone pole, suspended by a thick metal cord and stretched across the street, fastened to the opposite pole.

I bounce the cord a couple times with my foot, testing it. It should hold me…

But there's no time for 'shoulds.'

Wrapping my arms and legs tightly around the cord, I scramble across it like a nearsighted squirrel, just as the stagecoach rattles past underneath me. Then it passes right by.

I've missed it.

I cling to the cord, gaping at the coach's backside as it rapidly rolls away. Panic spreads hot in my gut. Turning my head, I look back toward the street below. The next float is passing underneath me. It's the enormous wolverine.

My last chance.

Gripping the cord, I drop my legs so that I'm dangling over the street. People start hollering and cheering, but I barely hear them. The wolverine float rolls directly under me. My window is now. I let go.

My landing is less than graceful. Both my hands slip off the wolverine's giant painted nose, and for a moment, I'm flailing at nothing but air. By the skin of my teeth I catch myself, digging my fingernails into the paper mâché as Merrick's glasses fall from my face. I roll over onto my back, the float thundering under me. Whistling cold air and applause in my ears, I rise into a surfer's stance on the wolverine's uneven head, still clutching its chicken wire skeleton, adjusting constantly to keep my balance. I can see the stagecoach's rear up ahead, rattling along about twenty feet in front of me. Still no glimmer on the roof. But for how much longer…?

It's now or never.

Jump now…

Or Merrick gets never.

I swallow hard. Gathering my muscles taut, I rock back and forth with three mock starts. Then I rocket into the air. I land on top of the stagecoach in a sloppy crunch, fire exploding through my knee as I tumble. But I'm not fried.

"IT'S NOW OR NEVER..."

The countdown display is right beside me. Now that I'm up close, I can see that the screen is made of metal, glowing like a grainy old film from some invisible projector. The screen shifts from '7' to '6.'

I give the screen two quick taps. No shock. No juice.

Looks like we're still in business.

With my axe, I begin hacking madly at the roof of that stagecoach. I chop. I rip. With all of myself, driven by the raw image of Merrick in the street, propelled by my panic, my raw hatred of Rascal Holliday. Finally, I've slashed a sizable hole.

Gripping my axe, I gather my breath and drop down into the coach, landing with a painful thump on the black silk seat inside. The blue computer screen bears a single sentence, in blocky white letters:

ABORT COMMAND: ENTER USERNAME

____

My stomach plummets like a rock.

It wants my ***name***.

Lord, no, not this...

Anything but *this*...

I rack my brain. I bite my tongue, slap myself in the face. I fumble frantically through the pages of my pink kitten notebook, dig through all the little pockets in the coach's interior, but none contain any answer. Empty, whistling caverns. Just like my brain.

My trembling fingers hover motionless over the keyboard, my breath coming in panicked gasps. I squeeze my eyes shut.

And I type my name.

My eyes pop open.

If you paid me a million bucks, I couldn't tell you what I just typed on that keyboard. If you placed my heart back in my chest, and threw in Holliday, hogtied in a red bow with an apple in his mouth, I still wouldn't be able to recall. It was a spasm of muscle memory, a fleeting resurgence of something mundanely familiar. An answer buried deep in the fibers of my hands, cloaked within the collective neural network connecting to Cl. Kyle's brain.

My eyelids contract. I can only stare at that blue screen.

USERNAME ACCEPTED.

Whatever it was, it's gone now.

And there's now a gray dot on my Icemaker.

When I stumble numbly from the stagecoach, my busted knee gives out. I collapse. Hank is there to catch me, and despite my bellyaching, I eventually let him hoist me up and drive me to the hospital. It makes me want to cry. Only Merrick is allowed to carry me. That was my rule. But I'm just too stinking tired to fight anymore tonight.

Hank maneuvers his compact car carefully through the crowd, a wall of grateful thunderous applause to our left and right. I lean my cheek against the seat of Hank's car and close my eyes.

I lost something precious today…but I reclaimed it.

I saved Merrick. For him, I secured a tomorrow. And tomorrow, I know I'll see him again.

I feel hollowed out, but not empty. On the contrary. That hollow space between my ribs never felt so warm and full. I savor the fading sound of the distant cheering. Their voices all meld together; I can't make out what they're saying. But in my mind, they're joyfully shouting the same thing.

My town. My town.

The only pulse I need right now.

*

Hank signs me into the hospital ER and then gently deposits me in one of the beds along the wall. Same bed I was in that first day, I note with detached amusement. That fateful day when I woke up in Carnival Creeke. The day I began this crazy epic adventure. I can even smell the lemon coffee cake, although I noticed they've now moved the desert, stashing it under the counter. No knife, either.

"Hey, Jedi girl." Hank chuckles. "Get you anything?"

I smile faintly. "Thanks. Actually, I'd really love a slice of that cake out there at the desk."

"You got it."

I gaze at him for a moment, my eyes falling on his name 'Hank' sewed onto his jumpsuit.

"Hey," I say, and he turns around. "I think my doppelganger might've killed you once. I've been meaning to say sorry about that."

"Okay, uh, well." Hank scratches his head, unsure quite how to respond. "Lemme go see about dat cake."

He swishes the blue privacy curtain closed and I strip down, tossing my clothes into a pile on the floor, slipping into the papery pink hospital gown before reclining back on the bed. I twist my ID bracelet around my wrist. It says "*Kyle, Cameron*."

No, I didn't miraculously remember my name again. I chose 'Cameron' only because I saw it on a box of CameronCo tissues on our way in. I'm just too tired to be clever or original right now.

Reaching down into my clothes pile, I pull the pink kitten notebook from my pants pocket, flipping to the last page. I stare at Holliday's message.

Hickory, Dickory, Doc.

What a weird thing to write.

Wonder what he writes in birthday cards…

I find myself tracing Holliday's handwriting with my finger. The same way I trace my circular heart scar at night, those nights when I'm perched above Lau Chow's, or lying quiet in my Red Rooster bed…

The curtain around my bed abruptly slides open and Sheriff Gammell enters. I quickly shut the kitten notebook and stuff it under my pillow. Without taking his eyes off me, Gammell scoots a plastic chair over to my bed and sits down. Looking at the floor, he puts both hands on his knees and draws a long, deep breath.

"When I joined up in the Marines," he begins without introduction. "I was seventeen. Just a kid."

So Gammell is a Marine. So that's how he was able to toss my sorry tail into his jail cell. Twice.

"Anyway," Gammell growls wearily. "When I got home, I felt like I could do anything. The world was my oyster, nobody holding my hand. Got my first little apartment. Then the sink broke. Nobody could convince me I couldn't fix the thing myself, but the swimming pool in my kitchen was a little much to ignore."

Raising his eyebrows, he reaches down and unclips his keys from his belt.

"This." Gammell slides something off his keychain and holds it up. A tiny, flat metal circle. Just an ordinary old washer, the kind you get from a hardware store.

Gripping the little object, he shakes it a few times.

"I keep this washer as a reminder...to never forget the little stuff. Be it good, or bad. 'Cause it's all important. Everything plays its part. Do you understand?"

He hands the washer to me.

For a long moment, I completely lose the ability to form the most basic of actions. Speech, breath, closing my fingers. I just sit there dumbly, the little washer in my hand.

Gammell leans back in the chair, his gravelly voice drained and soft.

"Don't ask me to explain how, but..." he hesitates. "I feel like I know you, Miss Kyle. Something inside me keeps saying I can trust you, even though I've got no cockamamie explanation why. Maybe I'm just old. And tired. But I will say this. We don't know how that stagecoach got here. And we don't know what was gonna happen when that countdown ended. But I believe you were acting with everything in your power to save Phil today. And save...Merrick."

My eyes burn as I look at the floor. Reaching out with his hand, Sheriff Gammell hesitates, then lays one rough pat on my shoulder. He leaves it there for a moment.

"You did good today," he says softly, gruffly.

It's not fully a smile, not under the weight of today's events. But Gammell draws his lips tight, and he gives me a firm nod. It's a nod I know well. Same nod he gave me that night on the roof of Lau Chow's, while all the townsfolk partied on Main Street below, sky-high with their levity of having narrowly averted turning into cows.

Then he says, "I won't forget what you did for this town."

There they are. Those words.

My most bittersweet consolation prize.

He gives me another nod then ducks out the curtain, letting it fall closed again. I squeeze the little metal washer so tightly my nails leave imprints on my palm. I've never had so much of nothing to say. Feels like I've got moths in my mouth. A warm haze swims inside my head.

I'm still smiling at the little washer when the blue curtain is slung back again. I'm expecting Hank with my cake, but this time Doctor Fairchild is standing there, a clipboard in his hand. His pink mole face puckers when he recognizes me.

"Oh, it's *you*. Lucky me." He cringes sourly from behind his glasses, hooking the clipboard onto the bedrail. "Pray we can get through this visit without you attacking me with a knife, hm?"

"Sounds like a hoot," I yawn with a smile.

Averting my gaze, Doctor Fairchild purses his thin lips and leans over, kneading my purple, swollen knee. He passes a small, palm-sized x-ray device along my leg.

"Alright, let's see what kind of mess you've gotten yourself into this time."

I roll my eyes. I know what the problem is. I've got an acute impact injury. Most likely second-degree, judging from the swelling. Rest, ice; compression, elevation.

Doctor Fairchild straightens, draping the cord of the x-ray around his neck.

"Well, you appear to have a second-degree impact sprain," he announces with a superior sniff. "Just keep it elevated and iced. And for goodness sake, stay off your feet."

Booya.

I point two fingers at him and make a thumbs-up, then lace my hands behind my head and shut my eyes. Doctor Fairchild just clears his throat in response and Velcros a cuff around my upper arm. I grimace.

Ugh. I knew they would try to check my pulse.

Typically, the vitals are taken by a nurse. I didn't think Doctor Moleface would be doing the honors. He's going to be more than a little freaked out when he sees I don't have a pulse.

There's no tricking these machines. As the cuff tightens around my bicep, my mind cycles quickly for a way to stall.

Should I fall over? Pretend to pass out?

Whatever. It's almost one o'clock, anyway. Worst case scenario, they'll try to put me on oxygen or something, and maybe some poor grunt gets chewed out for faulty equipment.

I watch as Doctor Fairchild's shrewd eyes squint behind his glasses. His forehead bunches up, mystified. He squeezes the bulb and air hisses, loosening the cuff. Suddenly his brow relaxes.

"Ninety over sixty," he declares smoothly.

Wait. *What?*

I jerk my head to look at him.

"A little on the low side, but otherwise, perfectly healthy."

Doctor Fairchild rips off the Velcro cuff. I almost fall off the bed leaning over to see his screen with those impossible numbers, but the doctor has already wheeled it aside. He unclips my chart from the bed like everything is as fine and dandy as apple pie.

"One more thing," he adds breezily. "I noticed something...*atypical*...on my x-ray of your knee. Nothing urgent... But when I return in a moment, I'd like a word with you."

As he's reaching to pull the blue curtain aside, he pauses, standing there with his arm outstretched. He turns his head, looking down at me.

"Do be a good girl and stay put, hmm?"

Then he smiles.

It should have been a normal smile. People smile all the time. So I'm not prepared when Doctor Fairchild's grin hitches up the corners of his mouth, stretching past his cheekbones, nearly splitting his head open ear-to-ear, a slender purple tongue flickering out over multiple rows of spindly, needlepoint teeth. His yellow eyes squeeze shut once, contracting like tiny sphincter muscles – then he slips out. The blue curtain falls lazily behind him.

The instant he's gone I lunge across the bed, seizing my Icemaker from my pile of clothes. I fall on my stomach and jam the button to open the screen.

Someone in town isn't who you think they are...

It's 12:44, a mere handful of ticks away from one o'clock. If I've still got a loose wildcard when that clock turns, even *one* wildcard, it's all over. Today sticks. Forever. And Merrick stays...

Merrick stays...

My gun's fan-shaped screen unfolds. Clear.

No red dots.

I stop breathing, rubbing my eyes. I gape at the screen.

The screen is clear. Doctor Freakface isn't a wildcard.

So what the heck *is* he?

Someone in town isn't who you think they are...

Skin vibrating, red alarms screaming inside my skull, I somersault helter-skelter off the bed, wincing and catching my breath sharply as hot pain shoots through my injured knee. My legs nearly buckle beneath me. I spring my Icemaker open into a full shotgun and slide it up under my hospital gown, holding it firmly under my arm against my ribs. Then I duck out from the blue curtain.

I glance at the clock on the wall over the nurse's station.

12:48.

"Doctor Fairchild?" I shout in all directions. "Where is he?!"

Nurses and orderlies leaning against the counter just shrug at me, then return to chatting in their hushed, careless tones. Not exactly the behavior of people who just saw a monster man in a doctor coat go running by.

He didn't show up as a red dot.

Did I just ***imagine*** *his face like that?*

I want so badly to know. I *need* to know if what I saw was merely my eyes playing tricks. The hallucination of a truly fried brain after a very, very long and sucky day…

I hobble rapidly along the hall, my bare feet padding silently on the shiny white floor tiles. I push through a set of double-doors into the maternity ward. There's a large rectangular viewing window decorated with festive pumpkin stickers. On the other side of the glass, a tightly-bundled newborn baby is being handed to a dark-haired lady in a hospital gown, her cheeks rosy and flushed. I immediately recognize her. It's that pregnant gal who gave birth to her baby on the Grim Reaper float, the night the wereteddy critters chased us. That night, she was smiling. Tonight, her face is *all* smiles.

And I recognize the father. It's Luv-Money. His shoulders hunch awkwardly as he catches his breath, he puts his arms around his wife, eyes shining, gazing at his tiny child. What did Merrick say his name was? Graham Sutherbee.

Guess he got my gasoline gift.

Tonight, he made it here in time to see his son born.

Pressing my palms to the window, I lean my forehead against the glass. A card on the baby's clear plastic bassinet reads:

"*Mother: Sutherbee, Minnie.*"

Sutherbee... LUV-MNY...

I glance back at the name card.

Love...Minnie?

Then it dawns on me. His license plate didn't say 'Love Money.' It says 'Love Minnie.'

The dang doofus loves his wife.

Folding my arms over my head, I sink down onto my knees, unable to take my eyes off the young family. I'm so tired. And somewhere, deep in the recesses of my chest, I feel something warm stir. A weight is lifting. For the first time since I woke up here, reborn here in this very same papery hospital gown, it feels like I'm carrying nothing at all. Like I'm breathing for the first time, only I hadn't even realized I'd been holding my breath all along.

A soft flutter. A haze is clearing.

I open my hand and look at Gammell's washer. I trace it lightly, smiling at the little metal circle.

I may not know who Cl. Kyle was...but maybe I'm finally beginning to catch a glimpse of who *this* Kyle is. Whatever Doctor Freakface found on that x-ray...

Keep it. I don't need to know. Don't *want* to.

I'm right where I want to be.

I'm finally home.

DAY 42: GOODNIGHT, MOON

I looked for Doctor Fairchild. Oh, you better believe I hunted him. But – surprise, surprise – nobody at the hospital had ever heard of him. There never was a Doctor Fairchild on staff. The pink-faced monster doctor was simply gone without a trace. He's a ghost story.

Like Holliday.

Like me.

*

Then came the day when everyone started flying. Pretty easy to spot, that wildcard. I didn't even have to check my Icemaker screen for red dots. People all over town would just be cruising along the sidewalk, munching their bagels, drinking their morning coffee, when the next thing we knew, everyone was floating around like balloons. Kicking their legs in alarm, grabbing at streetlamps and mailboxes and each other's shirts, until Mickey from the hardware shop came hollering back with about five miles worth of rope and cord. We instructed all our lostboys and lostgirls to hook on. Sam Dove donated all the kite string and bungee camping straps from his General Store. Gladys and her Bingo Brigade even chipped in with a truckload of yarn.

All of Carnival Creeke, for one gloriously silly day, tethered together like one enormous kite.

Merrick once again saved the day, cooking up a helium cocktail that canceled out the "balloon effect" and gradually lowered everyone back down to the ground.

At sunset, Sheriff Gammell ordered all the homecoming floats parked on Main Street and all the townsfolk gathered in the intersection, hovering around the float wagons like one big anti-gravity block party. It was just like a rerun of that day when all these folk were turning into cows – only instead of Dixie cups and anti-cow juice, everyone was lining up for a swig from Merrick's helium tank. With our feet in the air.

I'm okay with a rerun of Cow Day. That was a good day.

This one was even better.

The library clock tower declares it midnight, and although nearly everyone has been reunited with the ground, we're still partying loud and proud. Hot plates of food are set out on metal risers, amidst rows of thermoses containing Mrs. Moffatt's knockout warm cider and hot chocolate. Randy and his cronies are hooting like howler monkeys, doing back-flips in the air and pretending to slow-motion kung fu kick each other in the face. Jolly Phil is guffawing about something, throwing his balding head back and slapping Sheriff Gammell between the shoulder blades as he helps himself to a third slice of Merle's rhubarb pie.

Gazing at Gammell, I reach under my jacket collar. I've started wearing a necklace lately. Nothing fancy, nothing strung on that ten-dollar silver chain. But every time I look at Frank

Gammell, I see it – the little tarnished washer, hanging from his belt loop with his station keys. Sure, maybe he'll never actually hand that washer to me again. It will probably never hang on my necklace. But that's okay. Some things you only have to earn once. I know it's mine. And that's good enough for me.

We all look up as music starts booming through the huge pole-mounted speakers atop the homecoming floats. A low thrum of upright bass beats, followed by Frank Sinatra's lazy voice singing "Fly Me to the Moon."

"Very funny!" somebody yells out. Laughter ripples through the crowd. Sam Dove envelopes Julie in his long arms, dipping her back like a ballroom queen. Her embarrassed squeal is beautiful and so are her pale golden curls, spreading out like a fan across the back of her blouse.

Merrick twirls Jemma like a ballerina. Then he looks at me with a grin. "Hey, did you know this was the first song heard on the moon?"

I smile. "Oh yeah?"

"Yep. Buzz Aldrin brought a portable cassette player when he stepped off the Apollo Eleven."

"And?"

"And–" He raises an eyebrow slyly and extends his hand. "Shouldn't we commemorate this ironic occasion with a dance?"

I roll my eyes and grin affectionately.

"Just don't expect a repeat performance!" I call to him.

I grab Merrick's hand and he pulls me in a circle. Since we've spent all night escorting the kiddos and the elderly to the helium

tank, Merrick and I are the last two people who are still floating. We rise over everyone's heads, elevated to a different dimension, swaying to the music. I rest my cheek against Merrick's shoulder; smiling, my eyes slide shut. He's singing along with Sinatra under his breath. Merrick Cohen, doing that thing he does in that freaking brilliant voice of his.

"*In other words, hold my hand,*" he sings softly. "*In other words...baby, kiss me...*"

I keep trying to tell him he's a dork, but the boy just croons louder, belting out the words and cupping one hand over his ear like he can't hear me, smiling and shrugging. People have backed up into a circle around us, granting us center stage.

"So it's a show they want, huh?" I point a finger at Merrick. "You'd better catch me, Peter Pan!"

He grins and salutes. I hop into his arms and let him toss me up into the air, except I don't fall. The chilly night breeze lifts me up like a kite as I scissor my legs up over my head, arcing backwards. Merrick flips me upright; I grab him by the strings on his gray hoodie. The kinetic sway of our weightless bodies pulls me in, and I collide clumsily against his chest, prompting a wave of whistles and catcalls from our jubilant audience. Merrick catches me with both arms, embracing me a teensy bit tighter than might be platonic.

"Whoa, sorry," he stammers into my hair, red-faced.

"Don't be," I whisper. And I mean it. Sliding my arms around the back of his neck, I pull him to me. As far as I'm concerned, right where he belongs.

I'm sure now. Whatever Before-Kyle used to do, I'm sure she had a partner. No idea who it was...but now, it's Merrick. I've decided. As long as I'm still ticking, I will never again try to do this alone. And I'll never let him go again.

Sure, I'm still stuck in this loop. Sure, it's hard starting each day from scratch with everyone. So what's changed?

Me.

This girl, this Kyle? She's happy. Happier than I've ever been. My job, this town, these folk – never have I felt more at peace, more hungry for the next day's electrifying *wildcard du jour*. I can't guarantee what each day holds. But I guarantee, someday, I *will* give them a tomorrow. My promise to Merrick. I can't promise it'll be perfect. But I've learned to give myself a little grace. A little wiggle room. To fail. To grow.

You know what *is* perfect?

This.

Today, I'm one of them. Today, I belong. When this day resets, I know Merrick will still be here. And when I finally ring that bell and win this game? I'll find him again. It might be messy, imperfect, unknown. But until that after-party, I'm just living for the ride.

I feel Merrick take my face in both his warm hands, and I raise my eyes (was I intending to kiss him? Was he leaning in to do the same?) – but all we accomplish is a gracelessly hilarious bumping of noses.

I'm still laughing like a doof when I happen to turn my head. Glancing past the crowd, my eyes come to a sudden halt.

A figure is standing at the curb.

Arms folded across his chest, his slim body leaned back against an oil-black motorcycle. Even in the dark, I can see his fingers tapping rhythmically against the sleeve of his leather jacket. He might as well be a shadow, except for the way the overhead floodlights catch his studded belt, causing it to glint. No, this shadow has a face, and it's glaring at me through narrowed eyes, his expression frosty and calculating, like chilly ripples on a black pond.

My breath catches in my throat.

Unless this is a fantasy caused by the extra bacon I scarfed this morning, I am staring at Rascal Holliday. Everyone in their revelry seems to fade into the background, the music sounds as though underwater.

I open my mouth.

Holliday turns the instant I twitch a muscle. He springs gracefully onto the motorcycle, slipping a helmet over his wild black curls and taking off like a banshee, the roar of his bike's ignition noisily drowning out any ember of question as to whether I still think he's a bacon-induced hallucination.

I won't get this chance again. If I lose Rascal Holliday tonight, he becomes a ghost story again. Melts back into the hazy muck between my obsession and my finger on my empty pulse each night. No way…

Game over is not an option.

Not tonight.

I start pulling myself hand over hand down the speaker pole. My eyes dart through the crowd. Randy's sleek yellow-and-black Ducati sport bike is across the intersection, leaning up against a fire hydrant, a parking violation work of art. I immediately propel myself toward the bike. Fighting the lazy sluggishness of my limbs, I pause only to suck a floundering gulp from the helium tank. I can feel the anti-float serum start to take effect immediately, but the air still tugs my body upward as I grip the Ducati's handlebars and slam my rump down hard onto the seat.

"Sorry kid," I call over my shoulder. "I'll return it tomorrow, promise."

I wrap my legs around the bike and roar off, Randy hollering stuff behind me that would turn his granny's fine doilies yellow.

I don't know what I'm thinking. My good sense has been soaking slowly in gasoline, and seeing Holliday standing there lit my fuse. The sum of forty-two days just exploded. I'm coming up fast behind Holliday's bike now, and I can barely even see the buttons on my glowing dashboard. All I see is red.

We swoop through the streets like birds of prey, on the edge of disaster with every turn. Holliday keeps dipping left and right with his bike, disappearing behind oncoming cars then flashing out the other side. My breath catches as my elbows and toes brush the side of a swerving car, its headlights in my face, momentarily rendering me blind.

He's outmaneuvering me.

I don't care.

I'm not out to earn any style points tonight.

My knees gripping hard on the slim tank, I slide my butt back into the seat and press my chest to the bike. Every inch of my skin seems to be drawn to Holliday, like a paperclip to a super magnet. Spurring me headlong. Driving me faster...

I am incapable of losing him tonight.

The fire of my righteous fury won't *allow* it.

Holliday slices left onto Jackson Street, my rear wheel fishtailing wildly as I go skidding after him. I think I just demolished somebody's jack-o-lantern. My helmet visor is smeared with seedy pumpkin guts, but I got a glimpse at Holliday's bike.

He's on a Suzuki Dual Sport. If we were off-road, he would probably whup my tail. But Randy's Ducati is a higher-end Italian street machine. With twice the horsepower and torque, I'm on the faster bike, no contest. Give me a nice straightaway, and I would run clear over him before you could say 'trick-or-treat.' But here, confined to these back roads and alleys, straightaways last about as long as a sneeze. The brick streets are narrow, a crisscross grid of corners and sharp right angles, almost constantly slammed with stop signs, which Holliday blows through and I follow with gritted teeth. As long as we're squirting around downtown like this, Holliday is keeping me firmly under his thumb, and behind his back.

We zip past the diner, its windows dark, snug as a bug. Merle shut off the neon sign hours ago, before he finished off the last piece of grilled cheese and locked the door behind him. Gumby's

Toy Shop whips by. We cut diagonally across the Tuscany Mill parking lot, illuminated by a single streetlight.

I've never traveled through Carnival Creeke so fast. It's like flying through the pages of a storybook. *My* story. Holliday may have dropped me into this little snow globe life, but he forgot one key point –

This ain't his snow globe anymore.

You're on ***my*** *turf now, creep.*

Almost on instinct, my eyes swing over to the horizon. I see the water tower, its domed head peeping over the tree line, a hulking black shape silhouetted against the moon.

And at that moment, without warning, the memory hits me.

Thunk.

I landed on my back in the grass. My feet were still propped up on the metal bleacher that I was just sitting on a moment ago.

Did I doze off?

Remaining sprawled on my back in the grass, I gazed up at the sky. A bright blue expanse, a sheet of spun-sugar clouds, stretched over me and the empty baseball field in front of me. Stretched over the red brick elementary school, bathed in sun. Over the old, mint green water tower, squatting in the distance at the far back edge across the field. It should have felt peaceful. But it wasn't. A strange, nagging feeling gnawed the back of my head. There was something I was supposed to be doing. A task. Something important... What was it? Foggy...unclear. I probably just bonked my head when I fell off the bleacher. Hey, at least nobody saw me.

Lacing my fingers behind my head, I shut my eyes.

"Ye okay, then?"

My eyes popped open.

Who said that?

Springing up onto my knees, I looked around. The field was empty, save for the crickets. The baseball diamond was vacant. Not a soul in sight. One-hundred percent vanilla normal.

Then I looked up.

The black-haired boy was hanging upside-down, suspended from the top of the baseball backstop. Swinging up, he perched nimbly on the apex of the curved metal bar, causing the chain-link fence to rattle gently.

Curious, I gazed up at him.

He looked down at me.

And Rascal Holliday and I locked eyes for the first time.

"So," he repeated, a bit impatiently. "Are ye okay, then?"

I remember his Irish accent, feathery and musical. Made me sound like a goat with laryngitis.

"Oh, yeah, right as rain!" I blurted, hopping up and brushing the grass off my butt. "See? All internal organs intact."

"Well, that's fortunate."

Swinging his leg over the backstop, he dropped lithely down to the ground, like it was no more than hopping off a chair.

"I'm Rascal Holliday. And now, I've gotta ask ye a question."

Rascal? Weird name.

I watched him slink toward me, a bad feeling fermenting in the pit of my stomach. Something felt wrong.

It wasn't his sickly hospital pallor, or the way his hollow dark eyes set off his gorgeous pale face, giving him the appearance of a walking coma patient. It was the way he looked at me. Familiar, but not comforting. An icy, unsympathetic familiarity. His twitchy black eyes darted over me cockroaches, awaiting my next move with arctic hatred. I wondered what I could have done to him to make him look at me like that. A duffle bag was slung over his shoulder; he hovered one arm over it, protectively, as if there was a baby inside. Maybe there was. For all I knew, that bag could have held a demented little monster-clown-baby. But it didn't.

It was something much, much worse.

"Oh, a question, huh?" I plastered on my best cheesy clueless grin. But inside, my mind was racing. Calculating the distance from here to the edge of the field; the distance from my fist to his Adam's apple... "Cool. Shoot, I like questions. Questions are fun!"

He blinked icily, unamused.

Then in a slow, deliberate voice, he said, "Ever seen the stars come out in the daytime?"

Now, what the heck was ***that*** *supposed to mean...?*

My heart thumped faster.

Thump, thump. Thump-thump.

"Uh." I tried to act casual. I knew I was failing. "Sorry pal, I don't understand the question."

"C'mon, Doc. Think ***hard****."*

Though I was backing away, he was now right in front of me. Close enough to spit on. I should've spit. No...I should've run.

A red-hot command was screaming at me to run.

Why didn't I run?

It was like someone hit the reset button on my brain, wiped my ability to send neural muscle commands to my legs.

Run, Kyle.

404 error; file not found.

Run...what was my name again?

Strange...I couldn't remember...

I jerked to the right. He mirrored me, blocking me. I lunged left; he was already there, barring my path. I ducked, intending to kick out his knees, horror mounting in my belly when he dropped to the ground, catlike, the very same instant as me. For one burning moment, we just crouched there in the grass, frozen, staring at each other. A bulb was about to burst.

He cocked his head, raised one black eyebrow. "Is this inevitable? Do ye really wanna play this game?"

I swallowed. "Look, I don't want to play anything. Okay? So let's just go our separate ways–"

"Sorry. Can't let ye do that. But, I'll tell ye what." He grinned, that open-mouthed leer. "I'll give ye a head-start."

Yeah, right.

The next thing I knew I was tearing across that field, grass churning wildly under my flailing boots. The elementary school was a good thirty yards away. An island in a nightmare. I punched my limits harder, nearly outrunning my own legs, willing my muscles for breakneck speed. My skin prickled with dread. Not only for the sick spook occupying the unknown space behind me, but upon realizing why the field itself suddenly seemed full of terror.

What was I doing in a field?

How did I get here?

Funny...I just...couldn't remember...

Our bike engines rip and snarl as we loop back and find ourselves back on Main Street again. The intersection is now empty, cleared and devoid of homecoming floats, so there's nothing to slow us as we tear down the straightaway, our furious engines rumbling off the building walls. We roar past the library graveyard. The scaffolding tarp billows up and flutters, a delayed reaction after we've ripped by. Up ahead, the squat shape of the General Store is fast approaching, on the corner where the road splits off into a Y.

I catch my breath and hold it.

Go right, and it takes you back into the historic district, where we just cut a hot streak through.

Turning left would take us out of town. Farm fields, single straight road...and that endless void at the edge of town. Logically, anyone with two brain cells would expect Holliday to turn right, to hang onto his terrain advantage, to utilize that twisty street maze until he can finally give me the slip.

Only he doesn't.

He swerves left.

I exhale, shocked. Whether he meant to or not, that creep Holliday just handed me and the Ducati a winning chance.

We shoot up the steep slope. The moon flashes through the chestnut trees and briefly we're plunged into darkness, rattling across the covered trundle bridge. Our bike engines seem to be competing to drown each other out as we hurtle out the other side of the bridge like a pair of speed-drunk bats. The night opens up; the road stretching out in front of us like an arrow. Dark fields smear into a blur on either side of us. Holliday veers down the center of the lane. In disgust, I jerk out from behind him, and the instant I do, I flatten against my dash and punch the throttle as far as it will go. Speed envelops me as I shoot forward. A giddy laugh escapes my lungs.

I pull up alongside Holliday.

He turns his head and looks at me. I can't see his face behind that dark alien helmet. Bet he's surprised to find I'm still hanging with him. Impressed, even.

I hope so.

That's right, freak, I surge venomously. *Fear me…*

It's at that very moment that the memory decides to wallop me again. Like a waffle iron to the face, like running smack into a brick wall, we're back in the field again…

I vaulted over the chain-link fence into a small enclosed playground, running smack into the brick wall of the school. I flattened against the bricks, panting. An HVAC unit whirred obliviously. The mulch in this corner was slicked and wet. The sweet, coppery scent of blood was unmistakable. My head was throbbing. My pulse racing. A flutter of movement overhead jerked my eyes up to the roof, half a second too late to see his dark leather jacket sliding out of view. How did he get on the roof so fast?

Suddenly, the ground tilted. I lurched forward, confused. My head felt fuzzy… And where did he go? The black-eyed boy in the leather jacket, the one chasing me, the one whose name I can't remember. Name…my name…

What was my name again?

I tried again to remember. But I couldn't. It was like trying to remember a song, but all the instruments are missing, and all you hear is the dull, distant beat. Like all the files in my brain were tumbling out, spilling their blurred contents all over a slippery, ambiguous floor. Trying to recall my name was pounding blanks, my brain scooped clean, my dry skull plugged with cotton.

I clutched my temples, biting my tongue.

Hold it together. Names are inconsequential, momentarily knocked loose by stress. Freak out later. Now, just survive.

Panic engulfed me. I had to move.

Stay alive.

Beside me was a seven-foot tall chain-link storage cage, filled with playground balls and jump ropes. I kicked open the latch and the door swung open, spilling an avalanche of gym balls everywhere. My nostrils filled with their rubbery tang. I snatched a metal baseball bat from the corner of the cage and vaulted back over the playground fence, sprinting around the side of the school. Off in the distance, I could see the road, curving gently toward a little town, obscured by swathes of rusty brown oaks and fiery, red-orange maples. Naturally, Whatever-His-Name-Is would assume I would make a beeline toward that town. He would expect me to go screaming for help.

Good riddance.

I turned on my heel, running back toward the water tower...

I snap back to the present again. Keeping one hand on the Ducati's handlebar, I use my free hand to spring open my Icemaker. Outstretching the shotgun in front of me, I aim at Holliday, swerving the gun's barrel back and forth to keep his slippery shape in my crosshairs. I don't know why I'm bothering.

I can't shoot him.

No, it's not mushy mercy that has my finger frozen on the trigger throttle. I would happily blow Holliday to kingdom come. But then I would kiss my heart goodbye forever.

Of course, he might not die.

I don't know *what* Holliday is. The first day I met him, I saw him crawl up a wall like a freaking lizard. He's a different breed, for sure. Maybe he's like me. A super-healing freak. That would make sense. Well, about as much sense as any other element in this crazy-coated funhouse...

Then a strange thought kindles in my brain.

Is Holliday missing his heart, too?

The two of us, alike, a pair of creatures alone in the world...

I lower my Icemaker a fraction, aiming at the gas tank of Holliday's bike. Before I even squeeze my trigger he swerves sharply, dodging the shot I haven't fired yet. Never even a glance back. Like he just knew I was fixing to shoot at him.

He's anticipating me.

The creep is reading my mind again.

Gritting my teeth, I fire off a string of shots. The blue bursts of light sail harmlessly past his Suzuki's gleaming wheel spokes as he slaloms in an S-shape.

Let him dodge.

The edge of town stretches on forever, like an endless treadmill. He can't outrun me. Not as long as we're on the road.

So of course he drives off the road.

He jerks suddenly to the right, tearing up the gravel shoulder and skimming between two fence posts, streaking off across the field in a cloud of moonlit dust.

I literally feel him slip through my fingers like a fish.

"Oh, no you don't!" I scream.

Throwing my weight and yanking up on the handlebars, I pop my front wheels up the gravel shoulder and follow, landing with a muffled thump and bouncing over the hard dirt. My teeth chatter, my chin bopping the dash.

Remember what I said about his Suzuki spanking my Ducati off-road?

My high-performance street tires are merely spinning, unable to grip the grassy ditches, rendering the Ducati's powerful engine about as useful as a pogo stick in quicksand.

We plunge into cornfields. I go to choke the throttle and it bites back, skidding on the crushed silky cornstalks underfoot and throwing me forward. I hug the bike like a koala, fully expecting to kiss the dirt. But I manage to hold on.

I'm not running from you anymore, Holliday...

The mint-green water tower loomed at the edge of the field ahead, like some giant steel robot. I cut across the baseball field and skidded to a reckless halt, ducking behind one of the water tower's steel support legs. My heart was hammering so loudly I swear it would give up my location. A ladder appeared to lead up to a narrow catwalk around the tower's dome. Stuffing the baseball bat under my arm, I grabbed the metal rungs and started climbing. As soon as my feet touched the catwalk I scrambled around the opposite side of the tank, crouching, angling my body from view. There I sat, gripping the bat in both sweaty fists.

Deep breath.

Count to three...

Slowly, I leaned forward and peeked around the water tank. What's-His-Name should be coming across the field after me.

Any second now...

A moment passed. Breeze rippled the grass below. Crickets chirped. No sign of him. Maybe he was still on the school roof. Maybe by some miracle he actually didn't notice me run here...

"Tsk, tsk, Doc."

My muscles froze. I jerked my head up.

The black-eyed freak was leering down at me from the top of the water tower's tank.

This officially had become a horror movie.

How on earth could he have gotten here ***before*** *me?*

He would have passed me without me seeing him. How could he have guessed that I would hide here? Nobody's that lucky.

Unless he read my mind.

The thud of his boots landing on the catwalk sent a shockwave of terror through me. I turned in mid-run, colliding instantly against his chest, knocking my footing from under me. I felt the metal railing scrape past my hip as we flipped over it, and we fell from the tower, a tangle of limbs.

I hit the ground butt-first. A terrible way to land, and I knew it, but I wasn't given the luxury of choice as we were hurtling through the air. Jolts ran up my spine, slamming the air from my throat. He sat on my chest, pinning me, strong despite his slim frame, his boots grinding my arms into the soil. I fought him. Fought to keep the vomit down, to stay calm, even though every bone was likely broken, and all I could do was watch in rising dread as he unzipped that duffle bag and pulled out the thing, the unspeakable thing, the worse-than-monster-clown-baby.

The metal canister.

"What have you got there?" I asked him. My voice might have sounded downright casual if I weren't shaking like a leaf, and gargling on the hot blood pouring from my nose.

He averted his eyes. Wouldn't look at me.

"Ye seen those things at the bank drive-through window, right?" Calmly, he attached the three wires and positioned the canister over my chest. I felt the edges of it boring into my skin, a ring of tiny drills burrowed into the flesh over my breastbone. I couldn't lift my knee. Couldn't snap my arms wide, or buck to throw him off balance. He seemed to be predicting my every move, adjusting his body slightly to counter me before I even tried. So I did the only logical thing I had left.

I'd just gotten a good mouthful of spit when he wagged a warning finger.

"Shhh, easy, Doc." He grinned. "Stop wigglin'. It'll be less than silky if ye tense up."

The canister released a hiss, air-tight against my skin.

"This might be unpleasant. Would ye like somethin' to bite down on?"

Glaring at him, I tried to focus all my venom through my eyes.

"You can bite my–"

"That's a 'no' then. Okay. I'm gonna do this on the count'a three. One–"

"Hey, hey, wait!" I started to thrash wildly against his iron grip, the last futile attempt of a trapped animal.

"Two..."

Panting, I braced my back against the soil and swore on all that is and ever was that he would not hear me utter a sound when it happened...

Then he pressed the button without saying 'three.'

In retrospect, it probably wouldn't have made a difference if he had courteously tacked one more number onto his cruel countdown.

My back arched so violently that I saw mud fly up around me. I felt the back of my head bash into the ground as a cannonball burst through my sternum. Not like I'd been shot by a cannonball, but rather like it had come from inside my own body, blown outward, ripping through bone and muscle and flesh like it was nothing more than tissue paper.

"Breathe."

I heard a voice. Vaguely, I realized he was talking to me.

"Breathe, Doc."

He poked at me, like one pokes at a slab of dead meat.

Breathe, he said? How was I supposed to do that?

All I could do was jerk around on the ground, my clenched fists pressed into the dirt. My fingers going numb, I opened my mouth wide and gulped at nothing. It was terrifying, like trying to catch hold of a train car rushing past.

"Ye need to breathe, Doc."

I do. But I immediately wished I hadn't.

The air I finally caught hold of came barreling down my throat like shards of flaming glass. My lungs filled up quickly and turned inside out; I flipped over onto my face and coughed violently into the mud.

"What...did...you do to me?" I turned my head.

He was squatting over me, silhouetted against a blue sky of spun sugar, his wild hair slung over his forehead. He fiddled with some buttons on the side of the metal canister. I remember it had a narrow glass slit. A window, the glass smeared with red. Something was inside the canister. At first, I thought it was a chunk of raw steak. The horror didn't overtake me when I realized it was a human heart –

Only when I realized it was mine.

"You...took...my...heart? " I choked out. "You took my freaking ***HEART?!****"*

"Yeah, yeah, I took yer heart. Let's move on. We got more important things at stake here, Doc."

I craned my neck, an inexplicably morbid attempt to see my disembodied heart inside that demon tuna can. To see if it was still beating. But I wasn't able to steal a good look, because the creep had already stuffed the canister back into the duffle and swiftly zipped it up. Almost instantly his expression changed. His black eyes flicked rapidly left and right, scanning the field around us. Guess it should have made me nervous. But frankly, it was taking all my concentration to keep from passing out. Nasty black tunnels were closing in around my vision. I shoved a quivering hand up under my shirt, my fingers fluttering gingerly at the raw, stinging circle of jagged flesh over my breastbone.

I retracted my hand and stared at it. No blood...

"Can ye walk?" he asked impatiently.

Without waiting for an answer, he dragged me to my feet. As soon as he let go, I wobbled over sideways on my jelly legs. I dropped to my hands and knees.

"Why...me..." I sputtered, spitting dots of blood on the dirt. Holliday clapped a cloth over my face, and for a second, I thought he was trying to chloroform me. Then I realized he was wiping my bloody nose. I slapped his hand away. His black eyes stopped darting around and he stared hard at me, anxious and irritable.

"Ye ***really*** *don't remember a thing, do ye?" he pressed.*

Remember? Remember what?

He was asking too much of me, that's all I knew. Breathe, stand, remember... it was all too much. I was tired. Every cell in my body felt drained and empty. My forehead grazed the dirt. Out of the corner of my eye, I saw him stand, gazing down at me in disgust before stomping away. With effort, I reached my hand toward him.

"Wait...come back..."

He stopped and turned, his expression tentative. "Why?"

"Because..." I opened and closed my fingers in a grabbing motion. "'Cause I wanna tear out your heart, too." I gurgled weakly.

He just stared at me, cocking his head, a ghost of a smile.

"I wish ye were serious."

Really? He wishes that?

"Shh, don't worry. It passes. Ten minutes, ye gonna feel right as rain." He patted me on the head. In retrospect, I should have tried to grab his arm and flip him onto the ground, or at least bite him or something. But I was too disoriented.

"Sorry, Doc. I gotta go now. Keep yer eyes on the prize, okay? Find the device. I'll see ye again soon."

If I had just lifted my heavy potato head, I would have seen it. Instead, I heard it – a whooshing sound. Like water building up around a Plexiglas container...

A scuffle of feet...

Then a blue flash of light that spread across the ground I had my face buried in. Then silence. Birds.

Me, repeating 'Crap, crap, crap.'

When I finally crawled to my feet, the black-eyed punk was gone. Not a trace of him in a mile of field to my left or right. I wobbled around in a wild circle, flung my fingers onto my neck.

No pulse.

The moment your heart stops, you're on a countdown. Lack of oxygen to the brain causes your cells to begin breaking down. Nitric oxide is produced, and as your brain cells die, your brain tissue keeps on deteriorating. The hourglass is glued to the table.

How am I still alive?

I could make out the outline of a hospital just over the tree line. I should go there. Medical attention for a zombie? I had no choice.

Two drunken hops to the side, then I took off across the field, my jog now oddly strong, gaining strength with every stride, as I ran toward that hospital...

I blink, gasping, one hand clutching the Ducati's handlebar. My other hand clutched at the circular scar on my chest. Cornstalks are pummeling my legs and I'm ashamed to say it really hurts. Slowing, I weave through the path that Holliday cut in front of me. I can still hear his bike somewhere in the cornfield, but the throaty snarl is muffled, distant. I can't see him anymore.

And I'm being beaten up by corn.

The chilly air slapping my cheeks has cooled me a discouraging ten degrees. Right about now, my righteous fury isn't looking to be worth a roll of toilet paper.

I clench my teeth.

This isn't working. I could chase Holliday until my nose hairs bleed...but then what? What exactly did I plan to do? Jump on him like a panther girl? Hope he would pull over so we could have a nice civil chat?

Yes, I've rehearsed my showdown with Holliday. Rehashed it a thousand times in my head – my meticulously polished script, the punchy, righteous barbs that I would unleash into his smirky face... But here's the snag. Never, in any of my carefully rehearsed scenarios, did I pit both of us on high-speed vehicles.

I didn't think this through. Didn't formulate a plan. I just plunged in tonight with all my five-alarm emotions flaring.

I steer my bike through the cornstalks and bounce back onto the road, pointing myself toward the dotted lights of town.

Wish I could see Holliday...

My wish is immediately granted. About a hundred yards ahead of me, he bursts out from the cornfield and skids into the middle of the road. Then he spins in a circle and revs his engine.

That crazy son-of-a-gun is coming straight at me.

So he wants to play chicken, eh?

I crank my bike's gas and we zoom toward each other down the center of the road, our heavy metal gobbling up the white lines like tasty, tasty candy.

Can you read my mind, Holliday?

Can you hear me...?

My fingers uncurl from my chest, sliding up to my necklace.

My eyes darken.

I'm not going to swerve.

All those nights, lying in bed, begging for Holliday to show up… This town is *my* home. I've got a good thing going here. I hate Rascal Holliday for ripping out my heart… But at this moment, I hate that freak a hundred times more for waltzing in here tonight and reminding me how fragile my good thing is. With one smug glare, reminding me how easily he could mess it all up, send my happy silly little forged existence tumbling like a house of cards.

Suddenly, without wavering, Holliday yanks hard to the right. And I watch, in stunned euphoria, as he lays his bike down on its side, sliding toward me onto the pavement.

You've got to be kidding…

Did Golden Boy just wipe out right in front of me?

But it's a display of complete control as he leaps nimbly onto the screeching bike, crouching on it like a surfboard, riding the screaming, sparking asphalt. I can smell the scorch, our eyes meeting through our helmet visors just before we pass by each other.

I twist and look back over my shoulder.

Holliday is gone.

His bike is skidding down the road, spinning carelessly off into a ditch. Frantic, I whip my head from side to side, searching the inky-blue expanse blurring past me. But there's no sign of the rider whose bike is lying in that ditch.

I've lost him.

I punch my dashboard.

I don't know why that should surprise me. Holliday vanishes. That's what he does. Just like he went poof on that horrible, grisly day by the water tower. Gone in a flash of blue light, like smoke through my fingers.

The dark covered bridge is just up ahead and I roar toward it, alone now.

My eyes jump down to my glowing dashboard clock.

12:57.

There's only one thing to do now, and that is to swallow the bitter pill and accept it: This day is done. A mere fleeting grain of sand, preparing to slide down the toilet tubes. I've lost.

12:58.

It comes drifting into the back of my mind, for some bizarre reason, and I recall the day everyone was turning into cows. Simpler times...

But I just remembered something else about that day. When Sheriff Gammell was busting Randy's chops for slumming around Tannon's field in the middle of the night... Didn't Randy say he and his friends saw a weird blue light in the sky? They thought it was a UFO...

A blue flash. Just like when Holliday vanished that day after stealing my heart.

Some kind of interdimensional portal?

Is *that* how the slippery freak travels around so fast?

The covered bridge is looming up fast, its mouth gaping black and wide, preparing to swallow me whole.

If my theory is correct, and Rascal Holliday emerges from that blue flash over Tannon's farm, I need to be there when it happens. I need to be in that field. But Randy saw the flash sometime in the middle of the night. And the car alarm always wakes me at 6:11 each morning...

I need more time.

I need to wake myself up *before* that car alarm goes off.

Removing my focus from the bridge ahead of me, I thread every fiber of concentration into this single, urgent task for myself.

Wake up, Kyle...

I'm not bothering with steering and I've missed the covered bridge; the Ducati roars out from under me as I sail over the edge of the chasm into the creek below.

Wake up.

Wake up...

DAY 43: THE THIRTEENTH HOUR

I jerk myself to consciousness with a loud and unholy snort.

My eyes adjust quickly to the dark, the familiar angles of my four-poster bed taking shape overhead.

I'm in my Red Rooster room. The tin clock on the nightstand reads 1:07 am.

Hot diggity…

I did it.

Cold excitement prickles my skin as I vault from the bed. I grab my pants off the dresser and hurriedly hop into them.

Heck, I couldn't even be sure anything *existed* between the hours of 1:00 and 6:07 am. It was always like time itself kicked into action the moment that I woke. Part of me feels like I'm exploiting some sacred forbidden loophole. The other part of me wonders why I didn't try this sooner.

Holding my 8-ball keychain in my teeth, I squat and stomp into my boots, then pull on my jacket. Zipping up, my fingers bump against something cold and stringy.

My silver necklace.

I tug at the thin chain, frowning. This necklace shouldn't be here. I haven't bought it yet today. Yet here it is.

Just like that smashed record outside the gas station…

Well, add it to the growing list of ever-increasing weirdness.

I'll have answers soon.

I slip quietly from my room out into the hall. Gentle snoring emanates from the room where one of the Corgipoo ladies is sleeping. I don't want to wake anyone. They'll just slow me down, hammering me with typical middle-of-the-night questions. I hopscotch masterfully across the mine field of creaky wooden floorboards, bypassing the squeaktastic stairs and sliding down the banister into the foyer.

Downstairs, the breakfast alcove is dark. One dagger of moonlight streams across the corner of the floor-sized rug. Reaching under the table, I chug a bottle of orange juice and shove a packet of saltines into my mouth, even though I'm too nervous to feel hungry or thirsty. But I'll need energy. Don't want to run out of steam at the most crucial moment of this climax.

No, Rascal Holliday deserves my full, undivided attention.

And I will expect his.

I tiptoe into the kitchen. A smiling, cat-shaped clock above the microwave reads 1:15 am. I don't know the precise moment when that blue flash appears over Tannon's field. So I'll just have to make sure I'm there before it happens.

Tonight, I get answers.

If Rascal Holliday emerges from that blue flash, *he's giving me answers*. He's going to tell me why I'm stuck in his time loop game. He's going to tell me why he filched my heart.

By golly, he's going to answer every single one of my burning questions, even if I have to extract the answers from his cold black guts.

I grab a small, serrated steak knife from the wooden cutlery holder, and a pair of scissors from the drawer under the counter.

A standard attack is a three-step process. Fake, move, attack. Everyone knows that. Holliday knows that. So here's my plan.

A *four*-pronged attack.

I'll set up a nice little trap – something he'll expect. Something so obviously fake that he'll saunter right in, all smug and confident in his calculations, all the while expecting that my second and third moves will be actual attempts. Fake, move, attack. Then he'll assume I'm done. Big fat fail on my girlie face. That's when I'll hit him. Something he won't expect. A prestige. A wildcard.

I must become a wildcard.

Except this is Rascal-freaking-psychic-Holliday we're talking about. He's a mind-reader. Whatever I plan, he'll see it coming. He anticipated a loogie before I could even spit on him. Unfair…yes.

And yet, he *ran* from me last night. He bolted on his bike the moment I saw him in the crowd. It's delicious just how much this flatters me. I've always pictured Rascal Holliday as this diamond-plated trickster, invincible and omnipotent, laughing at me from his mighty lounge chair of perfectness.

But he ran from me.

The mere fact that Holliday reacted on the need to protect himself means that he has a soft spot. And if he's got a soft spot, I can shove a blade into it.

I stuff the steak knife inside the sleeve of my jacket, and the scissors down into the cuff of my boot.

As I'm headed back across the alcove for the front door, my eyes fall on the buffet table against the wall. I pause. A stack of clean plates sits on a corner of the lace tablecloth. Ceramic mugs are arranged neatly behind baskets, covered with checkered gray cloths that will be bright yellow in the morning light. Tiny Mrs. Moffatt will putter downstairs, fussing and filling that table with fruit. Sausages. Plump, ruffly waffles. And that whipped butter that smells like honey.

A pang of guilt hits me.

Sneaking around like this while everyone sleeps, warm and oblivious in their beds...feels somehow like I'm cheating on them.

But I'm not leaving them, I remind myself firmly.

I swallow down the feeling, and slip out the door.

*

It's colder than a gravedigger's butt outside. The moon is in exactly the same spot where I left it. Forty-five degrees east of north; a bright silver coin suspended on inky blue strips of night. The Quik-Pump gas station's single floodlight gleams on the road, illuminating the white lines on the rough pavement. Somehow the stillness makes it feels even more silent. Such stark contrast to when Holliday and I roared down this road. Hard to believe that was only twenty minutes ago.

I begin trotting down the side of the road at a brisk pace. My boots clomp dully on the dirt. The fence posts that shot past me at a blur last night now creep by at a considerably slower pace. Now that I'm out here, it's actually far from silent. From the blackness on either side of the road comes the steady singing of thousands of field crickets, punctuated by the occasional *'jug-o-rum'* croak of a bullfrog.

I press along at a controlled jog, glancing behind me every few steps, keeping one eye on the tree line ahead.

My palms are sweating. Not a good sign. If I rush in all hot and half-cocked, Holliday will rule me. I need to stay calm. Cool as a cucumber. Just like I rehearsed.

But I have another problem. Today's wildcard. It's lurking out there somewhere... Or it *will* be, soon. Probably won't surface for another few hours. No clue where. Not without my Icemaker.

I glance over my shoulder, back toward town.

I feel naked without that old shotgun. More naked than if I was out here in my birthday suit. But the bank won't open for another seven hours. And since I don't have time to hike back to town and stage an elaborate bank vault heist before dawn, I'm out of luck. I'll have to do this without my Icemaker.

I wipe my palms on my pants and jog on.

A pale, gauzy slip of cloud slides over the moon as I arrive at Tannon's three-level farmhouse. I hear Randy and his buddies even before I see them. The gang is camped out on the fence, by the gate to Tannon's field. Dumbest sneaks ever...I can clearly hear their hushed snickering and the sporadic crack-fizz of their beer can pop tops.

I roll my eyes.

Fishing out my mini-flashlight, I angle it at one of the bizarre weathervane contraptions on Tannon's lawn. My beam hits the dangling scraps of aluminum. It glints, throwing a nice reflected flash of light into the eyes of Randy and company. There's an abbreviated scuffle and the sound of hands smacking at each other, then the group goes scampering off toward the road, howling at the moon.

As soon as I'm sure they're gone, I make a beeline for the gate. My toe bumps something in the grass, causing a clatter of empty cans. I pick one up.

Smells like Fruity Pebbles soaked in thigh sweat.

"Keep drinking this junk and you're gonna grow a second butthole," I mutter after them in disgust. Their lord-of-the-flies hooting echoes down the road, thinning into the night until it's once again complete silence.

I duck under the fence and slip into Tannon's utility shed. The old soldier's hatchet is hanging in its designated spot on the far wall. Tannon very nearly chopped off my head with this axe, back on Cow Day, when I barged in here with Merrick, Gammell, and Deputy Scarecrow. I wish Merrick was with me right now. But he can't be. Not for this.

I remove the hatchet from the wall, gripping its long wooden handle, testing its weight in my hands. It's balanced differently than my battle axe, but whatever. I won't actually be doing any fighting with it. Holliday just has to *think* I will.

I take a deep breath.

This is it.

Final level. Big boss battle. The gentle whirring of the crickets seems somehow incongruous to the gravity of this moment.

I slip behind the shed and squat down, my back against the wooden wall. I lay the hatchet across my lap. There's a strip of dark woods along the far edge of Tannon's field. Picturesque in the daytime, by moonlight this field is a vast, cold sea of blue and silver mist.

I bounce on my calves. I keep wanting to reach into my jacket sleeve and pull out the steak knife, but I resist the urge. No, I have to keep those blades hidden. Can't even *think* about them. Holliday will know. And Holliday can't be allowed to know. No preconceived notions. I take another deep breath, trying to recalibrate. Focus on nothing. Set my brain to 'zero.'

I check my watch. It's 2:24 am. To pass the time, I spin the axe, alternating hands with a swooping motion. I pace along the fence. I watch the sky. Hours crawl by, slower than molasses running uphill in winter. Five o'clock rolls around, and still no sign of a stupid blue flash. I'm starting to think I missed it.

Or that it never happened.

Is it really so outrageous to think that a teenage boy would cook up a UFO story to cover the fact that he and his buds were out here underage drinking?

I let out a long, hot sigh, consulting my watch again.

This night is poised to go out with a yawn rather than a bang.

I slump my head back against the shed.

It happens the instant before I blink, so I only glimpse it for a millisecond – a blue strobe in the woods, momentarily illuminating the black tree line, like a pulse of lightning out across the distant sea.

I'm on my feet in a jiffy, gripping the hatchet by the handle and flying across the grass.

I enter the woods, and find myself standing in front of a burnt-down house. Or what's left of it. The house probably went up in flames decades ago, by the look of the weedy thorns snaking thick over the charred remains. Charcoal crunches under my feet. Only the chimney is still standing, a blackened stack of bricks, its decaying flue grinning like a gap-toothed corpse. Moonlight gleams on a large pit of broken ceramic tiles. Looks like this was once an in-ground pool.

I creep slowly to the edge, peering down into the sludgy concrete basin.

"What's up, Doc?"

I spin around.

Holliday is perched at the very top of the chimney. His grin glows at me through the dark like a Cheshire cat. His white teeth gleam. His belt glitters. Only his eyes remain black and unlit.

"Long time no see," he purrs.

My throat goes dry and my stomach does a somersault. My fingers tighten around the axe handle.

"Holliday, we need to talk. Come down from there, will you?"

He studies me, considering, his face amused. "Nah," he answers finally. "Don't think that would be beneficial."

"Oh?"

"Well, for one, yer lookin' to hack me into coleslaw. And that wouldn't be good for either one'a us. Would it, Doc?"

I slide the axe against the back of my leg, as if I were attempting to hide it.

"Just a precaution. Can you blame me?"

"No."

"Look, I just want to talk. I'll be good."

Until I'm not.

He steps off the chimney and drops nimbly to the ground, studded belt jingling. We stand four feet apart, surveying each other in silence. He's looking at me differently. Cautiously.

Just the fact that I'm here tonight has apparently moved me up a notch in his greasy book of importance.

I'm a new creature now.

"So," he drawls, honey dripping from his voice. "Have a good time last night?"

"Aw, come on, Holliday." I snort, pleased at how chill my voice sounds. "I would've figured you'd be flattered to have a girl chase you."

He grins. Then I realize he's not talking about our wild midnight motorcycle chase. He meant my anti-gravity tango with Merrick.

The back of my neck suddenly flares hot.

"LONG TIME NO SEE," HE PURRS."

"Back off," I growl, my voice low and guttural. "Whatever happens tonight is between *you* and *me*. You leave these people out of it, you understand me?"

I let the hatchet hang at my side, in plain sight. Holliday takes three steps toward me, catlike, shifting ever so slightly from one foot to the other. His face is inches from mine. He smells like leather and cherries. Weird. He doesn't smell like smoke. I thought he was a smoker. I watched him light up a nasty cigarette at Lau Chow's that first day...

"*You* and *I*? Fight?" Holliday grins, shaking his head. "Don't flatter yerself, Doc."

Then he turns and saunters off.

Just like that.

My jaw clenches involuntarily. Not only is he treating me like some dinky entry-level noob, but I'm pretty sure he also just corrected my grammar.

"Hey!" I bark.

He keeps walking into the woods.

For half a stunned second, I just stand there burning.

Then I lunge forward, swinging the hatchet at his back. The squirrelly punk ducks. Instantly he drops to all fours, without even bothering to turn around. Catching my balance quickly, I wheel the axe around in a figure-eight and hurl two swift chops at his back, both of which he leans his shoulders away from – *one, two* – swift, nonchalant dodges, almost lazy.

Did I mention he still hasn't turned around?

He snickers. "Yer swingin' that axe around like a piñata bat. C'mon, Doc. Yer better than this."

Better than *this?* Stars almighty, hasn't he been watching me? Have I not brought my A-game for the past forty-three days?

Despite all my better judgment and the red flags they're screaming at me, I mentally punch them away and channel all my rage into one hard swing with the hatchet.

Too hard.

I can't recover fast enough from the reeling weight of the weapon, and the next thing I know, Holliday has reached back and caught the axe handle in one gloved hand, jerking it fluidly from my grasp and kicking my legs out from under me. My back collides with cold ground. I immediately tuck my knees to my chest, reaching over my head and springing up onto my feet. I shove my hand up into my sleeve, grasping for the steak knife – but my fingers hit nothing but my skin. The knife isn't there.

Panicked, I plunge my hand into my boot.

The scissors are gone too.

"Lookin' fer somethin'?"

My skin jumps at the proximity of Holliday's silky voice. He's standing right behind me, his breath on my ear, dangling both the steak knife and scissors in front of my nose. Slippery demon. He must have swiped them while pretending to dodge my axe.

"*Tsk-tsk*, Doc." Holliday tosses my would-be weapons into the woods. "Surprise me, why don'cha?"

We spin around, facing each other.

Me, unarmed, breathing all hard like an idiot.

Him, with that grin.

That dark, bored smirk.

Holliday stops smiling and straightens. Then he starts circling around me like a shark. The hatchet gleams in his hand. My eyes drop. There's a jagged slab of broken pool tile, lying in the ashes at my feet. It might work as a weapon…

Who am I kidding? Holliday would skin me alive before I could even raise my pinkie.

I stand very still, hands clenched at my sides. The raw humiliation of my last four minutes hangs over me like a dripping, iron shawl. *Congrats*, it jeers. *You've just thrown Carnival Creeke down the drain. What would you like to do next?*

Merrick…Jemma…Sam, Hank…Graham and Julie Sutherbee, and their new baby… These people are helpless. They don't have a clue what's coming. Once Holliday kills me, once I'm dead and gone, I'll be unable to protect them anymore. All of them, laid out on the chopping block for whatever wildcard will eagerly gobble them up today – or tomorrow, or the next, if they manage to survive. With one swooping burst of folly, I just removed myself from the equation, all for the chance to lob rocks at the source of my own selfish predicament. A whopping fifteen-second tantrum.

And now it's over.

Feel better, Kyle?

I close my burning eyes. My skin jerks and braces in preparation for that hatchet in Holliday's hands to split me open. But he hasn't split me yet.

What's the holdup?

I squinch one eye open.

The son-of-a-monkey is back up on the chimney again. Axe across his lap, he's gnawing at his thumbnail, staring intently out into the woods. Ignoring me, as though I'm worth less than dirt. I feel my blood boil – if my blood even *can* boil, that old recycled ice water in my veins...

"Well?" I yowl. "What'cha waiting for, huh?! You slimy Irish mutant! You ripped out my heart – want my brain, too? My liver?! Why not?! C'mon, come and get me!! Piece by piece!"

Holliday pauses his skittish glance long enough to roll his eyes at me.

"Calm down. Neither one a'us are gonna lose any organs tonight. Ye came here 'cause ye wanna tell me somethin'."

I snap my mouth shut.

He's right.

Of *course* he's right, the dirty mind-reader.

My breathing slows. My fingers graze the necklace tucked under my collar. There *is* something I want to tell him. If Holliday cares so much about me fixing time in Carnival Creeke, then this juicy bit of info is sure to pique his skeezy interest. And if I can just exploit this one card, then I might gain a razor's edge of an advantage over him.

I take a deep breath. "Something weird happened."

"Ye don't say." He tosses a snide snicker in my direction, then turns away and resumes staring at the woods.

I glare daggers at him.

"I mean weirder than *usual*. Even for Carnival Creeke."

"...Keep talkin'."

I want him to look at me. I want him to see me as such a heavy factor in the future that he has no choice but to hang on my every word. I want this to be *his* problem, too. I want to make him feel it. I want to be the splinter under his fingernail.

"An old vinyl record I smashed days ago," I say slowly. "It reappeared. Showed up on the ground again. And people knowing things they shouldn't. Details from past days..." I pause for dramatic effect. "It's like they're *remembering*. Remembering things from yesterdays that never happened."

Holliday freezes. He glances at me.

"They started bleedin' over?"

"Yeah, you could say that." I shrug. "That's a good thing, right?"

"No. That's bad. Very, very bad. It means yer runnin' out of time, Doc."

He shuts his eyes and starts rocking back and forth on the chimney, muttering under his breath – dates and numbers. I want to ask him to speak up, but I know it wouldn't make a difference. I wouldn't understand.

Finally, Holliday opens his black eyes. Unnervingly calm.

"It means ***he's*** gettin' close," he hisses.

My stomach twists uneasily. "Who?"

"The name 'Lynch Luster' ring any bells to ye?"

I shrug. "No," I answer truthfully.

"How about the Gutsnake Gunslingers?"

I shake my head. Holliday smirks.

"Yeah, didn't think so."

"Care to enlighten me?"

"Not yet." He hops down from the chimney, axe still in his hand. My fists shoot up defensively – but he's not paying any attention to me. He's looking off into the woods again, his twitchy black eyes wholly unsettled.

"Ye gotta pick up the pace now, Doc. And by that, I mean *yesterday*. You're almost outta time."

I narrow my eyes. I won't allow him to toy with me. I solidly refuse to be puppetted into another of Holliday's games just because he spouts creepy warnings with some phony sense of urgency.

Except he doesn't seem to be faking.

"Fine," I cross my arms. "So this big bad *Lynch Luster* guy is coming to Carnival Creeke. Care to tell me what I'm supposed to do about it?"

Holliday snaps on me. "I already told ye!"

"Right. Fix the wildcard. Yeah. Check. I've been doing that *every day*, remember?"

"Forget the wildcard! The wildcard is just a symptom. Bacteria gatherin' around the wound. Ye gotta find the wound itself. Find a way to stop this day from skippin'."

"How?"

He shakes his head violently, as though trying to dislodge a swarm of bees.

"I shouldn't say this out loud. There's a device. Luster's hidden it somewhere...somewhere in town. It's been causin' a hiccup in time. But it's startin' to rot and it ain't gonna last forever. Ye been keepin' it under control by icin' the wildcard each day. But that ain't enough anymore. Ye seen the signs. Days bleedin' over. People with obsolete cookie crumbs leftover in their memory banks. It's gonna get worse. Ye gotta find Luster's *device*. Then ye gotta destroy it."

My eyes widen. My hands go numb.

Son-of-a-gun, I was right! Or at least *one* of my theories was right. A time-looping device. There's a *time-looping device.*

Hidden here, all this time...

"Well, gee," I sputter angrily. "Don't you think this might have been helpful to know forty-three days ago? Why didn't you just tell me sooner?!"

"Ye *know* why I can't!" he hisses back. "Ye just forgot."

"Okay Holliday," I chew my tongue. "I trash this guy's device, and you give my heart back. Sure. Piece of cake. So where am I supposed to find it?"

He remains silent.

"Hello? A little help?" I shout.

"I don't have that information," Holliday snarls. "I don't *know* where he's hidden the device. But *you* do." He hesitates. "Or...ye *did*. Ye had a hunch. That's all I can say. Luster's got ears all over this town. And on me. Each time we have these little chitty-chats, we're stickin' our heads on the chopping block. I can't do it. Ye need to find the device yerself, Doc."

My head is swimming. Those mystery notes… The image of Doctor Freakface and his monstrous, needlepoint grin flashes through my brain. The glee on his forked-tongued face when he saw whatever showed up on my x-ray…

Someone in town isn't who you think they are.

I stare at Holliday. "You," I utter. "You've been helping me?"

"Ring-a-ding," he retorts sarcastically. He gnaws at his thumb nail, flicking his eyes up and down. "Ye been usin' yer notebook?"

My silly pink kitten notebook?

"Sure, I've been writing in it."

"Good. Then keep doin' what yer doin'. If the days are startin' to bleed over, it ain't gonna stop there. This is just the tip a'the iceberg."

He glances over his shoulder, jigging one foot with sudden irritation. "I gotta go now. Ye wanna save their sweet little hides? *Find* the device, and find it *soon*."

"And what happens if I don't?"

"Best case scenario?" He shrugs darkly. "Everyone in town's head will explode."

*

I stumble my way back to town, my feet moving fast, my brain spinning faster. The stars dissolve and the sky fades from black to deep blue, but I barely notice. Only one thing burns my mind. Holliday's voice pounds in my head:

"I don't know where he's hidden the device. But ***you*** *do."*

Was he joking?

I close my eyes and revisit my tried-and-true adage. Weirdness always causes a ripple. If this guy's 'device' is the source of all weirdness, then it *has* been causing a ripple –

The wildcards.

The wildcard is just a symptom, Holliday said. *Like bacteria around a wound.*

Somewhere in Carnival Creeke, there's a wound. Festering. Infected. And the device is the bullet in the wound. All I need to do is remove the bullet that's jamming time in this town, and *voila.* I'll stop this Lynch Luster guy – whoever he is. And I may not trust Rascal Holliday, but I can't shake his chilling warning.

Best case scenario? Everyone in town's heads explode.

Just destroy this time-looping device. Then I'll get answers. A whole heap of answers. Holliday will give my heart back. And most importantly, everyone in town will be safe. For good.

Merrick...I'm so close.

Just find the device.

As I tromp along, I mentally draw a map of town. I begin replaying each day. Locations where the wildcards tended to appear most frequently. By the time I'm crossing the covered bridge, I've narrowed it down to one place –

Main Street.

The device must be somewhere on Main Street.

Sunrise bleeds feathery pink on the horizon, breathtaking colors reflecting in the glass of the storefront windows. The town is draped in its usual chilly morning haze. Over at the library, the workers are already up on the scaffolding, hard at their perpetual task of sweeping up the damage caused by the gargoyle's rampage yesterday. Their hammers clang and echo down the quiet foggy street. I hurry past them and try really hard not to picture their heads exploding. They have no idea what's at stake. Ignorance is bliss.

What does the device look like? How am I supposed to know when I've found it? I'm running out of time…

The library clock tower says 7:20.

I stop walking.

Staring at the library, it hits me like a brick in the face. My doppelganger, Deadhead Kyle. Last time I saw her, she was hustling up the library's clock tower steps. At that time, I thought she was just running away from me. Saving her own bacon. A logical conclusion. Right? But I should have known myself better than that. There's no way I would run into a one-way tower, trapping myself like that.

And neither would she.

No…she had another purpose. She had a *mission*. Only unlike me, *she* could *remember* her mission. That Deadhead shared all my memories. Including the reason I came to Carnival Creeke.

To destroy the time-skipping device.

Deadhead Kyle ran into the library. Whatever I'm searching for – the same device that Cl. Kyle came searching for – it must be somewhere in the library.

A muffled thudding sound in the background pulls me from my thoughts. Frowning, I look up at the construction workers. It's not them. This sound is separate from their banging hammers. I turn around. The rhythmic thumping is coming from down the street, around the corner from the bank.

Thud. Thud. Something big...

Oh, fabulous. My wildcard picked today to show up early.

Thud...thud...

It sounds heavy, solid...made of wood? I can't see it yet, but sounds like it's hopping.

What the heck *is* this thing?

One thing is certain – it's definitely getting closer.

I fly down the sidewalk. "Get out of here!" I scream at the construction workers, waving my arms. "Run away, *NOW!!*"

Wide-eyed, they drop their hammers and scramble down from their scaffolding, scurrying up the street. I sprint across the library's sprawling lawn just as something whizzes past my face, grazing my cheek, slicing me hot and sharp. I duck behind the granite monument, crunching pinecones under my knees. There I crouch, unarmed.

I'm being hunted.

I venture a peek around the cold stone. Sycamore trees block my view. There's another whistling sound; I jerk back as the tiny projectile zips by, chipping off a corner of the stone monument in a spray of crumbled grit. Something drops by my boot. I pluck it off the grass, examining it in my palm. The small bluish-black stone is sharpened into a tiny point. Looks like an arrowhead. The kind that Native Americans used to hunt...

I toss it back into the grass, hissing edgily through my teeth.

I don't have time for this small potato wildcard. Not when the solution to this whole twisted game lies just beyond my grasp. The answer is here. It *must* be here.

It's so close, I can taste its slick, salty victory...

I need to get into the library.

I grab a chunk of the broken stone monument and hurl it off in the direction of the graveyard. I hear it thud onto the ground, and when two arrows zing past in response, *thwack-thwack*, I bolt across the remaining lawn toward the library. Taking the stone steps in one bound, I heave the heavy wooden cherry doors shut, and slam the latch behind me.

The library is cloaked in shadows. Dark catacombs of corridors and shelves, the sole light source lent from a narrow cathedral window on the far back wall, casting a thin strip of early morning sunlight diagonally across the floor, swirling with dust. The rainbow kite rotates lazily from the rafters above.

Okay, here I am.

Now what?

I've visited this library nearly every day. Camped here, doing my Gray Time research. I never saw hide nor hair of anything resembling a time-skipping device. But again, I have no clue what the dang device looks like.

Where do I even start searching?

Deadhead Kyle knew where. It would have been peachy sweet of her to leave me a hint or something. Would that have killed her? Oh, that's right – *I* killed her.

I blow out a shaky breath. A sudden thud rattles heavily on the locked door behind me. I spin around.

The wildcard is bashing itself against the other side.

Let it huff and puff all it wants. I figure I've got at least until that door gives out to find what I'm looking for.

At least, I *hope* I've got that long.

I should find a weapon, just in case. I duck behind the empty book checkout desk. A life-sized bronze bust of Benjamin Franklin sits beside the dark computer monitor, his metallic lips pursed together in a bored expression. There's a flashlight under the counter; I grab it and click it on. The dusty beam of light slides past the dark alcove of slumbering computers, past the shelf with featured dinosaur books set on plastic display stands. A stocky, misshapen paper mâché triceratops smiles dopily from the shelf, scattered with plaster dinosaur "bones." I grab the largest bone. Feels fragile in my hand, but better than nothing.

Stupid Holliday. Wish I could feed him to a dinosaur…

Wait.

What was that he said to me?

"Ye been usin' yer notebook?"

Jerkface wasn't checking up on me. He was giving me a clue.

Hickory, dickory, Doc.

It wasn't a riddle. It was a clue, addressed to me. How does the rest of that old song go?

Whump. Whump.

The thing outside the door bangs harder.

Hickory, dickory, dock. The mouse ran up the clock…

Clock? Could he mean clock tower?

Whump! Whump!

I dash down the children's book aisles and crouch, thumbing through the rows of colorful, plastic-protected fairy tales. I slide a tattered orange book with gold lettering off the shelf, titled *Beloved Nursery Rhymes.*

Whump! The heavy door rattles on its hinges, this time sending a shower of drywall dust to the floor. The book tucked under my arm, I race up the narrow winding stairwell to the small bell tower chamber. The coffee mug sits cold and forgotten on the railing. Just like old times.

The steady, muffled thumping persists against the door downstairs. Quickly, I flip through the old book's water-stained pages until I find the nursery rhyme that I'm looking for.

'Hickory, dickory, dock.

The mouse ran up the clock

The clock struck one, the mouse ran down,

Hickory, dickory, dock.'

I frown. So...I'm supposed to run back *down* now?

Twisting, I peer over the wooden railing. Down past the long dark stairwell, at the very bottom, I can make out some kind of circular hatch on the floor. And there's something beneath the hatch. I click on the flashlight, shining it down. Something glints...

Did that thing beneath the floor just...move?

I freeze, squinting until my eyes ache. Wish I had Merrick's glasses...

Clutching the book, I propel myself down the stairs. My blood surges, tingling in my veins, doing that thing it does to compensate when my heart would be pumping fast.

I'm on the verge. I can feel it.

It's within my fingertips...

The circular hatch in the floor is slightly larger than a sewer manhole cover. Was this here the whole time? I never noticed it before. But then again, every time I've been in this stairwell, I always seem to be running for my life.

I clunk the nursery rhymes book on the floor beside me and drop to my hands and knees. Leaning closer, I examine the hatch. A sudden pain clamps over my head. Feels like a vice grip squeezing my skull...

I jerk back sharply.

The pain stops.

Cautiously, I lean forward again. The vice grip instantly tightens around my head. A dull force, pressing against my temples. My eardrums ache, my lungs feel compressed, similar to the sensation of diving to the bottom of a deep pool. It's as if the air in this spot is actually growing heavier, denser, the closer in proximity I get to whatever is under this floor...

Pinching my nose, I blow, popping the pressure in my ears. It brings momentary relief. Then, taking a deep breath, I lean forward and shine the flashlight down into the hatch. My whole body trembles, vibrating with anticipation.

The thing at the bottom of the concrete well is unlike anything I've ever seen, even in my bestiary of weirdness.

About ten feet below, in the middle of the room, is a fleshy, purplish blob. Sinewy tentacles stretch outward in all directions, clinging to the walls with suction cups, octopus-like. The tentacle tips have burrowed into the concrete, rooting the thing in place like a cancerous tumor. Goodness knows how long it's been here.

And in the very center, nestled in the fleshy maw, is a small mechanism. About the size of my fist, a ring of three ribbed, membranous coils squeeze and contract, like a life-support pump. A bulb throbs in its center, squirting tiny, rhythmic sparks outward. It makes a sound like a soda can opening, only sharper, cadenced.

Fzz, fzz. Fzz, fzz

Like a pulse.

Like a *heart.*

I've heard this sound before…

A shudder runs through me. Although outwardly nothing has changed, this place suddenly feels different. The cavernous pillars and long book aisles feel ominous. Gone is the familiar scent of cedar and peanutty-musk of old paperbacks.

Now it just reeks of death.

I push aside the feeling, and wipe my hand across my face. Alright, focus. How am I supposed to destroy this thing? It looks alien…magical…way out of my league, any way you slice it. I can't make a mistake now. I can't fudge this. This is no mere wildcard.

But there's something else on the floor. Something glinting in the murkiness. Must be what I saw from the top of the stairs. Moving the flashlight, I angle the beam around the chamber.

Scattered on the dingy concrete below is a large and odd collection of various items. An empty milk carton. A pocket-sized mirror, cracked down the middle. A tiny toy bear, with half of its face scuffed off. A tarnished 'best friends' locket.

Why is all this junk down here? It's impossible that someone could have dropped it by accident. Not all of this. But why would someone *intentionally* dump these down here?

I lean back slowly, realization sinking in.

A milk carton. Day One...when people were becoming cows. Then the broken mirror. That was Day Two, coughing up our evil twins. And the mutant wereteddy critters, no doubt represented by the mangled toy bear. I even spot a half-eaten gingerbread man.

Oh, freaking heckfire. This room, *this device* – it's been pumping out wildcards – and it's been drawing inspiration from this seemingly random junk. Like crazy dreams after eating a bad burrito before bed.

Bacteria gathering around the wound...

My mind spins. Ignoring the crushing ache in my eardrums, I run my hands over the galvanized metal hatch and wrench it open. Outside, the thudding is growing more frantic.

Whomp-whomp-crack!

That door won't hold forever. But as long as whatever-it-is stays outside, it's of no importance. All that matters is the thing at the bottom of this pit.

As I turn back to the hatch, I feel my knee bump the nursery rhymes book. Before I can grab it, it falls through the open hatch, landing with a thump on the concrete floor below. Right beside the device. The *wildcard-cooking* device. I just dropped a new ingredient right into the pot.

I gulp, staring at the book down in the pit.

"Oh, c-r-u-d," I hiss under my breath.

Maybe it won't cause a problem. Maybe the device won't realize it's there. Maybe –

But no. There it is. A slow, soft shuffling sound. The rhythmic *click, click* of footsteps, deep in the library, growing nearer... Around the corner of the cooking and baking aisle, stepping into the dim, dust-spackled light, comes a tall, beastly, bulging man. His silk pants swishing with each slow step, his fine latchet shoes clicking against the stone floor, the brass buttons glinting on his purple-and-green-striped tweed waistcoat. A rapacious grin spreads across his blue pockmarked skin, a fine gold monocle wedged into one eye socket. A newborn wildcard, cooked up from the nursery rhymes book.

Who is this bozo supposed to be?

He's holding a cane of some sort, swinging it lazily, purposefully...menacingly.

Oh, to have Icemaker in my hand right now.

Gripping my plaster dino bone like a baseball bat, I walk toward Mister Chuckles, my stride quickening into a jog. I raise the bone over my head.

"Hey buddy! I'm on a deadline here, so let's skip the battle royale and you just turn into a nice gray dot, okay?"

I swing the bone and smack him across his pockmarked face. The plaster bone shatters in my hands. His head spins a full 180 degrees, jiggling like a Jell-O mold, spewing a fountain of blueberry muffins that bounce in all directions across the floor.

I blink. "Um."

He's…the Muffin Man.

His bloated blue head twists back around, shooting me a piano-toothed grin.

I'm barely able to dive aside as his cane whistles past my cheek. I somersault through his bowed legs and spring onto his shoulders, locking my leg around his neck. He jiggles out from under me and dissolves into a cascade of muffins, vanishing. I hit the floor hard. Groaning, I roll over. Looks like I squashed a muffin under me. Mmm…this one has some kind of caramel drizzle. Briefly I wonder whether it's 'molten' enough to pass Lisa's seal of approval – but there's no time to mull over this vital conundrum, because that's when all the muffins start rolling across the floor, rolling toward each other, gathering together to take the shape of Muffin Man's ugly blue head, then his shoulders, rebuilding him like some bizarre pastry T-1000 terminator. My plaster dinosaur bone is in pieces on the floor, a heap of shattered powder. Clearly not my best weapon…

But I bet I could use that tall floor lamp to harpoon this freak before his muffins can finish rebuilding him.

I sprint toward the lamp, hurriedly unplugging it from the wall and grasping it by the metal pole.

Clickety-clickety-clickety –

I jerk my head around. Muffin Man is tap-dancing toward me with shocking speed, still wearing that twisted circus ringmaster grin, swinging his silver cane in an upward slash. I'm able to glimpse the head of the cane – a square metal hammer, like a meat tenderizer – half a second before it cracks me upside the chin. White starbursts explode in my face. I'm loosely aware that my feet have been knocked over my head, and I'm flipped backwards...falling...

Why am I still falling? The floor should be right behind me.

Where is the floor?

I can't feel the floor.

All I feel is the strange, sudden surge of pressure that clamps over my skull...

I jolt awake, swinging both fists wildly. But I never hit the library floor. Instead of cold stone, I'm thrashing against a downy gingham comforter, surrounded by warmth and familiar darkness. And I'm biting a pillow.

I spit out the pillow and jerk upright, utterly bewildered.

I'm in my bed. Back at the Red Rooster.

"Wha-a-a-t the–" I utter.

Did Muffin Man somehow *teleport* me back here?

But the tin rooster clock on my bedside table confirms that it's 6:11. Outside my window, the car horn starts honking merrily away. Just like usual.

Just like every morning...

My hand jumps to my chin. My fingers meet near-smooth skin. I frown. Muffin Man just cracked me in the chin not two minutes ago. My skin should be split like a banana peel…

I snatch the clock off the table, scrutinizing my reflection.

A faint half-moon scar on my chin. I can barely see it. This is no injury that happened two minutes ago. No, this is the result of an all-night snooze, my super-fast healing doing its super-fast healing thing.

Muffin Man didn't teleport me anywhere.

The day reset.

THE FREAKING DAY RESET.

SNACK BREAK!

Go grab some popcorn (or funnel cake, or gingerbread)

Ready? Let's return...

15

DAY 44: A PERFECT DAY

I sit amidst the tousled bedsheets, frozen and breathless.

The tin clock emits a steady *tick, tick.*

Why the frak would the device just **reset** *in the middle of the morning like that...?*

I slither quickly out of bed and yank on my pants and boots, hurrying downstairs into the breakfast parlor. The ceiling creaks overhead. Mrs. Moffat is still upstairs, setting out fresh towels in the bathroom. She'll be down any minute to start setting out breakfast. But I can't linger. No time for fluffy waffles.

Sliding an unsteady hand under the table, I pull out a bottle of OJ and chug it down. I also force myself to eat a packet of saltines, even though the crispy crackers taste like orange chalk. Or maybe that's the antacid tablets I just popped. My stomach feels like I just fell off a tilt-a-whirl.

I slink into the kitchen. The serrated steak knife is missing from the wooden cutlery holder. I slide open the drawer. The scissors are gone, too.

I frown, stewing over what this could mean.

The cat clock grins down at me from the wall, conjuring the image of Holliday's Cheshire grin in the dark.

"*Ye seen the signs,*" he said. "*Days bleedin' over...*"

So the knife and scissors are gone because I already grabbed them last night. Which means I've already chased down Holliday in our mad motorcycle street dash. And we've already had our little chat at the burnt house.

So all I need to do is go to the library.

Shoot, I already know where the device is…

I shut the drawer. There's a deli knife lying on a towel beside the sink. The knife looks dirty, but hygiene isn't my priority now. Maybe I'll give Muffin Man a nice infection. At least I'll be ready this time. This time, I'm not going in empty-handed.

*

I stumble numbly down the road toward town, keeping pace at a slow jog, my boots clunking on the pavement in the eerie silence. The cornfield rustles softly. My mind is whirling like a blender full of marbles.

Why would the day reset like that?

Option one: The device somehow *sensed* that I was there to destroy it. Sensed it was in danger, and it booted me out. A little far-fetched, I'll admit…but this is Carnival Creeke.

Option two: The device is growing unstable. If Holliday was telling the truth, then that evil hiccupping mechanism has begun to rot. And the more it rots, the more unstable it gets. An infected wound in time, spiraling out of control, hurtling us all on a one-way countdown to the very worst and last headache of our lives. And something tells me we won't have until one o'clock.

Despite my mental insistence that I'm cool, this erratic hiccup has really gotten me rattled. Normally I would get mad and blame Holliday, but now... I'm not so sure. My impression of him as some young nefarious puppet master behind this whole game may not have been accurate. So maybe he's not the one pulling the strings. He says he can't help me. Can't – or won't?

"I can't do it. Ye need to find the device yerself, Doc."

Why? Why me?

I can't shake this feeling. There's something he's not telling me. Something important. Something big.

"Lynch Luster." I say it aloud, shaping each syllable. Waiting for any brain twitches, any indications that I pinged a memory. For a second, the name tastes strange...rotten...but it could just be my gnarly stomach. I'm a tad jittery right now.

There's only one thing I know for certain: The playing field has changed. Variables have shifted. I need to be ready for anything. I'll need to keep my eyes open.

As if I planned on closing them, right?

My eyes are peeled so wide I can almost see my own brain.

*

I reach town at my usual hour, but today, it's anything but comforting. The familiar sleepy morning fog feels more like a haze, painting the library lawn like something from a dream as I crunch across the damp grass, the dirty knife in my hand. I stand for a moment, staring up at the old colonial building. The bell tower looms overhead.

Déjà vu.

Zip-thwack.

I spin around. A feathered arrow sinks into the grass. Rats, I'd forgotten about that mystery wildcard. I can hear it – whatever it is – thudding in the distance, hopping toward me. No idea which direction it's coming from. My fingers clench around the knife handle. I'll admit I'm itching to see what this thing is...but that device could reset again at any moment.

I don't have time to dilly-dally.

"Later, tater," I mutter, sprinting across the lawn, shutting the heavy doors behind me, making sure to latch them.

I make a B-line toward the bottom of the bell tower stairs. No hunting around in the dark like a clueless moron this time. And this time, you can bet I won't be a clumsy doofus and knock that nursery rhymes book into the pit. Heck, I won't even need to *touch* that book. And no book means...no Muffin Man.

It sounds almost too easy.

As I near the base of the narrow staircase, I notice that the hatch in the floor is already open. And there's something sitting by the hatch. My eyes widen.

It's the nursery rhymes book.

Whomp, whomp!

The library door rattles as the wildcard hurls itself again. The book wobbles precariously. Like the dumbest horror movie ever, I can only watch in helpless slow-motion as the book slips off the edge. I sprint toward it like a comet, but it's too late. I hear it hit the concrete below with a dull thud.

"Okay, okay, this is fine," I hiss insistently, running my hands through my hair.

Maybe some things are unavoidable. Like a choose-your-own-adventure story. Certain events will always happen, one way or another, no matter what. Like this book falling. And me versus Muffin Man.

Spinning around, I whip the knife out in front of me. I attempt to steady my breathing, despite every nerve being wound tighter than a guitar string. My eyes are locked on the cooking and baking aisle, waiting for Muffin Man to emerge. Waiting for the click of his ghastly dapper shoes.

A moment passes, then another.

Where the heck is he? Did he miss his cue?

I cock my head, listening, frozen in complete silence.

No Muffin Man.

I release my breath in a gasp of joyous disbelief. Whatever happened, I'll take it. I'll take it with bells on.

Shoving the knife into my boot, I turn back to the device. Alright, all I need is something to smash this thing. I jog around the perimeter of the library, scanning the dark shelves and cabinets. I'll need something heavy. I reckon even that big gray '*History of Rome*' hardback won't do the trick. No, I want to be sure. I want to crush that evil octopus into atom paste. I need something heavier. I'm considering unplugging and lugging over one of the computer monitors, then my eyes fall on the Benjamin Franklin bust on the checkout counter.

"Congrats Frankie," I muse with a wry smile. "You're going to save us all."

I hoist the heavy bronze head and make my way back toward the hatch, trying to ignore the steady whomping that's still going on outside.

Whomp away, I hiss in elated defiance. *You won't stop me.*

Nothing can stop me now. I'm so giddy, I swear I hear humming in my head.

No...not in my head.

I freeze. Please tell me I imagined that.

Soft, like a whisper, but plain as day, someone in this library is humming. I pivot, a knot of dread rumbling in my stomach. Tucking Ben Franklin's head under one arm, I slide the knife from my boot again. At the far end of the aisles, a shadow falls across the sunlit window.

Then it steps into view.

A little girl – no, she's huge, at least six feet tall – is making her way toward me from the shadows. Sticking the knife handle between my teeth, I yank out my flashlight. My beam of light illuminates the face of a porcelain doll. Her round face is caked in white stage makeup, lips and cheeks dotted with blood-red, batting five-inch curved eyelashes like spider legs. I try to guess who she might be, but then I see the lace bib she's wearing, her name embroidered in flowery lettering.

Little Miss Muffet.

Ladies and gentlemen, instead of Muffin Man, we now have Not-So-Little Miss Muffet.

She sashays leisurely, swaying her cotton candy puffball sleeves, the apron over her pink marshmallow Sunday salad teacup skirt smeared with goodness knows what. Her head lolls from side to side, causing her candy apple red ringlets to swing like the arms of a grandfather clock. And she's humming, because that's just what creepy girls do. All she needs is a knife, and – oh, there it is. A silver utensil, gleaming in her hand. Here I was hoping she might not be a walking stereotype of horror.

Then I look closer. It's not a knife she's holding. It's a spoon – serrated like a sawblade. Definitely could carve out my liver with frightening efficiency.

Did I mention I *really* miss my Icemaker right now?

I spin on my heel, turning my back on the big demon doll as I sprint towards the hatch.

Just destroy the device, and she'll go poof. She'll stop.

All of it will stop.

I skid to a halt at the edge of the hatch, clutching Ben's head.

This is it. Every day, every decision; all my failures and all my wins, every belly laugh and every broken bone, every blood-soaked all-night horror, every hug – it's all led me to this moment. Leaning over, I peer down at the device. The vice-grip pressure clenches around my skull, stronger and more intense this time. My palms are sweating. I quickly position the bronze head directly over the device below.

"Don't you dare reset!" I shout at the device. "Don't reset, don't reset. Just...say...nighty-night!"

I hurl the bust down into the pit as hard as I can.

My breath catches.

My aim is true. The bronze bust smacks right into the device.

And does nothing.

With a sharp snap of static, the bust bounces off, rolling uselessly on the concrete floor amongst the other junk. And for the briefest of moments, I glimpse a colorless, aqualine ripple moving over the device. A shimmer.

A forcefield.

Just like the stagecoach.

My mouth falls open and my soul deflates. I stagger backwards, catching myself against the wall.

This can't be happening. If *that* didn't even dent it...

Then what am I supposed to do?

I don't have an answer for that. Currently I'm a little focused on Miss Muffet, who decided that now would be a grand time to maul me. Giggling girlishly, she pirouettes around me, her apron swirling, slashing her saw-toothed spoon at my face. I counter and block, her spoon clanking against my knife. Hurling myself to the floor and rolling behind her, I ram the deli knife into her frilly pink back. The blade snaps off the handle, clinking melodiously across the floor and sliding under a shelf.

Well, that's not helpful.

Guess it was a discount knife. I can hardly fault Mrs. Moffatt for wanting to save a few pennies, but at this moment, I'm only focused on dodging and finding a plan B now that I have no weapon.

Strange...why is my head suddenly aching?

My eyes pop open.

My head jerks upright, as though waking from a dream. Frosty wind rips through my hair and face. I'm riding the Ducati bike, racing through the streets of the historic district. Shops flash past. The deafening snarl of the engine drowns my head, the punchy smell of gasoline and cold stinging my eyes.

Wait. I don't recognize this bike's glowing red dashboard.

Disoriented, I look down.

This isn't Randy's yellow and black Ducati. My legs are wrapped around Holliday's slim black Suzuki. And I've got an axe in my hand. Not my heavy metal battle axe, but a wood-handled hatchet – the very same hatchet that Holliday yoinked from my hands in the woods last night. I'd recognize the feel anywhere.

So the day reset again. But why am I –

THUNK.

The bike jolts to a sudden halt, pitching me airborne over the handlebars.

I somehow manage to save the skin on my knees, twisting into a diving roll and landing on the sidewalk. The Suzuki lies behind me in the gutter, its wheels still spinning. Guess I hit the curb. Face reddening, I spring quickly to my feet, hoping Holliday wasn't watching my Three Stooges moment.

Aside from my embarrassing spill, this day seems to be playing out swimmingly. This could be it. This could be *my day*. Bolting the library door, I jog over and peer down into the hatch.

The book of nursery rhymes and the bust of Ben Franklin are already down there.

I frown.

Looks like I'm late to the party today. And they aren't the only ones that beat me here. I catch a glimpse of Miss Muffet at the far end of the room, humming dreamily to herself, twirling her way past the computers like some big pink Wonderland reject. I recognize the tune she's humming. 'Hickory, Dickory, Dock.' Just for me, no doubt. How adorable.

She knows I'm here, so I'd better ice this device before she makes her way over.

But first I need to knock out that forcefield.

Electricity? That's how Hank diffused the stagecoach. Gave it a zap, punched a hole for me. But what can I use? A lamp? A computer? No electrical cords will reach far enough. And I didn't see an outlet anywhere near the hatch. Shame I don't have Gammell's trusty Taser right now...

Ducking low, I scamper quietly down the long corridor, slipping quickly into the next aisle. Miss Muffet is close. I'm keeping a few aisles between us, but I can hear her humming. A hollow, overly-saccharine sing-song voice, with a floaty, mocking edge. She's in no hurry. Stalking me like a walking meatsicle.

I pause. Curiously, I peer through a bookshelf.

Through a periscope tunnel of books, her tilted smiling mug is staring back at me. She makes a scooping motion with her saw-spoon, rubbing her belly with familiar delight.

I jerk back, my stomach doing flip-flops.

I swear she's being creepy on purpose.

Maybe she thinks I'll taste better if I'm scared...

I should go slice her babydoll head off right now. I've got an axe; she's got a spoon. Still, something in my gut is warning me not to underestimate the oversized Muppet. And I can't afford to die now.

I duck past the nurse's station, dark and locked. But the small glass cabinet on the wall swings open, and a small red backpack falls out. Crouching behind a desk, I unzip the pack and yank it open. A portable AED device.

A defibrillator.

Bingo.

In the distance, it sounds like Muffet has switched songs. Now she's humming 'Itsy Bitsy Spider.'

Wait, I think I remember this nursery rhyme.

'Little Miss Muffet sat on a tuffett

Eating her curds and whey.

Along came a...'

Oh, no. Lord, no.

And there it is. A scuffling and shuffling, the scraping of chairs toppling onto the floor...followed by a wet, rumbling, purring sound. From behind the children's puzzle table climbs an enormous Brown Recluse spider, the size of an elephant.

I have no beef with spiders. But look, this isn't a spider. And this is no sluggish, lumbering movie puppet, either. This sucker is *fast* – a massive crab from the hothouse of Hades, creeping twitchily across the floor toward me, its tent pole-sized legs clicking on the stones. Ugh, so many legs. I know it's supposed to be eight, but sure feels like a lot more.

I take one step and the creature hops clear over my head, landing behind me. The spider is assessing me with as much wary as I'm dishing out for it. Skittering in a circle around me, it pauses every few steps, a sort of stop-motion flinch, its body bouncing up and down like a hairy, overinflated football. It watches me through six glistening beetle-black eyes the size of silver dollars, its jaws sawing back and forth, its fuzzy, paddle-shaped chelicerae twitching and fluttering.

"Aren't you supposed to *scare* Miss Muffet *away*?" I wail.

Just my luck, I guess they went to couple's counseling and worked out their grievances so they could gang up on my butt. Can't argue with teamwork. Man, I wish Merrick was with me right now. Or Tannon with a bazooka, or Gammell, or even Twinkie Dad with a baseball bat...

No, it's better this way.

Stay warm in your beds, I resolve tenderly. *I'll handle this.*

Maybe I'll spill the whole tale to Merrick later over a bowl of turkey chili and a root beer float. But first, I need to survive this.

Chili and root beer later.

Finish this now.

Spurred by fresh hope from this small internal finish line, I sprint down the far side of the library, the hatchet in one hand, the defibrillator pack clutched tightly against my empty chest. The device hasn't reset yet. But it will. And when it does, I'll lose my progress. I need to prepare. When I get kicked back to start again, *I need to make sure* this defibrillator is right by the hatch when I arrive.

Darting out from the historical fiction shelf, I heave-ho sling the red bag toward the hatch as hard as I can. It slides across the floor – and promptly falls into the open hatch.

"*Frak!!*" I shout.

I shouldn't have yelled. But it doesn't matter. Muffet already knows where I am. She's camped atop the bookshelf right above me, swinging her feet from side to side, giggling and clapping with delight as her Bunyanesque pet spider scuttles towards me.

A bite from one little penny-sized Brown Recluse spider contains enough venom to dissolve tissue from the bone. A bite from *this* brute? Probably liquefy me into an Indiana Jones milkshake. No reset-day would bring me back from that.

I skid in a tight circle around the spider. It spins, mirroring me, its bulbous backside slamming into me like a massive sandbag, its prickly hairs shredding the skin off my hand like a cheese grater. I shake my hand, trying to ignore the searing pain, switching to a one-handed grip on the axe.

At least I wasn't bitten.

"Hey Cheeto! Bet you five bucks I can slice your legs into sushi before you can pump me full of venom!"

I don't wait for a response. I've already plunged in like a madwoman, hacking and chopping and screaming like a half-crazed wasteland lunatic, knee-deep in guts and glory. My axe whicks the creature's legs, chopping through them like a garden of bamboo, *snicker-snack.* The spider flops and flails, squirting a cascade of pea soup nastiness across the floor, splattering a colorful wall poster that says "*Reading is dreaming with your eyes open*" – until finally it collapses in a tangled heap of limbs.

Miss Muffet's porcelain face is stunned. Her lower lip juts out in a childish pout, as though I'd just confiscated her crayons.

"You want me, dollface?" I bark at her, axe poised over my head. "This axe is rated 'E' for everyone!"

She drops from the shelf and puts both hands on her hips. Then she marches over and plops down cross-legged beside the slain spider, folding her arms grumpily, and murmuring under her breath.

I lower the axe.

Well, since she's momentarily lost interest in disemboweling me… I seize the opportunity and tiptoe hastily back over to the stairwell. As I lean over the hatch, it's clear that the effect of the device has gotten stronger, even in this short amount of time.

Come on, Kyle. *Think.*

I could throw the hatchet. But if Ben Franklin's big bronze noggin didn't affect the forcefield, the axe is unlikely to, either. Plus, I'm not too keen on throwing away my only viable weapon.

I drop to my knees, hugging my aching skull.

Suffocating pressure hammers down on me. And not just my head. I'm surrounded by countdowns. I've got that mystery wildcard outside, a living battering ram against a door that won't hold much longer. Then there's this thrumming heaviness in my head, a constant reminder of Holliday's chilling warning to hurry. And then I've got Miss Muffet over there, still mourning the loss of her beloved or whatever –

I glance over at her. She just stood up.

What's she doing?

With a prissy sigh, she bends at the hips and reaches down, scooping up the big dead spider. Then she eats it.

I do a double-take.

Now, when I say 'eat,' I don't mean nibble or chew. I mean she literally shoves the whole dang thing down her gullet – legs and all, snorking and smacking, gobbling up the giant arachnid like a champion Coney Island hot dog eater. Daintily, she licks each of her fingertips, one by one. Then she turns and glares at me.

Uh-oh.

I turn quickly back to the device.

I need to crack this nut. Fast...

I tear my fingers through my hair, spinning in a mad circle before dropping to all fours. I throw my hands in desperation, jabbing a finger down at the device in the octopus blob.

"*WHAT DO YOU WANT FROM ME?!!*" I scream at it.

The blob twitches.

My breath halts in my throat.

Did that thing just *move?* Something just made it twitch.

Something...*I* did?

Swallowing, I lick my peeling sandpaper lips. Hurriedly, I reach my hand out toward the device, exactly like I did a second ago. Ten feet below in the gloom, the blob twitches again.

It *moved*. Unmistakably this time.

Shivering and breathless, I open my hand, slowly spreading my fingers. With a shudder, the forcefield over the device mimics me, peeling itself open like a flower. Then, like a screen shutting off, the shimmer ripples and vanishes. As if it's inviting me.

Permission granted...

Miss Muffet starts stalking across the library toward me, her geisha lips twisted in hatred. Her shoulder twitches. At first I think her arm fell off – but then I see her frilly pink sleeve rip at the seam, and a two-foot-long brown spike punches out from her shoulder. The spike unfolds, tripling in length – no, not a spike, it's a spider's leg. She keeps on tromping toward me, never breaking stride, even as hairy six-foot-long arachnid legs erupt from all over her body. I can't tell if that spider is trying to bust back out of her, or if she's somehow morphed herself with it, Frankenstein-style. Either way, I don't really care.

"Hey now, I've heard 'you are what you eat,' but, uh–" I grimace as another leg bursts out from her belly.

I know I said I have no problem with spiders. But *this?*

This is fresh from the Island of NOPE.

Let's see her keep coming at me with no head.

I run forward and swing the hatchet. The blade thunks into the side of her head, sticking there. Spider-Muffet stops walking, blinking her long insectoid eyelashes in surprise.

We stare at each other. Reaching up, she gives the axe handle a little tug, as if it's nothing more than a mosquito bite.

I take a step backwards. Then another.

Huffing a little '*hmph*,' Muffet resumes stomping toward me, her mouth smeared with spider guts, the axe blade still buried in her head.

"Uh, now would be a great time to reset," I hiss urgently at the device. "C'mon, reset, reset, reset!"

But it doesn't. Muffet is still charging towards me, walking on her huge, creepy, newly-sprouted spider legs, her slippered feet dangling in midair. I jerk left, I fake right – I could try to make a dash around her, but it would be a kamikaze run. She's too close now. She would easily catch me.

Her neck cracks, and right about the time that her head breaks off and rises up on an elongated, centipede-like neck, I turn tail and run the only place I have left.

Up the dang stairs.

I know what you're thinking. I know.

I swore I would never be stupid enough to trap myself up in this tower.

But like Deadhead Kyle, I have a plan.

I remember this bell tower. I remember every detail. Like that one window near the construction worker's scaffolding. The open window, the one with no glass, the same window that me and Deadhead Kyle took a tumble from. It's how I was able to climb up here on the day when this town was under ice.

And with any luck, that's how I'm going to escape.

"THE AXE BLADE STILL BURIED IN HER HEAD..."

I can hear my monstrous pursuer right behind me. My pace is slowing. But this staircase is narrow, and Miss Spider-Butt is massive, so I can only pray that her massive spider butt is slowing her down even more.

Up, up the endless curve of stairs, until my calves start burning and my breath gets short. I can feel it…that slow-seeping numbness in my hands and feet; that creeping itch under my skin. My heartless zombie body is nearing its limit. Exhaustion is sinking its teeth into me. Normally, this would be where I would need to stop and take a breather. But I can't stop. I press harder, yanking myself along the handrail to propel myself faster.

At last I've reached the top. The small, circular chamber is painted in a soft, sleepy, pink glow. Outside the semi-circle of windows, sunrise is spreading, spilling brilliant buckets of melted butter across the sky. Fiery orange reflects off the wooden floorboards, shining on the forgotten coffee mug on the railing, shimmering on the glass windowpanes.

All except one.

Wasting no time, I plunge out the open window, my belly scraping the underside of the sill, my boots skidding down the slanted roof shingles as I slide faster, faster. The edge of the roof comes quick. My fingers close around one of the scaffolding support poles just below the gutter spout, catching myself in a wild monkey swing. The platform below my feet rattles precariously. I drop to the next platform, as quickly as I can, descending catlike, trying to time each noise with the thunderous whomping I now hear plain as day, just around the corner, at the front door. Good thing the wildcard hasn't noticed me yet.

I'd like to keep it that way.

I drop to the grass, my stomach in my throat. Crouching, I risk a quick glance over my shoulder. Overhead, the bell tower windows are darkened by something mammoth and mad. There's a horrible, nail-splintering screech, and the open window vomits a cluster of spider legs, furiously waving and wriggling in the air, like enormous alien fingers reaching through a mouse hole.

Run, little mouse.

I run. I run for my life. My feet pound the leaf-covered ground, through the cemetery, skidding to a stop around the back of the library. Breathlessly, I survey my options. The lone cathedral window is about five feet up, on the stony wall.

Congrats. You just escaped the Box of Certain Grisly Death.

What are you going to do next?

Go back inside, of course.

I estimate I've got approximately thirty seconds, as long as Spider-Muffet is trapped up in the bell tower, and the wildcard hasn't noticed me –

The whomping just stopped. A clattering crash as the scaffolding collapses, followed by the unmistakable thuds of multiple creatures hopping across the ground toward me.

Make that fifteen seconds.

My breath comes in jerky gasps. If I can just break that window… They probably couldn't follow me. I'd buy some time. Get to the device. It's open. It's ready. I can actually do this.

I can do this…

No rocks big enough, but the pine tree branch that I'm hammering at the window does the trick. The ancient glass shatters like sugar. The thudding and hissing and clickings are getting closer. After a quick sweep of the branch to punch away any jagged glass stragglers, I grab the windowsill and pull myself up, feeding myself through the narrow opening, just as a flurry of monstrous movement catches the corner of my eye. I wriggle, kicking my legs, pouring myself through the window and falling towards the library's stone floor.

The floor…

The floor that just disappeared beneath me – I grab for the windowsill; it's gone, too – nothing to catch me as I pitch forward and fall, tumbling inside-out into the yielding emptiness of my own head…

My hands hit cold dirt. The sweat down my neck is dried, my sticky skin swathed in chilly night air.

I've been kicked back to start. Again.

"No, no, no…" I croak in disbelief.

Shuddering, I roll over and look around. Creaking trees, a cold blanket of stars overhead… I recognize those blackened chimney bricks to my left… I'm at the burnt house behind Tannon's field.

"If this is supposed to be funny, I'm not laughing!!" I scream to nobody in particular, punching the ground over and over. "I was *so close,* you piece of spit!! I was so close!!"

I stop punching. My breathing slows, realization sinking in.

I think I know why I'm here.

Crunching across the charcoal debris, I grab one of the broken ceramic tiles from the mossy edge of the sludge-covered pool. But this isn't a weapon. I angle the shard so it catches the moonlight, casting a beam into the woods like a makeshift flashlight. If my theory is correct, there should be three much better and much stabbier weapons around here somewhere.

Scissors, a steak knife, and the hatchet.

Now, where did Holliday toss them? It's way too dark to find scissors or a dinky little steak knife. Luckily, the hatchet is easy to spot. I grab it and sprint out of the woods.

I get it now. I need to connect the dots. Connect the broken threads. Maybe it's that simple. I just need to meet with where I picked up last time. Riding Holliday's bike, holding this axe.

I've got a date with a story that still needs a beginning.

Hatchet in hand, I break into a fast trot, my gaze sweeping the side of the road. Holliday's bike should be somewhere nearby. I saw it slide into a ditch when he vanished like a goblin.

Did I pass it? Maybe I ran too far…

The faint line of tire rubber is hard to see in the dark, but I follow where it veers diagonally across the road, cutting a sharp V angle before ending. I run to the gravel shoulder and find Holliday's bike, lying in a grassy ditch.

"Hello beautiful," I murmur, tucking the hatchet under my arm and hoisting the shiny black Suzuki from the ditch, rolling it back onto the road.

Two minutes later I'm streaking toward town at breakneck speed, leaned low over Holliday's bike, engine rip-roaring, the axe in my hand. A ribbon of deep blue morning begins to fade the velvet sea of stars on the horizon. Just up ahead, the black mouth of the covered bridge is approaching fast. I've never been more ready. That's probably why I don't even flinch when the pain clamps down on my skull.

I welcome it. I embrace it.

Gimme that pain. Let me finish this game...

My wish is granted. I'm back in the bell tower at sunrise, right where I left off. My hands are empty. Salty sweat slicks my face. My lungs are heaving, and I can't seem to remember what I need to do next. The room tilts unsteadily.

As if to answer my question, a furious tangle of giant spider legs suddenly fills the doorway. It's a tight fit, but squirming and thrashing, Spider-Muffet slurps through the doorframe. And she's mad as a wet hornet. Shaking spastically, she flings herself around like a rubber chicken between two walls, the axe still sticking out from her disheveled red ringlets. Her lower jaw broke off at some point, accommodating the fuzzy pair of chelicerae wiggling freely out of her mouth. She's tramping toward me, her head bouncing at the end of her long snake-neck, lolling back and forth like the weight of the axe is too much.

The window.

Snapping out of my brain fog, I hurl myself toward the open window – but Spider-Muffet blocks me, flailing her bulk in my path. So that's the end of that. I'm not escaping out the window this time.

With nowhere left to run, I climb atop the wooden railing of the belfry. The enormous bell hangs motionless above me, its Quasimodo rope dangling over a dark and bottomless expanse. There's no time to question my sanity as I take a flying leap off the railing, my stomach hiccuping into my mouth. I catch the rope with both hands, my weight prompting the massive pulley gears to grind slightly, enough for the bell to emit one deep, resonating peal. In horror, I feel my shoulder pop, that familiar stabbing fire as the weakened ligaments allow the bone to slip from its socket. A stifled moan escapes my clenched teeth. Clenching my sweaty grip on the rope, I steal a glance down at my dangling feet. I immediately wish I hadn't.

It's a dizzying drop.

Spider-Muffet swipes at me with her sawblade-spoon. Wonder what it's like to eat with that thing? It can't be very comfortable. Bleh, I've got metal-mouth just thinking about it. Or maybe it's just because I never brushed my teeth this morning. ...Or did I? It's too much to think about. At any rate, I don't think Muffet can reach me here. So that's good news.

The bad news?

I have no idea how I'm going to get off this bell. I'm just plain dry out of cards. Unless I can call down miracle lightning from heaven… My one good hand is tiring. My grip is slipping from the rope. And I'm tired. Lord, I'm tired. It's just a fleeting thought, fish flitting through my brain castle, how easy it would be to just let go. But I know that if I lose now, it's more than game over.

Fail now, and it was all for nothing.

To everyone in Carnival Creeke, yesterday was Gargoyle Day. To them, it was just one day, passingly seamlessly into this morning. Nothing in between. But to me… Land sakes, to me, I've got a lifetime sandwiched between those two calendar squares. And somewhere in the middle of it all, I stumbled into something special. Something like a home. Ain't that a kicker.

"I'm sorry, Merrick," I whisper.

But someone else has entered the room. Spider-Muffet hasn't noticed. She's so focused on killing me that she doesn't realize the bronze head of Ben Franklin just appeared behind her.

I blink hard. I must be hallucinating.

But Frankie is real. A bit comical, actually, since his lips are still pursed together in that bored expression. And his bronze head is attached to a bronze body, which is attached to four bronze arms. He's holding the defibrillator paddles – no, he's not holding them; the paddles are actually fused to his wrists where his hands should be. Spider-Muffet's insectoid eyes pop in shock as Frankie claps her head between those electrified paddles, zapping her with a river of buzzkill juice. Muffet collapses out of view behind the wooden railing, and I hear her saw-spoon clatter to the floor.

I choke a laugh in disbelief.

I can't believe it. Frankie's head. The defibrillator. Hot diggity, I cooked up my own knight of shining armor. And he showed up just in time.

"Thanks, pal!" I cough.

Frankie pivots, as though noticing me for the first time.

And he doesn't want my gratitude.

He thrusts one of his four arms out over the railing and I feel him seize me by the hair, yanking me across the expanse and slamming me to the floor. My back hits hard, his bronze hand clamped on my neck like a dungeon vice. Spider-Muffet is lying on the floor beside me, a lifeless heap of pink ruffles and bug legs, her candy-apple ringlets a sizzling mess of frizz. I struggle against Frankie's steely grip. It's hopeless. Might as well be pinned down by a car. And this is so, so much worse than a car. I'm pinned by a big bronze Mortal Kombat founding father monster. I manage to rip off a hunk of Spider-Muffet's hair and stuff it into his eyes, for all the good it does, since his unblinking eyeballs are metal. I know it's coming. I see those two defibrillator paddles close over me, eclipsing the light from both sides. I spit on his face. He never flinches. White-hot voltage plummets through me. My body bucks violently and my spine snaps into a rigid curve, then everything goes black.

I woke on the cold gymnasium bleacher. Merrick crouched down to a sitting position on the next bleacher below mine. I kept my eyes shut, so he must have thought I was still asleep.

"Hey...Kyle?" He'd paused, then continued softly. "Okay, you're sleeping. I'm glad. You deserve it. Plus, it makes this easier on me." He hesitated. "Kyle, I've gotta tell you something. I'm kinda glad you jumped out in front of my truck yesterday."

He laughed quietly. "Sounds crazy, right? Feels like ages ago. Another me ago. But if I'm honest with myself... Well, here goes. Kyle, I..."

Merrick's voice fades out, replaced by the gruff tone of Sheriff Gammell.

"*I know them all,*" Gammell's deep grumble echoes in my head, tinny, and far-away. "*Because the people in this town...they are* ***family*** *to me. Every single last one of them.*"

I think I need to wake up.

Wake up...

Wake up, Kyle...

My eyes pop open, my singed eyelashes sticking together for a moment. Four-armed Frankie is standing over me. With nothing left in this room to kill, he's now staring straight ahead, blankly, like a bronze statue. I roll upright, every muscle on fire, every joint screaming for mercy. But my arms move.

Frankie tilts his head and looks at me.

A slow laugh bubbles up in my throat, guttural and drained.

"Heh, heh...you were trying to stop my heart, huh?" I force a grin and drag myself to my feet, leaning heavily on the wooden railing behind me. "Well...hate to disappoint you, Frankie...but I'm one heart short."

My fingers brush against the coffee mug.

"Guess it's my lucky day."

In one swift motion I grab the mug, smashing it across Frankie's metal face. He barely blinks, but that's all I need. I take a step.

My legs move...

Today is my day.

Reaching down, I scoop up Spider-Muffet – not all of her, she's way too bulky and heavy; so I just grab legs and ruffles and anything I can get my arms around – and I hurl her hulking corpse at Frankie. It's enough to throw him off balance, and he tilts, erect, his own weight toppling him over the edge of the belfry railing, dragging Spider-Muffet along with him. I hear them hit the bell on their way, a chaotic metal-on-metal clangor that shreds my eardrums.

I drape myself over the railing and look down. The bottomless tower has a bottom after all. Both wildcards lie in messy pieces far below, crushed like fortune cookies. I didn't get to see their landing, but from the look of it, it was spectacular.

Turning away, I grip my injured shoulder and mechanically pop it back into socket. I know it hurts, but I barely feel it. All I feel is the creeping numbness. That sensation of ants crawling in my veins. I look at my hand, examining my blackened fingertips. I overdid it. Took my limit line and blew past it miles ago.

But not just that.

My ears are ringing, but not from the bell. This crushing pressure in my head... I reel back. The pain is immense. My head feels vacuum sealed. My eyeballs feel like two overinflated beach balls, my brain threatening to pop like a tube of toothpaste. I clasp both hands over my ears in an attempt to keep my skull intact. I gasp, struggling for air. It's intense, crushing; like a freight truck parked on my chest. I feel something warm trickle from my nose, and I taste the metallic tang of blood. This isn't the way it feels before a reset. This is the device breaking down.

Spreading.

I stumble over to the clock tower window and look down. Across the lawn, by the iron fence, the construction workers are doubled over in pain, clutching their heads.

My throat goes dry, my breath rattling in my chest.

If the device's effect has already reached outside the library, it's only a matter of minutes before everyone in town will be feeling this. This is it. We're moments away from our heads getting creamed into finger paint.

We're out of time.

If I can just get to the device… All I need to do is destroy that nightmare machine, and all of this stops.

I start dragging myself across the floor toward the stairs.

A gut-wrenching barrage of doubt pummels me. What if the forcefield turned back on? What if I can't make it open again? What if I can't destroy it, and it just keeps on pumping out an endless stream of nursery rhyme reject horribles until we all explode? What if the day resets again?

I'm so tired. And I don't have Merrick or Hank to carry me…

You'll see them soon, I firmly remind myself.

Just smash that device.

Finish this ***now****. Hurt later. Stitches and antiseptic later. Fluffy waffles and Merrick and Jemma and plastic horses and all the sunshine and sourdough and surprises in that jack-in-the-box of whatever lies beyond this closed loop. Just do this one last thing.*

I'm so close, Merrick...

Just destroy it. Even if I have to fling myself onto it.

"Hang on everyone...I'm coming," I whisper hoarsely. "I've got you... Almost there..."

I take a labored step toward the stairs.

Clunk.

Leaning heavily on the railing, I stumble, tripping down four steps, but managing to catch myself on the rail.

Just hold it together, Kyle. Almost there...

The air is getting hotter, thicker with each step. Regaining my balance, I take another step. *Clunk.* Weird...my footsteps sound loud. Echoing more than they should, even in this enclosed wooden tower. I stop moving.

I stand motionless.

Clunk.

My swollen eyes go wide. That sound isn't coming from me. Something else is in this stairwell. Making its way up... The wildcard from outside? Another fairytale freak? My vision wavers, the curving staircase swimming in and out of focus.

Clunk. Clunk.

My breath quickens. I'm a half-fried bowl of jelly. How can I fight this thing? What am I going to do? Bleed on it?

Sure. If that's all I've got left... Then let's do this.

Let's meet our final contestant.

Clunk. Step by step, it moves up the stairs into view.

Clunk. A rounded body, armless... *Clunk.* It looks like some kind of enormous egg, walking on two legs...

What vine-ripened hell is this?

Clunk. The thing stumps its way toward me, rocking its bulk from side to side with each step, its tiny, beady eyes burning from a puggish, troll-like face. My final contestant is...

Humpty Dumpty.

I don't know whether to laugh or cry. I think I might be doing both. All I know is this ridiculous bumpkin is standing between me and the finish line, the singular objective of my laser focused existence. *My town. My family.* My jaw clenches, grinding my teeth until my vision is streaked with smoking red. Distantly, I'm aware that someone is screaming – a primal scream of desperation and rage – and I realize the sound is coming from me.

I run at it. Straight at it. Slamming into the monstrous egg like a linebacker, sending us both tumbling down those stairs. Can't say what I'm thinking. Don't know what I expected. I'm a thing gone mad, my last wire clipped.

We tumble, somersaulting like crazy, reaching the bottom of the stairs in a matter of seconds. Humpty's big round body lands in the circular floor hatch, plugging the hole like a cork. I jump on him, putting the full force of my weight into my boots. It's not adequate. I jump again, and again, pounding the creature with my body until, with a crackle and a pop, Humpty slips through the hatch and we both fall into the opening. My hands scramble, catching the lip of the hatch, my busted shoulder screaming in agony. But I hold fast, my fingers curled around the metal grate, swinging haphazardly over the expanse. Twisting my head around, I watch Humpty fall, sailing gracelessly end over end, like a big flightless egg-bird, if birds looked like eggs. It lands on the device with a juicy, symphonic splat, bursting into a mushroom cloud of yolk, splattering my feet and the walls with glazed yellow. And at the epicenter of the mess, I see the device split in half.

My breath freezes.

The rhythmic sparking pulse goes dead. Still clinging to the edge of the hatch, I'm hit with a sudden updraft that blows through my clothes and hair, blistering and fusty, like a last breath of some ancient dying dragon. For a moment I half expect ghosts to fly out of the broken device and melt my face off – so I do the only thing I can do. Shut my eyes.

The wind subsides just as abruptly as it arrived, and when I peel one eye open, the smashed remains of Humpty Dumpty are also gone. No yolk dripping from the walls. Not a trace of shell. Just a grey, lifeless, broken device, sitting atop a mound of ash.

I did it.

I DID IT.

Still hanging from the hatch, I goggle in disbelief until the burning pain in my arms starts chomping at me and I remember that I'd rather not fall ten feet onto concrete.

I attempt to do a pull-up. My jelly noodle arms don't respond. Scraping the bottom of my strength barrel, I try again and again until, with an almighty roar, I manage to heave myself up over the lip of the hatch and tumble onto the cold floor. I lay there for what seems like an eternity, flat on my back, my chest heaving.

It's not even eight o'clock…and I can honestly say this has been the weirdest day ever.

A slow grin cracks my sweat-stained face.

I did it.

I feel my lungs spasm, but not to breathe. I'm laughing. My airway is already beginning to relax, my super-healing body going to work, knitting itself back together.

I did it.

Rolling my heavy clay body, I climb to my knees. Silence. Not just silent here in the library – outside, the whomping wildcard has stopped, too.

The roar of a car engine outside is followed by the screeching of tires. Someone is honking the horn. Frowning, I scramble to my feet. But I can't walk away. Turning, I look back at the broken device. I stand there for a moment longer, allowing the object of my last forty-something days one last, lingering gaze.

"Sweet dreams," I croak smugly.

I toss it a little salute before dashing across the library, across the clean floor that should be slicked with spider guts, and I stumble out into the blinding sunlight. The heavy front door is split down the center, hanging off its hinges. Looks like the arrow-wielding wildcard was about six seconds away from busting in and laying a lethal hurting on me.

What *was* that thing, anyway?

I turn my head, and I see it lying by the steps. It's Sam's wooden chief statue. Stiff as a board, lying lifeless on the stone porch, his pompous carved scowl frozen up at the portico columns. I almost laugh. Almost.

I'll definitely make a mental note to laugh about this later.

The car horn honks again. A gold 1969 Trans-Am is idling over by the cemetery, engine rumbling. I limp across the library lawn toward the car.

Rascal Holliday leans out the window as I approach. He's wearing sunglasses, so I can't see those black eyes flickering all over.

"Nice job, Doc." He claps his gloved hands in sarcastic approval. "Now hop in. Time fer a ride. An' it's time ye learned the truth."

A spastic jumble of emotions tumbles over me, from my head to my toes – shock, elation, disbelief. And all at once, I realize what he's saying to me.

I'm leaving.

I'm leaving Carnival Creeke.

Right now.

KYLE WILL RETURN

FOR HER FINAL HEART-STOPPING ADVENTURE

IN BOOK 3

KEEP YOUR EYES OPEN!

www.ingramcontent.com/pod-product-compliance
Lightning Source LLC
LaVergne TN
LVHW050927080826
845145LV00001B/238

* 9 7 8 0 5 7 8 5 9 3 0 7 4 *